T A SHELANO

The Doctor's Hidden Patients

Shelano Books

First published by shelanobooks.co.uk 2024

Copyright © 2024 by T A Shelano

All rights reserved. No part of this publication may be reproduced, stored or transmitted in any form or by any means, electronic, mechanical, photocopying, recording, scanning, or otherwise without written permission from the publisher. It is illegal to copy this book, post it to a website, or distribute it by any other means without permission.

This novel is entirely a work of fiction. The names, characters and incidents portrayed in it are the work of the author's imagination. Any resemblance to actual persons, living or dead, events or localities is entirely coincidental.

T A Shelano asserts the moral right to be identified as the author of this work.

Designations used by companies to distinguish their products are often claimed as trademarks. All brand names and product names used in this book and on its cover are trade names, service marks, trademarks and registered trademarks of their respective owners. The publishers and the book are not associated with any product or vendor mentioned in this book. None of the companies referenced within the book have endorsed the book.

First edition

ISBN: 978-1-0687275-3-5

Agent: Anna
Editing by Kieran
Cover art by Richard
Advisor: Amy
Advisor: Laura

This book was professionally typeset on Reedsy.
Find out more at reedsy.com

I dedicate this novel to all those who are neurodivergent. Just because we don't see the world the way they do doesn't diminish the value we add to it.

How much do we ever really know about others, even those who are closest to us? How far are we prepared to go to protect the ones we love? How quickly our lives can change, (for better or worse), and are often affected by circumstances out of our own control.

T. A. Shelano

Contents

Foreword

"The Doctor's Hidden Patients has a wonderful pace and feels like true escapism."
Intersaga Literary Agency

Set in Oxford, England in 1999, The Doctor's Hidden Patients is the stunning debut novel by T.A.Shelano.

It is a fast-paced voice-led crime thriller which immerses the reader in a world of nostalgic fiction intertwined with thought-provoking themes of political corruption and technological development relevant to our time.

We follow siblings Sarah and William Leidenstraum who are exposed to danger following the death of their father Robert who had been nurturing half-human half-robot hybrids in a warehouse.

The siblings battle to stay alive and establish the truth with support from a range of allies as it becomes increasingly difficult to know who they can trust to keep them safe.

"The pacing of the novel is impressive."
*****

"Intriguing premise. Inventive"
*****

"Strong Voice."
*****

Preface

I'd thought about writing a novel for a long time, but I had no concept of just how difficult it would be to complete one. It feels like an achievement to have completed a novel as I know so many people never reach the finishing line. I take my hat off to people who write them for a living, I really do!

I had the basis of an idea and a few thousand words from initial drafting when I attended a Writers' HQ writer's retreat in my native Birmingham in March 2020, shortly before... well we all know what came next. Developing this novel then became a key feature of my Boris lockdown time.

I wanted to write a page-turning thriller. Throughout drafting my focus was on keeping the narrative move at a strong pace which I hope readers will think I achieved. I wrote a book I'd enjoy reading and sought to add action and tension interspersed with occasional humour. Ensuring continuity and navigating to a conclusion required a level of patience I'm not renowned for.

I decided to write the book on the cusp of the millenium as a nostalgic reflection on the quarter of a century of incredible technological revolution that has passed with one eye on an AI future. This book was written, developed and edited by humans. A quarter of a century from now that concept will sadly be a work of fiction in itself.

Enjoy the rollercoaster ride that is 'The Doctor's Hidden Patients'!

Best Wishes

T. A. Shelano

shelanobooks.co.uk

Acknowledgement

I would like to start by thanking my wife Amy who has been nothing but supportive and encouraging since I first made the crazy announcement that I was going to write a novel. As the alpha reader, I will always fondly remember her response: "It's not what I was expecting, and it's a lot better than I thought it would be."

Thank you to family, friends, and colleagues who did not laugh when I said I'd written a novel, and who expressed genuine interest in reading it. I will always remember the following from my wife's friend Rachel when I said I'd completed a novel: "What, you mean reading one?"

I am grateful to the following people for their input and support in finalising this novel:

Laura C - Thank you for your support in agreeing to be a beta reader for the novel and for your advice in improving the first draft. I don't think this book will make you the million you were hoping for so you'll have to settle for thanks a million instead.

Richard H - Thank you for your support in designing the book's cover and for your all round technical skills in launching the book. You are the undisputed king of IT.

Kieran D – Thank you for proofreading and copyediting the final draft of the novel. Your support was invaluable in getting the novel polished and in great shape.

Anna K – Thank you for being the literary agent that gave me the feedback, guidance, and confidence I needed to improve my novel.

1

Chapter One: Revelations

Saturday 3rd July, 1999. 3.55pm.

It was a bright and sunny afternoon in a supermarket car park in Oxfordshire. Fifty-eight-year-old Dr Robert Leidenstraum, a German scientist living in the UK, gently pushed a heavy trolley. After numerous warnings from his GP about his blood pressure and cholesterol, he looked sheepishly at the wine and cheese filled carrier bags.

As he approached his prized black Audi A4 saloon, which he had got a good deal on just six weeks earlier, he noticed what looked like a sizeable scratch on the driver's side door which made his blood boil. As he bent over to get a closer look, pain permeated his left arm. He clutched his chest and fell to the ground, the trolley rolled back and rested almost lovingly on his head.

Dr Leidenstraum awoke in hospital and gazed at the ceiling of Ward Seven, wondering why he was not watching Wimbledon in his conservatory with Pimm's and strawberries. Then he remembered the car park. Who had scratched his beloved car? What had happened to his gorgonzola and merlot? Where was the fillet steak that he had planned to cook for dinner that evening? His pain and annoyance were exacerbated by the screaming of another patient, four beds along. The noise pierced his inner ear drum and penetrated his very soul. It was then that he heard a familiar and comforting voice break through the wretched wailing.

"Dad, thank goodness you're alive. I got here as soon as I could." It was Dr Leidenstraum's daughter Sarah, a twenty-year-old university student who hoped to become a doctor like her father, albeit by pursuing a career in medicine; his eldest child and undoubtedly his favourite. Whilst he loved Sarah's seventeen-year-old brother, William, he lacked his sister's intelligence, and though never short of effort, in Dr Leidenstraum's eyes he was never going to match her achievements, or be the son he had hoped for.

"I'm sorry, I didn't get time to pick up some grapes. I was in such a panic and rush."

"Don't worry, I should be eating strawberries right now. Grapes would only force me to accept my current predicament. Perhaps I could put them in my ears to shut him up," he said tilting his head in the direction of the screaming man.

Sarah chuckled. It was a fond reminder of how her father's

dry sense of humour had illuminated her childhood, when gloom could easily have prevailed following the death of her mother in a car accident. Sarah was four years old. Sarah's reminiscence was interrupted by her father's gasps for breath. Sarah shouted for help. Her father pulled her near and said meekly, "The lock-up. The keys are in my study. I'm sorry I never told you."

Nurses rushed to tend to Dr Leidenstraum, but all efforts were in vain. He was dead. Sarah reeled in shock. She was numb, overwhelmed with grief, and confused. What did her father's last words mean?

Sarah returned to the family home in a daze. She parked her beloved red Nissan Micra on the pebble driveway in front of the bay window of the semi-detached house. She climbed out of 'Joanna,' the name she had affectionately given her car in honour of her favourite actress, Joanna Lumley. The absence of her father's black Audi from in front of the recently painted white garage door was an instant reminder of her unfathomable loss.

Sarah opened the white UPVC front door, wiped her feet on the mat, and took her shoes off. Her father had told her a thousand times to take her shoes off. How she longed to hear him shout at her to take her shoes off one more time. Things would never be the same again.

Sarah called her brother's mobile, but he didn't answer. She contemplated her father's last words, and ventured into his study in search of answers. Family photos adorned the room, producing a flood of tears tinged with both sadness and joy as she pored over many cherished memories. Sarah's recollections paused as her gaze was drawn to a set of keys hanging on the wall.

Were those the keys? Sarah wondered. She snatched hold of them, three silver keys, each emblazoned with a different word: 'safe,' 'lock-up,' 'lock-up internal.' In the corner of the room, she was drawn to a small, wall-mounted safe and contemplated trying the safe key. Feelings of unease passed over her. This was her father's room; he had strictly forbidden her or Will from going in there. She recalled the rage he flew into when he had caught her in there during a game of hide and seek with Will. She had never dared set foot in there since. Being in there now felt like an invasion of his privacy, even following his death. If he had to wait for his final moments to mention these keys to her, what would she find? Then the phone interrupted her racing thoughts. It was her brother.

"Will, I need you to come home, ok?"

"What? Why? I'm in London."

"I can't say on the phone, but I need you to come home as soon as you can, alright?"

Concerned by his sister's tone, Will agreed to return on the next available train.

As the phone call concluded, Sarah took a sharp intake of breath and placed the key into the lock. The door opened. Her

4

trepidation was quickly met with a wave of disappointment. A few journals, a floppy disk, and some paperwork. She skimmed through the papers and happened upon documentation about the purchase of a warehouse, along with a photograph of it. She noticed the date was nineteen eighty-three, a few months after her mother's death.

Intrigued by this and, with her father's words ringing in her ears, Sarah opened the first journal. It felt wrong, but surely this is what he would have wanted, she thought to herself, as if seeking to justify her actions.

The journal commenced on the eighth of November nineteen eighty-three, the day the warehouse was purchased and highlighted plans to carry out biological experiments as part of an academic research project. Her father's notes outlined how his wife's death had devastated him. The emptiness and despair he felt had motivated him to use his skills to create and preserve life.

Skipping to the final journal, Sarah could see it had been written up until the previous day, the second of July, nineteen ninety-nine. The final notes were; 'the subjects continue to progress well. The new millennium can't come quickly enough.'

Sarah was studious in nature, but couldn't motivate herself to begin trawling through her father's extensive diaries, particularly given the fact she was struggling to hold back more tears. Instead, she decided a visit to the warehouse would kill the proverbial two birds with one stone, as it would serve as a welcome distraction whilst satisfying her curiosity as to what her father had been doing there.

It was a warm and bright evening after a beautiful sunny day. The opposite of how Sarah felt. Sarah drove 'Joanna,' and listened to FM radio. The pub beer gardens bustled with sun scorched revellers who had lapped up the rare glorious British sunshine. It would probably be raining next weekend. Britney Spears *Baby One More Time* was played. How many times had she heard that song in the last few months? Sarah preferred Christina Aguilera to Britney, but she had often found it impossible to resist the temptation to warble to Britney. *No Scrubs* by TLC followed. Sarah loved that song. If her friends were in the car with her, they would sing loudly with the song on full blast.

As her twenty-minute drive concluded, she found herself immersed in an industrial estate which contained several warehouse units. The DJ played Baz Luhrmann's *Everybody's Free (To Wear Sunscreen)*. The lyrics were just too painful. Sarah switched the radio off. All the businesses on the estate were closed so Sarah felt confident her visit would go unnoticed, and more importantly unchallenged.

Sarah recognised the warehouse from the photograph in her father's study. It was the last warehouse along on the right-hand side of the estate. She saw that the windows to the side of the building were tinted. As she approached the front door, she saw a small sign inscribed with 8B. The emptiness of the industrial estate made her feel distinctly uneasy, but she plucked up the courage to climb out of her car. She tentatively placed the 'lock-up' key into the lock, and gradually opened the front door. Sarah was underwhelmed by the sight of an empty wooden table and chair surrounded by brick walls from the floor to the ceiling. However, she noticed there was a steel door behind the table and chair.

Sarah placed the 'lock-up internal' key into the lock of the steel door. She turned the key and pulled the handle down. Hesitantly, Sarah walked into a completely darkened room. As she switched on the lights, she gasped in shock at what she saw before her: twelve glass cubicles, six to her left and six to the right. Each one contained what appeared to be a person facing in her direction. Sarah froze in fear, her mouth opened wide as her eyes popped metaphorically out of her head. She saw what appeared to be six males and six females of differing ethnicities, all around her age.

Sarah was stunned. "What is this? What the hell has dad been doing?" she whispered to herself as she walked tentatively along the centre of the room and gazed at each specimen like a tourist in a museum. Sarah's wonderment was disturbed by a tap on the glass of the cubicle that was fourth along on her left. She screamed and fell to the ground. Tentatively, she looked up anxiously, gripped by paralysing fear. The figure inside looked human, but was attached to a tube from the back; they all were. The figure waved at her and smiled. Sarah was aghast and screamed again, a few decibels louder than the first time.

Sarah scrambled to her feet, and turned to run back towards the door. As she did so, she heard a voice say, "Sarah," which stopped her dead in her tracks. She glanced cautiously over her right shoulder, and looked directly at the figure.

"Hello Sarah," the figure said.

It felt like time had descended into slow motion, as Sarah fell to her knees unable to digest what had happened. Sarah crawled furiously towards the door like an energetic baby, climbed through the gap, jumped to her feet, and slammed the steel door shut, like an angry gaoler. She sat with her back up against the door and caught her breath.

Sarah's attention was diverted by the sound of her phone ringing. It was her brother. Shaking uncontrollably, she answered the phone.

"Sarah, my train gets in at half nine. Can you pick me up?"

"Y-Y-Yee-Yes," Sarah stuttered.

"What's going on? Are you ok?"

"I'll see you soon Will. I'll see you soon. I've got to go." She locked up the premises, got into her car and drove to the train station.

Sarah was elegant, short, and slim with shoulder length, mousy brown hair, piercing blue eyes and a prominent, upturned nose. She cut a lonely and somewhat pitiful figure as she sat on the square brick wall surrounding the giant green clock on the concourse and waited anxiously for her brother to arrive. Sarah watched the countless people scurrying through the station. She struggled to process the many emotions that whirled around her mind like a washing machine on full spin. How was she going to explain the last few hours to her brother?

Will emerged from the distance, his unmistakable gait on display. His toes scraped along the ground as he walked purposefully yet awkwardly to meet his sister. Will was tall and slim with long unkempt brown hair and sullen brown eyes. His appearance was in stark contrast to that of his sibling. As Will approached, the look in Sarah's eyes instinctively told him what the news was.

"It's dad, isn't it? He's..."

Sarah nodded.

"...been nicked because of the bodies in the warehouse?"

Sarah reeled in shock. Her brother knew about the warehouse?

"No, dad's dead. He's dead. I'm sorry Will. I'm sorry. The warehouse. How did you...?"

"Dead? Dead? He can't be? No, he can't be?"

Sarah hugged her brother and they shared a tender moment in grief that was in contrast to their usual sibling rivalry.

Having let the moment pass and allowed for the news to begin to sink in, Sarah probed her brother. "What were you saying about a warehouse?"

"Nothing."

"I know too."

"How? And how did dad die?"

"I was there at the hospital. He'd had a heart attack. He told me about the warehouse just before he died."

"How much did he tell you?"

"Not a lot, but..."

"But what?"

"I've been there. Just before I came here to meet you."

"What. Why?"

"Curiosity. I was in shock. I am in shock. I didn't know what I was going to find. I don't know what I found."

Realising his sister was battling with her emotions and that he hadn't yet processed his own, Will displayed an emotional maturity beyond his years and calmly suggested they carry on the conversation at home.

Will poured a large measure of his father's best whisky into a fine crystal spirit glass, a glass he'd never been allowed to drink from. He took a tentative sip and looked up to the sky as if to acknowledge his father would be watching him angrily.

"Even in the circumstances, dad wouldn't approve of your drinking, especially his best whisky, and in one of his special glasses," Sarah said.

Will ignored his sister and took a substantial swig of the fine single malt. "This is so smooth it soothes rather than burns the back of your throat, unlike that cheap stuff they sell in the Old Crown at two quid a double." Will then reluctantly updated his sister on what he knew about the warehouse.

"A few months ago, I was with my mate Tariq when he went to get his Fiesta fixed at a garage on an industrial estate. We had a bit of spare time and went to grab a coffee. I saw dad's car pull into the estate and park up by this warehouse which I thought was odd. I made an excuse to Tariq that I needed to make an urgent call and snuck down to the unit. Dad hadn't locked the door so I entered and found him in that room with all those people in glass containers. Obviously, he was shocked and wasn't best pleased to see me. He became angry and paranoid; he accused me of following him. I didn't know how to react, but I shifted it back towards him and what he was doing in this warehouse. I demanded answers and couldn't believe what I heard. He swore me to secrecy. I'm sorry you've found out about it like this." His recollection was disrupted by an unexpected knock at the door.

"I'll get it," Sarah said.

It was Alice, a well-meaning but annoying neighbour. Alice was forty-eight years old, short, and slightly overweight, with shoulder length, dark hair tinted with patches of grey and emerald green eyes. Alice, who had long displayed amorous intentions towards Dr Leidenstraum, stood in an ill-fitting low-cut black and white striped knee length dress, and jet-black heels.

"You look nice Alice. Are you going out for the evening?" Sarah said whilst thinking Alice resembled a chubby Zebra.

"Thank you, Sarah. It's new. I'm loving the fit. It's just on the right side of cosy, so I will have to watch my calorie intake. Anyway, is your father in?"

"No, he isn't. You'd better come inside."

"Hello Will. How are you?"

"Hi Alice."

Sarah and Will looked at Alice, both struggled to contemplate what to say to her.

"There's no easy way of saying this, Alice. Dad died this afternoon," Sarah said, swallowing hard as she conveyed the devastating news.

Alice was momentarily rendered speechless and sat down on a chair. "I love him, loved him. Dare I say it, more than I love my Dave."

"I'm not sure this is the time," Will said.

"You're right. I'm sorry. I'm intruding. I'll go. I'll come and see you in the morning."

After Alice left, Will cut his sister a puzzled look. "It's a bit late for her to be coming around, isn't it? Where were we before we were interrupted?"

"The warehouse."

"Dad told me he'd bought the warehouse after mum died. To carry out experiments related to his work."

Sarah listened intently, scarcely able to believe what she was hearing.

"He was looking to a future where advancements in technology would see humans gradually replaced, so he was creating half human, half machine hybrids in an attempt to try and help preserve the species, as it were."

Will hesitated and then gave Sarah the earth-shattering news that their father had commenced his experiments by extracting DNA from babies in his work touring hospitals.

"No, no, he couldn't. How could he? Are you saying the people or whatever they are in those cubicles share DNA with teenagers out there in society; they are their robotic twins? And you've kept his secret. You haven't tried to stop him?"

"Actually, I've been helping him. As I'm studying IT at college, he asked me to conduct research for him into software development. He thought it would help me to improve my academic results. You know I've always been a bit of a techie geek, so it's like I'm part of building real Transformers or something."

"Can you hear yourself? How unethical all this is. Well, it's stopping now. Do you hear me?"

"Dad said you'd react like this. It's why he never told you. He wanted to. He wanted you involved. That journal he's written about the work he's done was for you, not me. In the event of his passing away or getting locked up, I think he thought you'd be able to follow his work because he knew I wouldn't be able to."

"I don't want to follow his work. This is insane. You can't be serious. I'm not doing it." Sarah stormed angrily upstairs.

"We can't just leave them there, they'll die. They must be tended to every few days. There's a process. I can't do it. I will need your help," Will shouted up the stairs after his sister, but she didn't respond. All he heard was the sound of her bedroom door slamming firmly shut.

The next morning, the atmosphere was tense as Sarah walked into the kitchen and was confronted by Will demanding the keys to the warehouse. He was evidently determined to take control of the situation and wear his sister down.

"I think we should go there together this morning. We can't start making any funeral arrangements until tomorrow anyway. We need to do this."

"Ok. Ok. We will go there together and we need to stick together. Not that I forgive you or dad for what you've done. Don't think that for a second. I'm thoroughly ashamed of the pair of you. Anyway, what is this process you were shouting about last night? To keep them alive I mean? What will we have to do?"

Sarah's reluctant willingness to get involved brought a wry smile to Will's face.

"Each of them is fed and watered through a tubing system and powered by a rechargeable battery pack. I don't know much about how it's done, but I know dad undertook these procedures every seven days without fail. He told me they'd be dead and unable to be saved if this wasn't done at least once every nine days. I guess it explains why growing up we never went on holiday for more than a week at a time."

Sarah forced a smile at her brother's humorous remark.

"I know you really don't want to, sis, but I think if we, if you take his journal, you will be able to work through it."

"His final diary entry was Friday so I guess that was the last time he fed them or charged them or whatever. We won't need to do that today, but I agree we should still go. I will put the journals and paperwork from the safe in a bag and take it with us."

Whilst travelling in 'Joanna' to the warehouse, *No Scrubs* came on the radio. Sarah turned up the volume dial much to Will's annoyance.

"I hate this song," Will said.

"It's better than that Slipknot rubbish I've heard coming from your bedroom. It's just not music, Will."

"That's what dad said. He kept telling me I should listen to the Beatles."

"Well, it would be an improvement."

"Trust you to side with him as always."

"Shush, I love this rap part of the song," Sarah said as she tried to mimic Lisa "left eye" Lopes, much to Will's amusement.

As TLC faded back to the DJ in the studio, Sarah turned the volume down and attempted to establish what had driven her brother to get involved in their father's work.

"I'm a bit surprised you wanted to help dad with this?"

"I've always been a disappointment to him. You are... were, his favourite. He'd always made that abundantly clear. This gave me an opportunity to work with him and prove my worth. I don't necessarily agree with it, but he's put a lot of work into this project and I think we should see it through."

They arrived at the site and parked up. "Hang on. When I was here yesterday one of them said my name. How is that possible?"

This resulted in an awkward silence as Will hesitated to respond. "It's part of the programming. They've seen photos etc."

"That's creepy. I don't like it."

"I thought you'd be flattered. I thought inanimate robots were your type, judging by that guy Simon you were seeing. Dad needn't have bothered with all this. He should have just experimented on him."

"Thanks a lot, Will. I take it the closest you've managed to get to an intimate relationship is still with your right hand?"

"I've got loads of interest. I'm having to turn them away. And I'm left-handed, remember."

"So, you've worked on these things?" Sarah said, anxious to move the conversation away from their squabbling and back to the important task at hand.

"No. Dad wouldn't trust me to work on them, but I've watched him working on them."

They got out of the vehicle and entered the building. Will tried to reassure his sister that all would be ok. Sarah and Will walked along inspecting each pod, with the same pace and attention as Her Majesty the Queen meeting entertainers after the Royal Variety performance.

The figure that had greeted Sarah the day previously said: "Hello Sarah. You came back."

"He..Hel...lo Hello," Sarah said.

As they reached the last two cubicles, Sarah noticed a black curtain covering a small square area behind a locker, like what you'd find in a leisure centre changing room.

"Have you ever been behind that curtain, Will?"

"No, I can't say I've ever paid it much attention before."

Sarah felt apprehensive and proceeded towards the curtain slowly. As she reached it, she placed her left hand on the dusty fabric and pulled it across quickly.

"AAARGH," screamed a voice at her from within a glass pod. Sarah responded in kind. Will grabbed hold of his sister and pulled her away from the pod, but then stopped abruptly.

"Oh my god. I don't believe it."

Gathering her composure, Sarah looked up and was as equally aghast as her brother.

The figure in the pod was a human robot hybrid of Brett Sadler, their next-door neighbour Alice's son.

Sarah and Will didn't recognise any of the others, but this freaked them out, as it was someone they knew. This felt personal. The figure in the pod was perturbed by Sarah and Will's gawping.

"What are you two looking at? Where's Dr Leidenstraum?" Sarah swiftly pulled the curtain across. The figure continued to remonstrate as they tried to comprehend that it was a clone of Alice's son.

For Will, the shock forced him to think more about the ramifications of his father's work. He'd minded a lot less when it was people he didn't know. This was different, he knew Brett. Whilst Will was slightly older, he'd grown up with him.

Sarah recognised her brother's anguish. She caringly placed a hand on his shoulder and they embraced, marking another rare tender moment between them. Will asked his sister what they should do, his earlier confidence and determination had seeped away in a heartbeat.

"We must grieve for him and plan the funeral. We need to talk to relatives and friends. I don't think either of us can deal with this right now."

Will nodded and they left the warehouse.

Sarah sat on the rusty brown leather couch in silent contemplation. She looked forlornly to her left at the matching empty chair and footstool. A white mug emblazoned with 'I Love Tenerife' in red letters, and a sky-blue coloured cereal bowl were on the glass table next to her father's chair. Sarah had bought the mug for her dad from a tacky gift shop whilst on holiday the year before. He had cherished it ever since. She smiled as she remembered parting with a few pesetas whilst her friend Megan complained about the sunburn on her arms, and wittered about how the waiter at the restaurant the night before was clearly in love with her. They had apparently locked eyes for at least four seconds when he served her paella. How much would the mug cost this year, now Spain had adopted the Euro as currency? Sarah wondered.

Will paced anxiously up and down the well-worn oatmeal carpet. He asked his sister if the revelations had changed her opinion of their father.

"I don't know. It really hasn't sunk in yet. I'm still in shock. I don't want it to, but I fear it might. I'm not ready to deal with that yet."

The pair discussed contacting various people to break the news of their father's death. Then the doorbell rang. Will opened the door and was confronted by a ghost. It was Brett Sadler.

"I've come to send my condolences," he said. Brett was fifteen years old, medium height, slim build with a mop of light brown hair. He was an unassuming young man, of a quiet disposition, and academic by nature.

Will was rooted to the spot, but then began to shake like the branch of a tree in a light breeze. He was speechless. Sarah walked through the lounge door, took one look at Brett, and froze also. Brett was perplexed by their reaction to him, but attributed it to grief.

"I'm sorry I probably shouldn't have come. I'll go."

"No. Please come in," Sarah said.

"I appreciate this is an incredibly tough time for you both, but I wanted to say that I'm very sorry for your loss. He was a great guy and I'll miss him too."

"Thank you, Brett. That's so very kind of you," Sarah said.

"If I can help with anything please let me know. Anyway, I'd better get going."

"Thanks, mate," Will said.

Brett left and Sarah gently closed the door behind him.

"Thanks, sis. Seeing him has really brought it home. I didn't know how to react or what to say to him."

"I know, it's hard to comprehend. My head hasn't stopped spinning."

2

Chapter Two: Choices

<u>Monday 5th July, 1999. 8.15am.</u>

Breakfast in the Leidenstraum household was always consumed sat at the oval-shaped mahogany table in the dining room. A grainy photograph of the family of four hung on the wall in a large, brown frame. It was perfectly placed to watch over the table. Will loved and hated the photograph in equal measure. He loved seeing them all together, which predated his own earliest memories, but he despised the bright green romper suit populated with teddy bears his parents had chosen for him to wear that day.

Sarah and Will's mother adored the table in the dining room. She had convinced their father to spend five hundred pounds on it at a specialist furniture store in Abingdon. They had suggested to their father it was time for something more fashionable, but he'd refuted the idea. He had joked it was because he wanted to continue to get his money's worth. The look in his eye suggested he just couldn't bear to part with it.

Will was sat at the table eating cereal and drinking a glass of orange juice. His sister joined him with a slice of toast smothered in marmalade and a steaming hot black coffee.

"Be careful not to spill your coffee, sis, this table cost five hundred pounds," Will said and chuckled.

Sarah smiled. "Dad did love talking about how much this table cost, didn't he? I think he begrudged her that five hundred pounds. He probably wanted to use the money towards buying a new car."

Their gentle reminiscence was interrupted by the faint sound of a phone ringing and vibrating. The sound appeared to be coming from a drawer in a tall wooden cabinet stood to the right of the picture frame. They looked at each other bemusedly. Will opened the draw and answered the phone.

"Hello Dr Leidenstraum. How are you this morning?"

"Hello. It's his son Will here."

"Oh. Well may I speak with your father please?"

"Who is speaking please?"

"I'm a friend. My name's John."

"Well John. I'm very sorry, but I'm afraid my father passed away on Saturday."

"Oh. I'm so sorry for your loss, Will." The phone then went dead.

"Hello? Hello...?"

"Who was that?"

"A friend of dad's called John."

The phone then beeped. It was a text message.

John: "Meet me outside the cathedral at eleven thirty. Don't be late."

"This is odd. What are we going to do?" Will said.

"Nothing. Aunt Janice is coming this morning and we're going to make the funeral arrangements. Reply to this John and tell him that."

Will drafted the message as per his sister's instructions and sent it to John.

The phone immediately beeped in response.

John: "Warehouse."

Sarah and Will stared at each other in shock and Will began to panic.

"Oh my god. Who is this guy calling himself John? How the hell does he know about the warehouse? This is freaking me out. We're going to have to meet him."

"No, we can't. Please try and stay calm, Will. Tell him we'll contact him later after we've sorted everything out and once aunt Janice has left. We'll then arrange to meet him."

Will: *"John. This is going to have to wait until later."*

They paused for a few moments in anticipation, but a response was not forthcoming. The doorbell then rang. It was Aunt Janice, their mum's sister.

"I'm so sorry, you two. Come here and give your Aunt Janice a big hug." Janice was fifty-three years-old, medium height, very overweight, with curly dark brown hair; she was twice divorced with no children. Janice was a fun-loving and a deeply caring person, but somewhat naïve. Individually, Sarah and Will had both been very close to their aunt growing up and were relieved to see her.

They talked things over and Janice offered to assist with the plans and reduce the burden for them as much as possible. Janice went out to her car to bring in her suitcase and bags as she'd planned to stay with Sarah and Will for a few days. Whilst Janice was doing this, the phone rang and Will answered it. It was John.

"Who is the fat woman collecting her belongings from the Punto?"

"How dare you talk about my Aunt Janice like that. Wait a minute. How do you...?" The phone then went dead. Will looked at his sister with sheer terror.

"AUNT JANICE," they both said, and ran outside to see a man approaching their aunt.

"Hello. Is it Janice?" John said. He was a tall man of athletic build, middle aged with receding blonde hair and the facial features of an inquisitive hamster. He was immaculately dressed in a light grey suit, white shirt and claret coloured tie with pristine brown shoes.

Janice turned around and smiled. "Yes. Do I know you dear?"

"No. I'm John, a friend of Dr... I'm a friend of Robert's. He'd talked about you and I'd seen some old photos. I've come to pass on my condolences to Sarah and Will." Both stood on the driveway looking anxiously at John, alarmed by what was going to happen next.

"Come in, I'll make you a nice cup of tea or coffee," Janice said.

"A coffee would be lovely, thank you. Milk and one sugar

please." John offered his sympathies to Sarah and Will; their faces were etched with fear and apprehension. Whilst Janice made the drinks, Sarah and Will accompanied John into the lounge.

"You're in danger. I'm concerned your father's death wasn't an accident. Stay away from the warehouse until I tell you otherwise –" he cut short what he was saying as Janice walked in with the drinks and asked John how he knew Robert.

"Through the medical profession. He was a great man who will be sorely missed. You don't have any biscuits, do you? Sorry to be a pain."

"Yes, we've got some digestives," Sarah said.

"Wonderful. They're my favourite."

"I'll get them," Janice said.

"They're in the cupboard next to the fridge, Aunt Janice," Sarah said.

"Clearly, I can't get into this right now with your aunt here, but I need to speak to you as soon as possible. Please give me a call." John stood up to leave.

"What about your biscuits, dear?" Janice said as she returned to the lounge.

"I'm going to have to run, unfortunately, but I'll gladly take two with me, or maybe three. Thank you very much for your hospitality." John nodded at Sarah and Will as he departed.

"What a lovely man," Janice said. Sarah and Will remained silent, unsure what to make of their surprise visitor. The trio then commenced the task of formalising funeral arrangements.

Later, Janice suggested she go shopping to get some food for the next few days.

"I won't be too long," Janice said. As she left, she noticed an envelope addressed to Sarah and Will lying on the porch floor. "There's a letter for you two. I'll put it on the table."

"Thanks," Sarah said as she and Will discussed calling John.

"We've got to find out more from him about what's going on," Will said.

"I agree, but he seriously scared me. He had a strange demeanour about him."

"I'm going to call him." Will dialled the number. As he did so, Sarah opened the envelope.

"Will, it's a letter from John. He must have left it on his way out."

At that point, Will's call was accepted. "Hi John." Much to Will's surprise, a female voice answered.

"Where's John? Who are you?"

"I'm John's colleague, Rachel, John's busy."

Sarah glanced intermittently at her brother, trying to establish what was happening whilst continuing to read the letter.

"Ok, well we're supposed to be arranging to meet with John."

"You can arrange to meet with me instead."

Sarah finished reading the letter and waved it at Will in a frenzy. The letter read: 'Don't speak to anyone else except me. If you receive contact from anyone else, don't trust them. If you contact me and reach someone else it means I'm in trouble. Do what you can to help me, but please don't endanger yourselves.'

"O... ok... Rachel.... Yes.... I guess we'd better meet you," Will said, whilst trying to digest the information.

"Meet me at the coffee shop with the blue sign on the High St in an hour. Don't be late."

"Yes, ok. We will see you there, Rachel." The phone line went dead.

"I thought I was scared, now I'm petrified. Do you think we should be meeting her?" Sarah said.

"I'm not sure what choice we have, sis."

Sarah and Will left a note for Aunt Janice and went to the coffee shop. They sat next to each other at the furthest table in the far left-hand corner of the shop. They sat facing the front door of the shop, with Will sat nearest the wall. There were about a dozen customers inside and two busy staff behind the counter. The toilets were on the opposite side of the shop. Sarah and Will were sufficient distance from prying ears. Will fidgeted nervously. He leaned on the edge of the table, accidentally smearing his arm with the remnants of a custard cream slice messily discarded by a previous patron.

"For goodness' sake, Will. Please watch what you're doing," Sarah said and handed him a tissue from her bag.

"It's not my fault the table is dirty, is it?" Will said as he wiped his arm.

"Keep your voice down. We don't want to draw attention to ourselves because of a bit of cake."

A thirtysomething, tall, attractive female with flawless skin, finely plucked eyebrows, and pearly white teeth entered the shop. She had rich and luscious dark hair. She wore a designer black suit. The fashion choice combined with her stern and humourless demeanour conveyed the appearance of an upmarket undertaker who had become separated from the cortege.

Rachel surveyed the shop with her ocean blue eyes. The way Sarah and Will stared at her gave themselves away immediately. That and the fact none of the other patrons were a day under thirty-five. Apart from a little boy in a pushchair nursing a rusk as his mum chatted on a mobile phone. Rachel walked over and sat down opposite Sarah.

"Where's John? How do we know we can trust you?" Will said. He was more scared than his sister, but desperate not to show it.

"A simple hello would have been a start. I'll get him on the phone if that puts your mind at ease."

"Hi John, it's Rachel." She passed the phone to Will.

"Hi John, it's Will. Are you ok?"

"Hi Will." Will felt relieved to hear John's voice, but then considered he didn't know John any more than he knew Rachel and remained guarded.

"We found your note, John."

"Yes. Sorry I was being very cautious. I wanted to make sure that should anyone contact you, you would be wary and challenge it. I'm sorry my colleague Rachel has had to meet with you in my place. I'm dealing with some urgent business. I'm sure you understand?"

"Ok John. No worries."

"Rachel will explain everything. I'll see you soon." The phone call ended.

Sarah and Will looked at Rachel with trepidation.

"Your father's work had obviously been kept top secret, but unfortunately there's been a leak. It is thought a security cleared IT contractor sold details of your father's work to a rogue foreign state. We've found out about it and need to protect you, as well as the important work your father was involved in."

"Rogue foreign state? What are you trying to say, that Saddam Hussein is after us?" Will said.

"Not quite, but you need to be aware that you're likely to be targeted as they don't appear to know the location of the warehouse."

Janice loved her Punto. It was a shade of purple, subject of a few repairs, and had clearly seen better days. Janice recognised the Punto was in many ways a reflection of herself. As she parked on the pebble driveway in front of the white garage door, Janice was completely unaware her every move was being watched. Janice unloaded the shopping from the car, but felt uncomfortable as she became aware of someone approaching her. She turned around. It was John.

"Hello John, you startled me."

"Sorry to frighten you, Janice. I can't find my wallet and thought I may have left it here earlier on today. I couldn't have a look for it could I?"

"Of course, you can, John. You don't need my help do you? I'd like to help but—"

'No, I don't need any help thank you. You focus on unloading the shopping."

They entered the house and John headed straight for the study. He rifled around, but was disturbed by Janice.

"What are you doing? You didn't go in here earlier. Why would your wallet be in here?"

"I didn't, did I? Silly me," John said, as an angry expression covered his face. They walked out of the room with John behind Janice. He reached into his pocket.

Rachel sipped her strongly caffeinated beverage, leaving a bright red lipstick mark on the side of her cup.

"I do love an espresso," Rachel said.

"If we're in danger, what are we going to do?" Sarah said. She didn't want to appear rude, but this wasn't the time for a polite conversation about coffee.

"Don't worry we will take steps to protect you."

"What about Aunt Janice? She's at our house. She could be in danger," Will said.

As Rachel was poised to answer, the sound of sirens could be heard approaching, followed by the screeching of tyres as several vehicles pulled up outside the café. Rachel jumped to her feet.

"Oh my god they've found us. Quickly, follow me to the fire exit." Sarah and Will did as Rachel instructed. As Rachel burst through the door, she was apprehended by uniformed police officers, wrestled to the ground, and placed in handcuffs. Sarah and Will froze and placed their hands compliantly in the air.

"William and Sarah Leidenstraum?" A female wearing a stab proof vest with her fist clenched firmly around the baton extended by her side said. "I'm Detective Sergeant Clare Stevens from Oxfordshire Constabulary. We need to have a chat. You can put your hands down." Clare Stevens was short to medium height and of slim build. She had a strong Scottish accent and possessed a facial expression and demeanour that would send a rottweiler into retreat. She had cold, squinting eyes, a convex nose, and nicotine-stained, uneven teeth. She exuded an aggressive authority and evidently commanded respect.

Sarah and Will looked at each other puzzled, stunned, and scared. They gradually lowered their hands.

"It's such sad news about my brother-in-law, John. I guess you just never know when your time is up," Janice said whilst walking to the kitchen.

John retrieved a taser from his pocket. He was about to strike Janice when the doorbell rang.

"I'll get it," Janice said turning to look at John as John hurriedly hid the taser behind his back. Janice answered the door to two uniformed police officers as John scurried out of view behind the kitchen door.

"Hi, madam. There's been an incident involving Sarah and William and we're here to make sure everything is ok," one of the officers said.

"Incident. Are they alright?"

"Yes, they're absolutely fine. Please put your mind at ease."

"Well, I'm fine, thank you. There's just John here looking for his wallet," Janice said, blissfully unaware of the peril the knock at the door had saved her from.

Both officers looked at each other anxiously upon hearing this and reached for their batons. One officer spoke into his radio. "Female at the location is safe and well. A possible suspect may still be at the premises," he said.

John listened intently from the kitchen as he desperately contemplated his next move. He noticed a key was in the back door. He slowly turned it to unlock and gently pulled the handle down, ensuring he made as little noise as possible. John darted down the side passageway into the back garden, and ran as fast as he could along the recently mowed lawn towards the rear fence, which he climbed with the vigour of an army recruit tackling an assault course.

As one of the officers entered the kitchen, he saw the open door and looked through the kitchen window at the exact same moment as John's legs cleared the fence. He was then able to make good his escape along the alleyway behind the fence.

"HE'S GOT AWAY," the officer said.

A frustrated DS Stevens heard this on the radio. "Ok, secure the scene and wait for another car to collect the female," she responded. She informed Sarah and Will that their aunt was ok and they would be taken to the station to be spoken to.

Officers provided Janice with vague information about what had happened and questioned her about John. All three were unaware that John was now in the vicinity of the front of the house. He carefully entered his car parked opposite, desperately trying not to attract attention. He reached into the glove compartment for his gun and contemplated returning to the house, even with the officers in attendance.

As John was about to step out from his car, another marked police car appeared in his rear-view mirror, drove past his vehicle, and parked a short distance in front of him. He hid from view as two visibly armed officers got out of their vehicle and rushed towards the house, where one of the officers present let them in.

John concluded the situation was now too risky and instead seized the opportunity to get away. He started his engine, which alerted officers in the house. Janice looked out of the window.

"That's him. That's John."

The armed officers rushed outside towards their vehicle as John sped away. They identified the registration details of the vehicle and commenced pursuit, but they were too far behind and quickly lost his trail. John had escaped.

In a car on the way to the station, Stevens heard the news. "I don't believe it," Stevens said, and punched the steering wheel in annoyance. "ALL UNITS IN THE LOCAL AREA, FOCUS ON FINDING THAT CAR NOW," Stevens transmitted across the radio. Sarah and Will looked at each other, both equally scared and bemused by the rapidly unravelling circumstances they found themselves in.

Stevens turned to Sarah and Will. "Everything will be ok. We'll get things sorted. Try not to worry." The tone in Stevens' voice and feigned look of hope in her eyes did very little to reassure them.

Sarah and Will were led through a corridor to a small room with a brown windowless door. The door had a small silver-coloured sign in the middle of it, with 'Witnesses' inscribed in black letters.

"I've never been in a police station before. It really does look just like Sun Hill Station on The Bill," Will said.

Stevens rolled her eyes. "Most offices look the same, William; this is just an office with people who wear a uniform. Please take a seat," Stevens said and closed the door behind them.

Sarah and Will again sat next to each other facing the door; Stevens remained on her feet. The table was somewhat sturdier than the one in the coffee shop. Will instinctively checked the table for cream; he wasn't going to make that mistake twice in the same day.

The door opened and in walked Janice. Sarah and Will both jumped to their feet at the sight of their aunt. They hugged her tightly. Janice was still none the wiser about the facts surrounding the unfolding drama.

"I'm glad you're both ok. What on earth is going on?" Janice said.

Stevens interrupted the reunion, introduced herself to Janice and shook her hand.

"I'm Detective Sergeant Stevens, Clare Stevens, and I need to speak to Sarah and Will privately. There's been some confusion around some of Dr Leidenstraum... Robert's work, and where he kept some keys to his laboratory. Nothing to be concerned about."

"Ok dear," Janice said, as she was ushered away by some other officers and taken to another room.

"Tell me what you know of your father's work, then I'll explain to you what's happening and what will happen next."

"He's been making human-robot hybrids that are clones of real humans and keeping them in a warehouse. We don't know a lot more than that," Will said, resigned to the fact the truth had to emerge.

"It's been going on for a very long time, since the eighties," Sarah said. "My father's not a bad man, is he? Please tell me he's not?"

Stevens took a deep breath. "I'll give you both a full overview of events. You will have to decide for yourselves the ethics and morality of your father and his work. I'd be grateful if you could save any questions you have until the end." Stevens proceeded to read from a briefing document:

"Dr Robert Leidenstraum was commissioned by the British Government in nineteen eighty to be a long-term scientific advisor in the development of interactive technology and software. This was with the objective of assisting humans in overcoming a variety of medical conditions and ailments. He would be a leading specialist in his field which would be known as biotechphilanthropical studies."

Sarah and Will raised their eyebrows. "No, me either," Stevens acknowledged.

"Dr Leidenstraum has conducted research and produced numerous papers for official purposes within government, scientific and medical circles. What he didn't communicate was that he had been conducting experiments outside of the scope of his brief for many years. In recent times some of your father's conclusions had drawn scepticism from other experts in medical, scientific, and technological fields and suspicion was raised as to how he was generating the results of his research. A top-secret undercover investigation was launched into your father. You'll appreciate that due to the sensitivity of the operation not many people were aware of it. However, rumours of a leak within the investigation started to circulate and a counter investigation was initiated which established that details of your father's work and the existence of a warehouse/laboratory had become known by,

shall we say, hostile countries who would be interested in these developments. The counter investigation established that the man you know as John, he himself a scientific advisor to the top-secret investigation, was likely responsible for the leak. At this point, we don't know if he's been paid for this or how he came to leak the information. Investigations into John have so far led us to the female you know as Rachel, but nobody else. The plan was to allow John to contact your father and take it from there, but your father's death has altered events and leaves you and the legacy of his work vulnerable to exploitation by dangerous individuals. Had your father survived, we would have been looking to arrest him for his actions."

"What happens now and what about his funeral?" Sarah said, as tears streamed down her face.

"We need to protect you and those closest to you, including at the funeral. We will take all necessary steps to do so."

"Once John found out dad was dead, why did he come to the house?" Will said.

"At the moment our working hypothesis is that John hadn't managed to establish the location of the warehouse. He was trying to obtain information about that and anything else of significance to your father's work. We're going to keep you in an apartment and you will have security twenty-four hours a day. Your home will remain under armed guard. We'll also be looking to put in plans to covertly guard the warehouse once we know where it is."

Sarah and Will looked at each other and nodded. "We know where it is," they said.

"Ok, I'll talk to you about that later. In the meantime, I can arrange for some of your things to be collected, but you won't be able to go back home for the foreseeable future. I know this must be difficult for you, but I'm sure you'll appreciate your safety is paramount."

"What about Aunt Janice?" Will said.

"She's going to be taken to her own house and will have officers covertly monitoring her address. She mustn't be told what's going on. The less she or anyone else knows the better. We'll let you speak to her on the phone later."

Sarah and Will were then taken to an underground car park at the station, placed into an unmarked van and escorted to the secret location.

In a quiet street near a country park, in a neighbouring town, a male sat anxiously in his car. His face and body were drenched in sweat. Tears filled his eyes. It was John. He took a photo from his wallet of a woman and two children. "I love you. I'm sorry," he whispered tenderly. A solitary tear dripped onto the photo. He reminisced about the many times he'd parked in this street to take his family to the park. His children loved the adventure play area almost as much as the sound of the ice cream van that inevitably appeared on cue, much to the delight of the swathes of children playing joyously. John was partial to a ninety-nine with raspberry sauce himself. Would he ever come here and buy his family ice cream again? Then his phone rang. His eyes widened with fear.

"Hello. Who is this?" his voice trembled.

"John, I'm not sure if you know, but Rachel has been detained. I hope you have obtained the information we require?" a male voice said.

"No, the police turned up. I was fortunate to get away without being arrested."

"This isn't good enough, John. I'm going to give you two days to resolve or else."

"Two days. How?" The phone line went dead.

John head-butted the steering wheel of the car four times in sheer frustration. He then received a text message from a number he didn't recognise which read:

Unknown: "To help you with your mission. Meet me at the coffee shop on Argyll Street tomorrow morning at nine. Don't be late."

Magnolia paint covered every wall of the sparsely furnished, but sizeable apartment. It had a cosy kitchen diner with white table and chairs which camouflaged into the matching clinical kitchen cupboards, work tops, and electrical goods.

"It could be quite a nice apartment, this," Sarah said. "With some different paint on the walls, and maybe some wallpaper and some pictures. The police protection budget clearly doesn't stretch far where furniture is concerned."

"I don't care about the colour of the paint and the fact there's no coffee table. I can't believe we're stuck here, it's ridiculous," Will said as he paced up and down the lounge.

"What else did you expect from dad pretending to be a modern-day Frankenstein? You thought it was cool and exciting him playing God. And you, trying to impress him by helping him. I just wish he were her to experience this, I just wish he was here."

Sarah held her head in her hands and cried what little tears she had left. Will hugged his sister; their father's death seemingly continuing to bring them closer together than ever before.

3

Chapter Three: Danger

Tuesday 6th July, 1999. 8:55am.

John had grown to like the coffee shop on Argyll Street. It was cosier than the one on the High St and unlike the one on the High St his wife's cousin wasn't the Duty Manager. She didn't like John and would invariably tell his wife if he dared to treat himself to a luxury chocolate brownie to accompany one of their delicious tuna and cheese melt toasties. John's wife didn't understand why the toasties weren't satisfying enough. She lectured him about the outrageous calorie content of consuming the unnecessary sugary snack.

The shop on Argyll St looked relatively quiet this morning. John entered and ordered a flat white with an accompanying packet of biscuits. He sat on a table with two seats in the corner. As he proceeded to melt a biscuit over his hot beverage, a tall attractive female in her late twenties with brown hair, wearing a smart grey suit jacket and skirt approached him.

"Good morning, John," she said smiling. She hugged John warmly which made him feel distinctly uncomfortable. "My name is Laura. Pretend we know each other and be convincing," she whispered.

John did as Laura instructed and awkwardly reciprocated the hug. "It's lovely to see you, Laura. What can I get you?" His greeting sincerely lacked any tangible authenticity.

"Skinny latte please, John. I'll pass on the biscuits," Laura said, as she elegantly took a seat. John stared intently at Laura with his face scrunched up in thought.

"What are you staring at? Go and get my coffee. We haven't got all day."

"It's just... well, you remind me a lot of Rachel. Only greyer. The suit I mean, not your hair, or personality or anything."

"Coffee. Now, John."

Upon his return with the beverage, Laura retrieved an envelope from her handbag and discreetly opened it to reveal photographs of Rachel's meeting with Sarah and Will leading up to the police raid and Rachel's apprehension.

Laura sniggered at the shocked expression on John's face. "Staying one step ahead is very important if you wish to succeed, John." Astonished, John merely nodded in acknowledgement.

Laura showed John a photograph of Clare Stevens taken during the arrest. "This is Detective Sergeant Clare Stevens. She announced her name during the arrest and Rachel slipped it to her solicitor in custody."

"The solicitor's corrupt?"

"Keep your voice down. Yes, of course he is. Do you think our employers would expect us to use the duty solicitor if we're nicked?"

"They're not my employers."

Laura smiled. "The Leidenstraum household is going to be off limits now. To complete your mission, you're going to need to figure out where they've taken Sarah and Will and the best solution to that is Clare Stevens. Now you know what she looks like, I suggest you stake out the police station, and follow her when she leaves."

"You want me to carry out surveillance of a police station and of a police officer? Are you mad? I'll get caught."

"John, you're displaying a very negative attitude. I suggest you show a bit more positivity about what you need to do and focus on the consequences of failure. That should help you to explore the art of the possible," Laura said, as she leaned in close to John. "If you know what's good for you, you'll do as you're told and you'll do it well." She kissed John on the cheek delicately and laughed.

"Thank you for the coffee, John. It's been lovely. See you again soon."

"I hope not," John muttered under his breath. He stared at the photo of Clare Stevens and worriedly contemplated the day ahead.

Will paced up and down the beige carpet of the living room. Every carpet in the apartment was beige. Magnolia walls and beige carpet. Sarah looked out of the window at the car park. Thirty-four parking bays, fifteen in use. Four of the cars were red. None of them were 'Joanna.' They both grew increasingly restless. Fear and grief had been fleetingly substituted with tedium.

Will received a text message from his friend Tariq:

Tariq: "Hi bro, what's happening? I've not heard from you and thought we could play Snooker later? Txt bk."

Tariq was eighteen years old, medium height with a stocky build and was a bit of a joker. He was one of Will's best friends.

Will responded: *"Hi mate, sorry I've not been in touch, my dad has died and things have been a bit crazy. My head is all over the place."*

Tariq replied: *"Sorry, bro. We must meet up soon."* Tariq turned to his sister Shabeela, aged thirteen, and said: "That's sad, you know?"

"What is?"

"My mate Will. His dad has died." At this point their father Tanveer entered the room.

"That is sad news, Tariq. How old was he?" Shabeela said.

"I don't know, to be honest."

"How old was who? What are you two talking about?" Tanveer said. He was a short, rotund man with an even shorter temper.

"My mate Will's dad has died."

"Will who? Not a name I've heard you mention much of before, son."

"I met him at college. We went to different schools so I didn't know him from before. He's got a strange surname. I think his dad was German or something. It's Leivenbaum or Leidenbeam, or something like that anyway."

"Is it Leidenstraum?" Tanveer said, with a look of horror etched on his face.

"Yes, that's it. How did you get that dad?"

"Well, it sounds German, doesn't it? It was obvious," Tanveer said sheepishly.

"Are you ok dad? You've gone a bit pale," Tariq said, perturbed by his father's odd reaction.

"I'm fine, son. I'm fine. I just need to get some air." He then went outside and sent a message on his phone:

Tanveer: *"WE NEED TO SPEAK NOW."*

The phone rang instantly. "What is it?" a male voice said.

"My boy knows Leidenstraum's son."

"Why the hell have you never said anything before now?"

"I didn't know, I've just found out. I had no idea."

"Ok, see what you can do through your boy to track him down. I've got someone else working on it as well."

Tanveer walked back into the room. "You should get back in touch with your mate Will and see if you can help him with anything, like the funeral."

"Why are you so interested all of a sudden?" Tariq said.

"I'm not, just trying to teach you some manners and respect, boy, which you're clearly lacking. Maybe you should arrange to meet up with him."

"I've made that offer, just got to give him some space to let him grieve I think and let him decide if he wants to get in touch with me."

"You're right, son. Just be there for him if he needs you."

Tariq and Shabeela glanced at each other, both suspicious of their father's unusually caring attitude.

John sat in his car watching the comings and goings of Oxford's boys and girls in blue. Who carries out surveillance of a police station, he thought to himself as he peered through a pair of binoculars that would be more suited to birdwatching. Is this what officers did when watching suspects? It wasn't a job John would want to do. A good friend of his from secondary school had moved to London and joined the police cadets. The last he'd heard, he had been promoted to Inspector and had married a sergeant. They'd had twins and were living in a leafy Surrey suburb. If only he could see John now.

John observed DS Stevens leaving the station in a car and started to follow her, but soon got caught up in traffic at a red light. In a split second he decided to swerve around the car in front and jump the red light, turning right onto the dual carriageway to maintain his pursuit of Stevens. Cars beeped furiously at John as a collision was narrowly avoided.

Unbeknownst to John, the beeping horns and his actions were witnessed by Stevens in her rear-view mirror. She realised the car matched the description of John's, thought it was too much of a coincidence and requested back-up. So as to not alert John, she maintained a steady speed, but amended her route away from the journey to the location of Sarah and Will.

Continuing to give her position and with back up units not far away, she pulled into the residential car park of an apartment block and parked up. John drove behind her and parked a few spaces further along. Stevens pretended to search for something in her bag and did everything she could so as not to alert John or arouse his suspicion. This caused John to panic and he became caught in two minds as to how to react. Impatiently, he got out of his vehicle and approached hers. She locked herself in. He banged furiously at the window, pulled out a gun and pointed it towards her. Stevens screamed and, with exquisite timing, police cars swarmed the car park. John turned around with the gun still poised. This was perceived as an act of aggression by armed officers who immediately discharged their weapons. John fell to the ground, blood trickled out of him and under Stevens' car. She got out of the car and tended to him on the ground.

"My wife and kids, please. You've got to help me. They've got my wife and kids. I'm not the bad guy," John said as he gasped for breath.

John was rushed to hospital by ambulance. Stevens accompanied him. Drifting in and out of consciousness, Stevens encouraged John to expand on what he'd said. She gripped his hand firmly. "Stay awake. Speak to me. Come on, tell me about your family."

"Kidnapped. They've been kidnapped. I was forced to do this," he said as he became increasingly weak.

"Who has kidnapped them? Come on give me something that will help me find them?"

John gasped and reached towards his trouser pocket. "Phone. Numbers in phone. Photos. Rachel."

"I know about Rachel, but I need other names. Anything you can remember."

"Laura. Laura," he said.

"Laura. Who is Laura?" Stevens said. She pressed John for more information, but he became unresponsive. As a paramedic tended to him, Stevens removed the phone, wallet, and keys from John's pocket. The ambulance arrived at hospital and John was rushed immediately into surgery. Stevens opened John's wallet and found the picture of his wife and children. She prayed that John would survive his injuries, but vowed to find them no matter what.

Detective Chief Superintendent (DCS) Paul Johnson was a domineering figure, very tall and stocky with broad shoulders; a talented rugby player in his youth, he was renowned for his expensive but ill-fitting suits and receding hairline. He was carrying a substantial beer belly and double chin; his reliance on alcohol evident in the angry capillaries that adorned his face like intertwining lines on a map.

Stevens entered the CID room and headed straight for Johnson's office. He was the senior responsible officer for the investigation and had trained her when she first became a Detective Constable. Clare had full faith in him as both a superior and a trusted confidante.

"Sir, I need to debrief you on this afternoon's events," Stevens said.

"Come in, Clare, and close the door," Johnson said.

DC Marcia Reynolds watched intently from her desk. She was a tall, well-built mixed-race female in her mid-twenties, very smartly dressed, and a recently qualified, but ambitious and eager detective who had asked to shadow DS Stevens as part of her development. DC Reynolds admired Stevens and had sought advice from her when she had sat her exams and applied to be a detective. Something in Stevens' demeanour made Reynolds think this could be a good opportunity.

"Sir, the subject who was shot. I don't think he's the cause of the leak in the investigation into Dr Leidenstraum."

"Clare, I find your response a bit of a surprise. All evidence points towards him and he's just followed you armed with a gun," Johnson said.

"Sir, whilst laying on the ground having been shot, he told me someone had taken his wife and kids. In the ambulance he again reiterated they'd been kidnapped. I think he's been set up."

"He'd just been shot. He probably didn't know what he was saying."

"Sir, honestly I am convinced he's telling the truth."

"Ok, I will assign some resources from here to work with you. It is best we keep it secret between us, Clare. I'm not convinced we can trust the others in the counter investigation."

"Thank you, sir. I appreciate it, but are you sure that's wise? It's a breach of protocol. The counter investigation was set up—"

"Clare, I'm well versed in the protocols of such matters, but this is an unusual case. I'd rather be confident in my own command and control, if that's ok? I will be completely responsible for this. I don't want you to feel I'm placing you in a compromising situation."

"Thank you, sir. I respect your decision." As Stevens turned around to leave the office, she saw Reynolds through the glass. Reynolds looked at Stevens with a willing smile. Stevens stopped and turned around to face the Chief Superintendent.

"Was there something else, Clare?"

"Actually sir," she pointed at DC Reynolds, "maybe Marcia Reynolds can help me. She's new and really keen. It could be a good learning opportunity for her."

"Errr no," Johnson stuttered. "She's still relatively new as you say and I think you need more experienced detectives for this. Please leave it to me."

"Sir, I'm sure she would benefit from—"

"Clare, Marcia has other things she needs to do. She will no doubt be able to support you on something else when she's more experienced. Trust me, I will find you some resources."

"Yes sir. Sorry. Thank you." Clare was disappointed in the response, but respected his decision gracefully. As Clare left Johnson's office, she looked at Reynolds and said: "I'm sorry, I tried. We'll definitely work together soon, I promise."

Reynolds smiled and nodded at Clare. "Thank you, Sarge. I appreciate it."

It had been frowned upon when Tanveer had put his mother

into a care home a few months ago. Tanveer's family, friends, and the wider Muslim community were disgusted with him. It was perceived as a shameful and selfish act not to take an elder into your own home and care for them as they had cared for you. Some people at the mosque had shunned Tanveer ever since. Tanveer wished he'd had a sister to take care of her; he had two brothers, but they were both overseas. If neither of them were prepared to give up their lives and return to the UK to look after her, why should he? Besides it was a nice care home, although culturally his mother had struggled to adapt, as her English wasn't very good. He was sure she was happy enough though.

Tanveer's phone rang. "I'm going to have to take this, Mum," he said. He stepped out of her room into the nursing home corridor and answered it.

"Has your boy got in touch with the Leidenstraum boy yet?"

"Give me a chance. I don't want to arouse any suspicion."

"You need to get a grip of this. Time is of the essence and I'm currently having trouble getting hold of the person I had looking into it. You need to show a bit more urgency, do you hear me?"

"Ok, ok. I will speak to my boy."

"You've got twenty-four hours." The phone went dead. In a panic, Tanveer phoned his son.

"Hi dad."

"Hi son. Are you at home?"

"Yes, why?"

"No reason. I am just with grandma and was going to have a chat with you when I get home. I haven't spent much time with you lately."

"Are you ok, dad?"

"Fine son, fine."

"Ok, I'll see you in a bit."

Tanveer said goodbye to his mother and drove home. He walked in the front door and shouted Tariq's name repeatedly and impatiently.

"Dad, what is wrong?" Tariq said as he walked out of the lounge.

"Nothing's wrong, boy. Can't a father be interested in spending time with his boy."

"Sure, but–"

"But what?"

"We don't spend a lot of time together, do we? We haven't

done for a long time. Not since before mum went to Pakistan."

Tanveer looked Tariq directly in the eye. "That's what I want to change. Even just having a chat. Let's sit down and have a chat in the lounge now," completely ignoring the reference to his estranged wife.

"Ok, dad." They sat down, Tariq on the sofa, Tanveer on a chair. There was an awkward silence.

Tariq's phone beeped. He instinctively retrieved the phone from his pocket.

"So, I say I want to talk to you and you're more interested in your phone."

"Sorry. What do you want from me, dad? It's a message from Will. Ok?"

"The Leidenstraum boy?"

"Yes, and can't you just call him Will?"

"How is he doing?"

"Why are you bothered?"

Tanveer looked at his son angrily.

"Ok. He says he wants to meet me, but he can't at the moment."

"Perhaps you could go and see him. Say that you'll go and see him."

"Do you think I should? Maybe he just needs time."

Tariq: "I'll come to yours if it's easier. We'll go to Snooker another time."

Will: "I'm not at home."

Tariq: "Ok, maybe I can meet you somewhere?"

Will: "That'd be good. Let's meet at the Snooker Hall actually. Give me two hours, ok?"

Tariq: "Ok bro. See you there."

"I'm going to meet Will at the Snooker Hall in two hours," Tariq said to Tanveer.

"Ok, son. I think that's a great idea. It's very caring of you for a friend in need of support at a difficult time. I'm proud of you." Tanveer then stood up to leave the lounge.

"Where are you going? I thought you wanted to spend time together," Tariq said.

"I do son, but–"

THE DOCTOR'S HIDDEN PATIENTS

"But what dad?"

"I've got things to do and you're going to be meeting your friend soon anyway."

Tariq stood up from his seat angrily, brushed past his father and left the room to go upstairs. Tanveer went outside into the garden and took out his phone. Tariq slammed his bedroom door and stared out of the window. He saw his father in the garden and opened the window ajar. Tanveer made a call, unaware his son was listening to him.

"My boy is going to meet the Leidenstraum boy at the Snooker Hall on Chamberlain St in two hours' time. I need reassurances for my boy's safety. Please tell me my boy won't come to any harm, please. Hello... HELLO." Tariq watched his father pacing and holding his head. As Tanveer turned around to face the house, Tariq dropped to the floor in his room to ensure his father didn't see him. Tariq messaged Will:

Tariq: "Yo bro, not sure about Snooker innit. I hurt my arm in the gym, you know? Meet me in the coffee shop opposite. Can you make it half hour earlier?"

Will: "Hurt yourself in the gym. A likely excuse. You need to stop watching porn, but yeah ok, I'll meet you in the coffee shop."

"I'm feeling a bit tired. I'm going to have a lie down for a while," Will said to Sarah.

"Ok, no worries. Are you ok?"

"Yeah, I'm fine."

Once inside his bedroom, Will opened a window and climbed out. He managed to hang out of the window by his fingertips and shuffled along to drop to the balcony below. He then climbed over the balcony and lowered himself until it was just a short drop to the ground.

Johnson sat in his plush glass fronted office and squeezed a bright red stress ball. He had a lot of outstanding paperwork to complete, but the sports section of his favourite newspaper sprawled out in front of him was competing for his attention.

DC Simon Lyle and DC Natasha Herbert bounded confidently into the CID office and knocked the door of Johnson's office. Clare Stevens briefly looked up from her paperwork.

Johnson slid the sports section out of sight and beckoned them in. "Tell Clare Stevens to join us, Natasha," Johnson said.

"Sarge," Natasha said, as she poked her head out of the door and planted a fake smile in Clare's direction. "The guv has asked if you can join us."

Clare Stevens put down her trusted black biro, walked to the office and closed the door behind her.

"Clare, I've spoken to DI Taylor and DS Simpson and they're able to release Simon and Natasha to help you review this potential kidnap," Johnson said.

Stevens wasn't particularly pleased with the resources Johnson had allocated to her, but didn't wish to appear ungrateful to a superior officer whom she held in high regard. Whilst she'd never worked closely with them, she was aware Herbert and Lyle both had mixed reputations at best amongst colleagues. "Thank you, sir. I have a plan of action in mind which Simon and Natasha can assist me with."

Simon Lyle was in his late twenties, a conventionally good-looking male who was fully aware of that fact, tall with blonde, perfectly styled hair. He swaggered, with a confidence bordering on arrogance, was streetwise, opinionated, and often aggressive. He was a challenging character who revelled in his polarising reputation.

Natasha Herbert was a cold, cunning, vicious, manipulative, short and slim female in her mid-twenties with shoulder length dark hair. Her persona made her less popular than Lyle with her peers, but she was respected by seniors for her demonstrable intelligence and diligence.

Stevens placed the items retrieved from John's pocket on Johnson's desk and listed actions to be taken. "I've noted one number from John's phone that's been in touch with him recently, but isn't stored as a contact. I think that must be a starting point. Natasha, can you please cross reference it with the phone seized from Rachel when she was brought into custody? Simon, we need to go to John Paterson's home and do a search," Stevens said.

Three miles away in Chamberlain St, Will occupied a wooden seat looking out of the window of the coffee shop. He ordered a latte and waited for Tariq.

A short while later, Tariq appeared. Tariq was clearly nervous and on edge. He had a worried look on his face and was fidgeting. A concerned Will asked him if he was ok.

"I'm fine. Do you mind if I sit facing the window? I've got a headache and need to get some light."

"Bad arm, bad head. I thought you were the one supposed to be cheering me up," Will said.

"Sorry, bro, how are you? I'm sorry to hear about your dad."

"Thank you. It's tough. I'm trying to come to terms with things, but I'm finding it hard."

"I can imagine. I know it seems a strange thing to say, but are you in some sort of trouble mate?"

"How do you mean? Why would you ask that?"

"I'm sorry, man, ignore me."

"What do you know?" Before Tariq could respond he saw his dad's silver-coloured Mercedes C Class car pull up outside the Snooker Club.

Tariq grabbed will. "We need to hide, bro. Stay away from the window."

"What the hell is going on, Tariq?"

"It's my dad. He mustn't see us."

"Your dad. Why, what's up with him?"

Tariq and Will squatted. Their eyeline was level with the bottom of the window. This drew stares from the barista and other patrons. To reassure them, Tariq laughed and said: "I'm hiding from my dad. I didn't wash the dishes as I promised." This convinced nobody and they looked away from them shaking their heads disapprovingly.

"The youth of today, they are a waste of space," one patron muttered under his breath.

"What aren't you telling me, Tariq?" Will said as quietly as possible.

"I don't know mate, I really don't, but something's not right.

My dad was pushing for me to meet you and I couldn't figure out why. Then, after I agreed to meet you at the Snooker Hall, I overheard him on the phone and he was talking about you, the fact we were going to be meeting at the Snooker Hall and talking about guaranteeing my safety. I was freaked out, which is why I asked you to meet me here. There's nothing wrong with my arm. I'm just a bit shook up by it. I said to come here so we could scope out the Snooker Club."

Will reflected for a moment and looked at Tariq. "I know what it's about, but I don't know where your dad fits in." At that moment, Tariq and Will's attention was drawn to two vehicles, one car and one van pulling up outside the Snooker Club. As two men got out of each vehicle, Tanveer got out of his vehicle and confronted them. A short exchange took place and all five men entered the Club. Tariq and Will looked at each other. Both were bemused, neither said a word.

Apart from a smattering of lights hovering above the rows of illuminated green baize cloth covered tables, the room was pitch black. Tobacco smoke filled the air. Stephen Hendry and Steve Davis wannabes eyed up their next pot with cues in hand. Snooker tables didn't look this big on television, Tanveer thought. What did his son find enjoyable about this game? Where was his son?

"Tariq isn't here," Tanveer said.

One of the men asked the owner if they'd been in. He responded he knew Will and Tariq, but hadn't seen them today. All five men left the club. As they did so, one of the men nodded to the others. Tanveer was set upon, punched repeatedly, placed in a headlock, and dragged to the van.

Tariq got up in an apparent attempt to leave the coffee shop to help his dad, but Will stopped him. "What do you think you're doing?"

"I've got to help him."

"You aren't going to help him by getting kidnapped as well. We need a plan."

The car and van started to pull away, leaving Tanveer's vehicle behind. "I've got it. I've got the spare key to his car. I've been driving it without him knowing sometimes. I did it to impress the girls at college because they laughed at my Fiesta."

Reluctantly, Will agreed. They left the coffee shop, got into Tanveer's car and began pursuing the car and van from a distance, with Tariq in the driver's seat and Will in the passenger seat.

"In the coffee shop you said you knew what all this was about?" Tariq said.

"My dad's been doing some weird science experiments for years. It turns out he attracted the attention of some dodgy people not long before he died, but I don't know where your dad would fit in. We had this guy John come to our house and then me and my sister met with this woman who knew John, and then the police turned up. It's been crazy, Tariq."

"No way, bro, I didn't know your dad was a scientist. But wait a minute, my dad is a scientist too, you know."

"What? I didn't know that."

"This John you were talking about. What does he look like?"

Will gave Tariq a detailed description of him.

"That sounds a lot like my dad's manager. This is crazy, bro."

The black leather two-seater sofa was ripped in no fewer than three places. It had at least four cigarette burns. How many people had sat on this sofa confronting their deepest fears and staving off monotony as Sarah was now? Sarah moved one of the cushions and could see some paper poking through the sofa seat. It was a five-pound note. Sarah pocketed it and smiled to herself that she'd found it and not Will. She'd use it for petrol money for 'Joanna', if she ever saw 'Joanna' again.

Sarah knocked on Will's bedroom door and called his name a couple of times. "I've found a fiver down the side of the sofa," Sarah said. Receiving no response, she entered and saw that he'd gone.

In a panic, Sarah immediately called Clare Stevens who was at the Paterson household. "Clare, my brother has gone."

"Gone, gone where? Have you tried calling him?"

"No, not yet."

"Don't worry. I'll call him now," Stevens said.

The pursuit continued as Will's phone rang.

"Who is that?" Tariq said.

"It's the police."

"Don't answer it."

"I've got to. Hi Clare."

"Don't you 'hi Clare' me. What the hell do you think you're playing at? Your sister is scared witless. Where are you?"

"We're in a pursuit. Someone has kidnapped Tariq's dad. I think it's all connected in some way."

"A pursuit? Who the hell is Tariq and who is his dad?" Lyle heard the conversation and sent a message on his phone, unbeknownst to Stevens.

"Look, I've got to go, Clare. I'll update you as soon as I can."

"Problem, Sarge?" Lyle said.

"Isn't it always?" Stevens said before calling Sarah back to try and allay her fears.

"Your brother's ok, I think. He's with Tariq, if you know him. You stay where you are and I'll update you as soon as I can." Sarah bit her fingernails and seethed with anger at her brother's recklessness.

Stevens and Lyle continued to search the Paterson home. Herbert then arrived at the property. Surprised by her arrival, Stevens asked Herbert why she had attended the address.

"All I can say is sorry, Sarge," Herbert said. Lyle then approached Stevens from behind and tasered her, causing her to fall to the ground in a heap.

"Now what are we going to do with her?" Herbert said, as DCS Johnson arrived.

"Let's ask the guv," Lyle said.

As Stevens writhed in pain, Johnson walked in. "What are we going to do with you, Clare? Always like a dog with a bone, you just can't let go," Johnson said.

Stevens looked up to see Johnson hovering over her with Herbert and Lyle watching on unsympathetically.

"W-w-w-hat is going on, sir?" Stevens said.

"Clare, I'm so sorry that I have to do this." He retrieved a gun from his pocket and ordered Herbert and Lyle to wait outside.

Both did as they were instructed.

"You're one of, if not the, best detectives I've ever trained, Clare. I trained you too well, if anything. It breaks my heart to have to do this, it really does, Clare."

"SIR, WHAT IS GOING ON? WHY ARE YOU GOING TO SHOOT ME? I'VE LOOKED UP TO YOU MY WHOLE CAREER. I NEVER HAD YOU DOWN FOR BEING CORRUPT. YOU'RE NOT A KILLER, I DON'T BELIEVE IT."

"I wasn't, Clare, but since Sharon divorced me, I've been really struggling for cash. I've got serious debts, and needs must, I'm afraid."

"What about Herbert and Lyle? Where do they fit in? There's always been rumours about them?"

"They both joined the police on behalf of organised criminals. I only found that out since I—"

"Became corrupt. You disgust me, Paul. You don't deserve to be called sir."

Outside the address, Herbert and Lyle heard a single gunshot.

4

Chapter Four: Bravery

Natasha Herbert admired the immaculate charcoaled block paving on the driveway of the Paterson's house. "I wish my driveway was like this," she said.

"You can't beat good old tarmac if you ask me, Tash," Lyle responded.

"It's a lovely street this, Si. There's a Porsche on the driveway over the road. I could see myself living somewhere like this."

"Never mind the old Porsche, can you believe the gaffer has shot–"

The door opened and Johnson shuffled out of the address. He was barely able to look Herbert and Lyle in the eyes.

"Are we going to just leave her here?" Lyle said.

"For now, yes," Johnson said. He instructed them to both

write up their pocketbooks and pretend to be continuing with enquiries. They were to say they'd found no evidence of kidnap at the Paterson address. He ordered them to follow him in his car.

The car and van followed by Will and Tariq pulled up outside a residential address. The van parked on the driveway and Tariq's dad was quickly bundled inside.

Will phoned Clare Stevens, but there was no answer. He left a voicemail with details of their location. Frantically worried about her brother, Sarah sneaked out of the same window as he had. She hid behind a tree in the car park and called him.

"Where the hell are you?" Sarah said.

"Relax, sis, I'm with Tariq on a stakeout," Will said with a smirk.

"You're out of order. You should have stayed at the apartment." Sarah's focus on chastising her brother was distracted by the arrival of two cars in the car park. It was Johnson, Lyle, and Herbert. They entered the apartment block.

"I've got to go, Will," she said ending the call abruptly. Her phone then rang. It was Clare Stevens.

"Are you still in the apartment?" Stevens gasped.

"No, I'm by a tree in the car park. Are you ok?"

"Can you see a taxi pulling into the car park?" Stevens said whilst fighting for every breath.

"Yes, why?"

"I'm in it. Get in it."

Sarah ran quickly and climbed into the taxi.

"Oh my god you've been shot," Sarah said. "We've got to get you to the hospital."

"That's where we're going," Stevens said.

"Why the hell did you come to get me rather than go to the hospital? Who shot you?"

"Get my phone, I missed a call. You're in danger. I had to come and get you. The guy that came to your house, John. He's been shot as well."

"What? Is he dead? Who shot him?"

"He's in hospital. Still alive as far as I know. He was shot by armed police. As was I, but by other police... who aren't and shouldn't be armed... but were?"

Sarah was confused, but retrieved the phone. "The missed call was Will. There's a voicemail."

"Play it."

Sarah shouted at the taxi driver to go faster.

"We're almost at the hospital," the driver said.

Sarah listened to the voicemail. "Will and Tariq are at an address."

"Help them. Don't call the police whatever you do," Stevens said.

Upon arrival at Oxford's main hospital, Sarah and the taxi driver took an arm each and carried Stevens into the Accident and Emergency Department. Blood dripped out of Stevens and onto the floor, like raindrops landing on a window ledge.

"HELP! HELP!" Sarah said. "She's been shot." This drew gasps from staff and patients alike. Two nurses ran over to help. One of the nurses called for a trolley and instructed a receptionist to press an alarm.

"I can't believe we've had two people shot on the same day," the nurse said as she stemmed the bleeding and held Stevens' hand.

"How am I getting paid?" the taxi driver said to Sarah.

"Are you serious?" Sarah said.

"My cab is covered in blood and I can't now work, so yes, I need paying. It's not my fault she's been shot. She should have called an ambulance instead of a taxi in the first place."

Stevens pointed to her handbag, which Sarah was holding having brought it into the hospital from the taxi. "There's money in my purse," she said faintly. Sarah retrieved the purse from the bag as Stevens was placed on a trolley and raced to theatre for surgery.

Sarah stared at the driver. "You want paying. I've got another address for you to take me to. Then you'll get paid and then you can clean your precious cab."

"Ok, that's fine by me."

As the lift pinged, a bead of sweat worked its way down the constable's brow and onto his nose. DCS Johnson emerged and walked along the plain turquoise carpet towards him; the buttons on his elegant blue shirt fought to hold back his paunch.

"Vanished. How can she have vanished?" Johnson said. He furiously berated the officer guarding the front door of the apartment.

"You heard nothing? Well, hopefully you'll be able to hear the sound of your P45 dropping through your letterbox." Herbert and Lyle followed him into the apartment. He closed the door, taking a final angry look at the guarding officer as he did so.

"Now what are we going to do, guv?" Herbert said.

"Try and find her. She can't have got far."

"What about Will and this Tariq?" Lyle said. "Are you going to tell—"

"No, we need to find them," Johnson said. "And we're the Police. So, let's get everyone on the force looking for them, shall we? You focus on finding Sarah for now. I'll go back to the station and brief the CID room."

"What about Stevens?" Herbert said.

"Wait for it to go dark and then remove her from the address. Make sure you clean up properly."

Will and Tariq were fixated on the address, completely unaware someone was approaching their vehicle from the rear. They were startled as a door opened and Sarah climbed onto the back seat.

"Where the hell did you come from?" Will said.

"I came in a taxi. It's not nice when people do things you don't expect, is it? Listen to me. Stevens has been shot and said we can't trust the police."

"What? Can't trust the police, can't trust my dad. What is going on?" Tariq said.

"Stevens has been shot. Is she ok?" Will said.

"I don't know. They've rushed her into surgery."

"We need to get to your dad, Tariq, find out what he knows. We reckon John is Tariq's dad's manager, sis."

"I'm afraid he's been shot as well," Sarah said.

"Too many people getting shot. I just wanted a game of snooker, bruv. I can't cope with this."

Tanveer was tied to a chair in the kitchen. A phone was placed to his ear.

"Now, Tanveer I don't know what your stunt was at the Snooker Club, but you won't outsmart us, do you understand?"

"I'm not trying to. They were supposed to be there. I don't know what happened or where they are. Honestly."

"I want to believe you, Tanveer, I really do. I need to make sure you're telling me the truth, ok?"

"O... o... oh... Ok," Tanveer said.

The man holding the phone to his ear took the phone away. Another male struck Tanveer with a baseball bat so hard his chair fell backwards with him still tied to it. He then struck Tanveer once again in the ribs with the bat which caused him to yelp in pain. Tanveer was untied from the chair and taken into the lounge where he saw a female and two children who were blindfolded, gagged, and tied to chairs. While restrained, the phone was placed to the ear of a very distressed Tanveer.

"You know that woman and those children, don't you, Tanveer? Well, you tell your son and the Leidenstraum kid to meet you at your house in the next hour or I'm going to give you an alternative. Their blindfolds will be removed, you will look them in the eye, and you will shoot them. If you don't, you can consider the baseball bat as a starter to the main course and dessert that'll be served to you. Don't even think about asking me not to hurt your son again either. It's your daughter you should be asking me not to hurt. I do love the wallpaper in your lounge." The male placed Shabeela on the phone, she was screaming. The phone then hung up. Tanveer started wailing and was dragged back into the kitchen and retied to the chair.

Tariq, Sarah, and Will considered their next move. Tariq's phone rang. It was Tanveer.

All three looked at each other in a panic.

"You've got to answer it," Sarah said.

"Sarah's right. Answer it, Tariq."

Caving into their pressure, Tariq tentatively accepted the call.

"Hi dad, how's it going?"

"I need you to come home as soon as possible son and bring your friend with you."

"Home. What for? What friend?"

"Don't argue with me, boy. I need you and the Leidenstraum boy to come home within the next hour, do you hear me?"

"Yes, dad. Is everything ok?" The line then went dead.

"I don't get it. He's asked me and you to meet him at home in the next hour. What is going on?"

"It's a trap," Sarah said. "It has to be."

"What are we going to do, sis?"

"We need Clare Stevens," Sarah said.

"She's fighting for her life, sis. I'd like to be optimistic, but I don't think she's going to be out in the next hour to help us somehow."

"Hey, look over there. Jehovah's Witnesses are knocking on doors," Tariq said.

"What's the plan then? For them to help us?" Will said.

"Wait, maybe they could help. I've got an idea," Sarah said.

Johnson strolled up and down his office. He ran his sweaty, shovel-like hands through what little hair he had left. He looked at the framed photo on the wall of him in pristine uniform that fitted like a glove; a full head of jet-black hair. It was oh so long ago when he had joined the force, with youthful exuberance and the best of intentions to protect and serve. His contemplation was disturbed by a knock at the door.

"Come in," Johnson said.

DC Reynolds entered. "Sir, there's been a report of an unidentified female turning up at the hospital with a gunshot wound. Uniformed armed officers are in attendance, but do you want me to go and find out who she is and see if it's connected to the guy shot by armed ops in any way?"

"Thanks Marcia, but.... no, I'll get Herbert and Lyle to go," Johnson said. "Why do you think it would be in any way connected to the armed response incident?"

Reynolds couldn't help but notice Johnson was behaving sheepishly which she found odd. "We don't ordinarily have many firearms incidents sir, and what with this investigation involving DS Stevens... I don't know the finer details but−"

"Thank you for letting me know and for expressing your thoughts Marcia, but assumptions can be dangerous things to make. Like you, I don't expect to see Oxfordshire turning into the Bronx, but as police officers we must maintain an open mind and learn to expect the unexpected. Now, if that's all? I'm busy."

"Yes, sir," Reynolds said and left the office perplexed by Johnson's attitude. She sat at her desk and contemplated what to do.

Johnson called Lyle: "You and Natasha need to go and clean that house up now and then you need to get to the hospital."

"Why, what's the rush?"

"I think Stevens is still alive, that's why."

"WHAT? How can she still be alive? You shot her. You did shoot her, didn't you sir?"

"Yes, yes. Of course, I did."

"Well, why is she still alive then?"

"I shot her in the body. I thought it would be enough."

"Sir, without wishing to state the obvious, why didn't you shoot her in the head?"

"I couldn't. I've known Clare a long time. I'm not a hitman."

"You're weak, sir. I'd have shot her in the head. As would Tash. We hate the bitch."

"I'm your superior officer, how dare you speak to me like that."

"You're corrupt, like us. Nothing superior about you, sir. Nothing whatsoever."

"I'd have no problem shooting either of you in the head, believe me. Now, clean up that house. And then get to the hospital and finish the job."

"Don't worry, sir. We'll finish the job and clear up your mess."

From her desk, Reynolds witnessed the body language of Johnson through his office window and became increasingly suspicious about what was going on.

"You can't be serious, sis. This is dangerous," Will said upon hearing the dynamic plan of action Sarah had outlined.

"I agree, but what choice do we have?" Tariq said.

The Jehovah's witnesses gradually moved closer to the address containing Tariq's dad. Then the garage doors opened. Sarah, Will, and Tariq's view was obscured by the van on the drive which now had its rear doors opened towards the garage. The van and garage doors were then closed. Two men climbed into the driver and passenger seats respectively, and the van drove off.

"We need to follow that van," Tariq said.

"No way, Tariq," Will said.

They both turned around and looked to the back seat for guidance. It was empty. Sarah had gone. They turned to the front. She was already talking to the Jehovah's witnesses who had reached the address next door. Will and Tariq looked at each other and contemplated what would happen next.

"Hi, my name is Sarah." She shook hands with the male and female who looked bemused. "I want to find out more about what you do. Can I watch you as you knock on the next door?"

"You're a Jehovah's witness?" the male said.

"Well, yeah. I mean no. Sort of. I want to be."

"Of course, you can watch us knock the next door. Maybe you can help us keep the door open," the female said.

"I hope so," Sarah said. She smiled, but then rolled her eyes as they turned their backs towards her and walked towards the door. They rang the doorbell and waited in anticipation.

A scary looking, tall stocky skinhead answered the door. "What do you want?"

"To inspire you with religion," Sarah said with a flirtatious wink.

"You what?" the male said.

The Jehovah's witnesses looked disapprovingly at Sarah and tried to engage the male more traditionally. He attempted to close the door, but Sarah placed her foot in the way.

"She's learning quickly," the female said to her colleague.

"Get your foot out of the door, NOW," the skinhead said.

"Give them a chance. Whilst I quickly use your toilet." She barged past the male as a second, equally intimidating, male appeared.

"What did you answer the door for? Who are you and where do you think you're going?" the second male said to Sarah.

"I need the toilet. Please. It's my IBS."

"IBS?" he said with a confused look etched on his face. "Ok. You can use the toilet. You deal with them," he said to the first male.

The male escorted Sarah upstairs as she observed the doors to the downstairs rooms were closed.

"Look, nothing against you people but I'm not the religious type so on your way," the first male said.

"We need to wait for Sarah."

"You can wait for her. At the end of the drive."

As the Jehovah's witnesses turned to walk away, a car screeched onto the drive and they leapt out of the way to their right-hand side onto the lawn. The car ploughed into the front door as the skinhead dived for cover. Will and Tariq crawled out of each side of the vehicle.

"Allahu Akbar," Tariq said. The Jehovah's Witnesses, holding each other tightly, looked up at him. "Or whatever works best for you."

The second male took out his gun and barged through the bathroom door. He was sprayed in the face with deodorant by a prepared Sarah. This left him disoriented and allowed Sarah to push him firmly out of the door, causing him to fall backwards down the stairs dropping his gun as he did so. At that moment, the first male got up to confront Will and Tariq. Will jumped off the bonnet at him as he reached for his gun.

Tariq also jumped in to help his friend, but they struggled against his superior strength. He fought them off and again reached for his gun. He pointed the gun in their direction and prepared to pull the trigger. As he did so, he was shot in the arm and then in the leg... by Sarah. He dropped his gun, which was quickly retrieved by Tariq. The second male tried to clamber to his feet at the bottom of the stairs. Sarah shot him in the foot. Will and Tariq froze in shock.

"Don't just stand there. Tie them up, get their phones and belongings, and we'll search this place carefully," Sarah said. Adrenaline coursed through her veins.

"You're scaring me, sis."

"And me," Tariq said.

"And me," both males said through gritted teeth as they writhed in pain.

"Good," Sarah said.

"What about the Jehovah's witnesses?" Will said.

"What about them?" Sarah said.

"They witnessed this. The irony," Tariq said.

"I don't care. You've just drove into a house and I've just shot the Mitchell Brothers. There are going to be plenty of people in the street who are witnesses and calling 999. Tie these pair up and get a move on so we can get out of here. We need to get to Tariq's house."

"Maybe there's something in the kitchen we can use to tie them up with," Tariq said.

He and Will moved cautiously towards the kitchen door. Will turned the handle gently; Tariq pointed the gun.

"I'll cover you, bro," Tariq said.

"Are you kidding? Get that gun away from me. I'm more likely to get shot by you than anyone else." Will pushed the door open and then dived to the right by the stairs. Tariq pointed the gun as his hands shook uncontrollably.

The door opened to reveal Tanveer sat tied to the chair with a gag in his mouth.

"Dad," Tariq said. He ran into the kitchen and immediately removed the gag.

"Hi son, I'm so pleased to see you. I will explain later, but we need to get out of here."

Will opened the lounge door and saw a woman and two children tied up. "Tariq, sis, you've got to see this."

"Untie me, son," Tanveer said.

"Hang on a sec, dad."

"I'm watching these two. What is it? We need to get out of here," Sarah said.

"There's a woman and two kids tied up in here," Will said.

"Then untie them Will and we'll use the rope for these two. Come on, hurry. Tariq, get the belongings off them. Which one of you has the keys to the car?" Sarah said as she desperately tried to take charge of the situation.

"Untie me, son. We can use my ropes to tie them up."

"Yes, dad. Good idea."

"No Tariq. Don't untie him. We can't trust him," Sarah said.

"Son, ignore her. They've got your sister and we need to get home."

"WHAT? No. Not Shabeela," Tariq said. He paused and became visibly upset.

"We really haven't got time for this," Sarah said.

Tanveer's phone rang. It was on the kitchen work surface. Tariq answered it.

"Hello, Tanveer speaking," Tariq said as he executed an uncanny impression of his father, much to his father's annoyance.

"Your boy Tariq and the Leidenstraum boy haven't turned up yet. I'm growing impatient and I've had a change of plan. I think it's best your daughter comes with me and I think it's best that I deal directly with your son. You will be killed. It was good working with you." The line went dead.

"They're taking Shabeela and they want you dead. What the hell have you done, dad?"

Tariq saw the baseball bat by the fridge. He picked it up and started to beat his father furiously with it. He was stopped by Will who dragged him into the lounge. As Will tried to calm him, Tariq couldn't believe his eyes.

"Mrs Paterson," Tariq said.

"You know her?" Will said.

"It's John's wife Cheryl and their kids Lucy and Robert." Will and Tariq untied Cheryl and the kids. Cheryl hugged her children tightly.

"Tariq, what are you doing here? What's going on?" Cheryl said.

"There's no time to explain. We need to go," Will said, seeming to have learned from his sister's dynamism.

They entered the hall; Will and Tariq grabbed the rope and started tying up the men. Cheryl noticed Tanveer tied to the chair in the kitchen.

"Tanveer. What are you doing here? Are you ok? Let me untie you."

"NO. DON'T UNTIE HIM," Tariq said. "He's somehow involved in why you've been kidnapped."

"WHAT?" Cheryl said, before slapping Tanveer around the face. She reached for the baseball bat, but was restrained by Sarah who had now made her way from the stairs to the kitchen.

"I'd like to have a go baseball batting him as well, but we've really got to go," Sarah said.

Tariq faced his dad. "When the police get here you do the right thing, dad, you tell them the truth, you hear me?"

"Come on Tariq, we've got to go," Will said as he placed a supportive hand on his friend's shoulder. Sarah, Will, Tariq, Cheryl, Lucy, and Robert all left the address and climbed into Tanveer's battered car as sirens could be heard approaching. They left the scene and escaped out of sight with seconds to spare.

5

Chapter Five: Confusion

Tanveer's Mercedes was far from the ideal conspicuous get-away vehicle as it had sustained significant, if not irreparable, damage. As Tariq navigated the suburban Oxford streets, other drivers and pedestrians watched shell-shocked as the bumper dragged along the floor. It generated the same display of bright orange sparks you would expect from an enthusiastic welder. The bumper finally fell off as Tariq turned right into Greenwich Avenue. It would weld no more.

Sarah's adrenaline levels overwhelmed her central nervous system. "What are we going to do now? Where are we going to go now? Did I just shoot two men? Is this car going to break down?" she said.

"Calm down, Sarah," Cheryl said. "Tariq, drive us to my house. John might be there. We can call the police."

Sarah, Will, and Tariq remained silent which did not go unnoticed by Cheryl. "What aren't you three telling me?"

she said.

Sarah placed a hand on Cheryl's arm. "We'll speak when we get to your house," Sarah said glancing in the direction of the children as she spoke. Cheryl nodded at Sarah with a terrified look on her face in anticipation of the news that awaited her.

As they entered Windleberry Close, a male and female were leaving the Paterson household. The male placed a bin bag in the boot of a car parked on the drive.

"Who the hell are those people, and what were they doing in my house?" Cheryl said. She grabbed the door handle, but was stopped by Sarah.

"NO CHERYL. THEY ARE POLICE." It was Herbert and Lyle. Sarah recognised them from when they had driven past her earlier at the car park. Everyone in the car looked at Sarah.

"Tariq, pull over and park on the other side of the road. Keep your head down everyone," Sarah said.

Herbert and Lyle then drove past them without realising. As soon as they were out of sight, all six occupants exited the vehicle and entered the house.

Back in the safety of her own home that she thought she would never see again, relief flooded over Cheryl and she embraced eight-year-old Robert and four-year-old Lucy, tearfully hugging, and kissing them furiously. Cheryl was a tall, slim, stunningly beautiful, elegant, and well-educated woman with glowing shoulder length auburn hair and piercing brown eyes. She took the children upstairs to their rooms, and then returned to talk to Will, Sarah, and Tariq in the living room.

"I want to know everything. Now! Including why my house smells of bleach."

"That's probably the one question we can't answer," Will said.

"I think we need to hear your story first. They have got my sister," Tariq said.

"Oh no Tariq, poor Shabeela. I'm so sorry. On Friday evening, I had been food shopping with Robert and Lucy, and decided to drive the scenic route home along Renfrew Lane. A black car sped past us and pulled in front of me. It stopped suddenly which forced me to brake harshly. I saw in the mirror that a van had stopped immediately behind me, so I had nowhere to go. Masked men with guns jumped out of both the car and the van and ordered us out. We were bundled into the back of the van, bound, gagged, and blindfolded." Cheryl became emotional again and was comforted by Sarah, who put an arm around her and held her hand.

"You must have been absolutely terrified?" Sarah said.

"I thought we were going to die. I was so scared for my children more than anything."

"Did they say why they were taking you?" Tariq said.

"No, they said absolutely nothing. We were driven for what felt like an eternity and then taken out of the back of the van. They put John on the phone to each of us to prove we were alive. I heard them say that if he didn't do as he was told he would never see us again."

"And you haven't heard from John since?" Will said.

"No, I hope he's ok. Is he ok?" Again, Cheryl sensed an awkwardness in the facial expressions and body language of Sarah, Will, and Tariq. "What has happened to John?"

Sarah, Will, and Tariq all looked at each other forlornly.

"TELL ME," Cheryl said.

"He's been shot," Sarah said.

"Oh my god," Cheryl said. She fell to the floor and wailed hysterically.

"As far as we know, he is still alive," Sarah said.

At that moment, Robert and Lucy entered the room.

"Where is my daddy, I want to see my daddy," Lucy said.

"What has happened to dad?" Robert said.

Cheryl embraced her children and held them tightly. They were both visibly affected by their mother's hysteria. Cheryl looked up at Sarah, Will, and Tariq. "We need to see him. We need to see John."

"I think the best option is for us to all stick together. I don't think it's particularly safe here, so maybe we could go and see him," Tariq said.

Cheryl asked her children to return to their rooms, which they reluctantly complied with.

"We need to speak to DS Stevens. If she's still alive, that is," Sarah said.

"DS Stevens? I thought you said we can't trust the police. And where does Tanveer fit into all this?" Cheryl said.

"The only police officer we know we can trust is Clare Stevens. And she's also been shot," Sarah said. Cheryl looked perplexed.

"As for my dad, we don't fully understand his involvement in this but he was trying to hand over Will to the same people who kidnapped you. We think it's all connected to some of Sarah and Will's dad's scientific work."

A phone rang in Sarah's pocket. She took the phone out and looked panicked. "It's the skinhead's phone."

"Give it to me, I'll deal with it. They've got my sister, remember." Sarah reluctantly passed the phone to Tariq.

"Have you disposed of the problem?" the voice said.

"If you're referring to my dad, we've left him for the feds. Now, where's my sister. You'd better not hurt her, you hear me."

"Or what, Tariq? Are you and Will going to pay me a visit? Are you a gangster now, Tariq?" the voice said, and laughed. "Tariq, you have a choice to make and the choice is between family and loyalty. If you want to see your sister again, alive and in one piece that is, you're going to have to work for me."

Tariq listened intently. The others stared and gesticulated at him in an attempt to establish what was being said.

"Are you listening to me, Tariq? You need to pay attention, do you understand? If you've left your dad, and Dean, that's the guy whose phone you have, and Terry, for the police, then good for you. It shows a lot of courage to make decisions, but going forward, I will make the decisions, and you will do as you're told, or Shabeela will pay the price, and you can have your sister's death on your conscience. You will lead me to that warehouse and you will make sure the authorities, and the Leidenstraums are none the wiser. If you make that happen, I'll release Shabeela to you unharmed. I'll be in touch." The call ended abruptly.

Tariq stood in contemplation for a moment whilst the others looked at him for answers.

"What did he say?" Cheryl said.

"It was the guy that's got Shabeela. I think he's in charge. He said he'll be in touch, but if we go to the police, he'll kill her." Tariq looked devastated. He was comforted by a sympathetic Sarah and Will.

The constable wore a high-vis jacket. She attached the blue tape around the lamppost on one side of the street, walked casually across the road and tied it to an adjacent lamppost. A few hundred metres along, this was replicated by a colleague. The cordon was in place.

"We saw everything officer," the Jehovah's witnesses said to an officer. They were ushered to the other side of the thin blue line, by the thin blue line.

"We will take your statements, but we need to secure this area for public safety, and sweep for forensics," the officer said.

Police evaluated the scene, and attempted to obtain information from Dean and Terry. Both were in too much pain to answer any questions. Tanveer was somewhat more forthcoming in his response.

"I am so glad you are here, officers. Please untie me. These racists kidnapped me, and said they were going to kill me."

Dean and Terry grimaced at each other in bewilderment.

"You're going to be safe now, sir," an officer said.

"Thank you, officer. I can't thank you enough," Tanveer said. He dropped to the floor and prayed.

"Sir, witnesses said that some teenagers crashed a car into the address, and left with hostages they'd freed. Why did they leave you?" another officer said.

"It is because I'm Asian, and a Muslim. The hostages they released were white."

"Can you tell me why you think these racists who kidnapped you would also have white people as hostages?" the same officer said.

"I don't know. Maybe the racists are loan sharks, and they owed them money or something."

"Sir, witnesses have confirmed one of the rescuers was Asian. Would they not have been keen to free you?"

"I'm not sure, maybe he was a Sikh. Discrimination exists between Asian communities, you know, it's not just for white people. Haven't you done your diversity training?"

"Ok, sir. I think we need to get you checked over by the ambulance crew. You've clearly suffered a deeply traumatic experience."

DC Reynolds updated her pocket notebook at an untidy desk in the CID room. She looked around and noticed every desk in the CID room was untidy; the whole room was untidy, and it had an obnoxious scent. Why did her predominantly male colleagues feel unable to dispose of old newspapers, crisp packets, sweet wrappers, and takeaway boxes, or wash up cups and plates? Did they expect her to do it because she was a woman? Marcia concluded there was undoubtedly a stench of misogyny to accompany the stale smell of sweat, doner kebab and chips.

DS Patel walked in. "I don't know what's going on today, Marcia. It's crazy out there," he said.

"Why, what's happened now?" she said.

"Apart from these shootings, some teenagers have drove a car into a house, and rescued some hostages. They shot the kidnappers and left them tied up at the address, along with another unconnected hostage, apparently," he said.

"Oh, I see," she said.

"Oh, I see too, DC Reynolds. I see OVERTIME. Kerching," DS Patel said. He strutted happily to his desk.

Reynolds felt more uneasy than she had done earlier that these events were not purely coincidental. None of this made sense. She decided to ignore Johnson, opting to visit the hospital to find out more about the female who'd been shot.

The Petersons had a beautiful home. As a stranger, you could walk in and instantly find it as welcoming as your own home. It gave you a warm, fuzzy feeling of comfort and peace. This was largely attributable to Cheryl. She had remained friends with a man named Latrice, who she had met at university. Latrice was a passionate interior designer and a slave to the art of Feng Shui.

Aside from scepticism for harmonising your domestic environment, and a total lack of interest in extortionately priced soft furnishings, John had originally demonstrated jealous tendencies towards his wife's friendship. That was until Cheryl pointed out it was more likely that Latrice would be romantically interested in John than her.

On this day, the Paterson's home had been violated, and wasn't its usual inviting, friendly space. As the group continued to deliberate over what to do next, the smell of bleach lingered heavily in the air. Latrice would be furious.

Tariq and Cheryl eventually persuaded Sarah and Will they should go to the hospital.

"We can't go in that wreck," Cheryl said.

"It got us back here, didn't it?" Tariq said.

"It's badly damaged, and will draw attention to us at a time when we need to be as discreet as possible. It is also about a mile's drive short of catching fire," Sarah said.

"That's a fair point. My mate Rizwan's brother is a taxi driver, but he's not working at the moment because he injured his foot playing football. He's got one of them six-seater vehicles. I'll ring him now. Whilst I do that, you'd better tell the kids their father is in hospital." Tariq called Rizwan.

"I'll tell them John is ill, but I'm not telling them he's been shot. I don't want to scare them any more than they already are," Cheryl said. She composed herself before going upstairs to speak to Robert and Lucy.

It was an ordinary Tuesday night at Oxford's main hospital; medical staff tended to their patients. Unbeknownst to each other, Will, Sarah, Tariq, Cheryl, Robert, and Lucy arrived in the hospital's car park driven by Rizwan, at the same time as an ambulance arrived with Tanveer, Herbert and Lyle parked up in their vehicle, and Reynolds arrived in hers.

"Which one of us is going to kill her?" Lyle said.

"I thought we'd both do it to be honest. Although I'm not sure how we'll get past the armed uniform," Herbert said.

Lyle chuckled.

"What are you laughing at?" Herbert said.

"One of them muppets shot himself in the foot last week. Didn't you hear about it? I'm sure between us we can outsmart whichever wannabe Rambo they've got in there tonight. The one thing they like looking at more than themselves, and their gun, is the ladies, so I think you might just have to use your charm...s, Tash," Lyle said. Again, he chuckled to himself.

"Well, if he's gay, I imagine you'll take over then," Herbert said.

'GAY? There are no gay armed officers. It's a job for the macho heterosexual alpha male," Lyle said.

Herbert rolled her eyes. "So, the last update was that they hadn't identified Stevens, right?" she said.

Lyle nodded. "The officers who attended weren't from our nick as the hospital falls on E nine's patch, and fortunately didn't know her."

"So, we're going to have to declare that we know her and incorporate that into the plan somehow," Herbert said.

"If we do, I think we both need to act really shocked, and you need to cry, Tash."

"I'm not going to cry, Si, don't be ridiculous. We're supposed to be hardened detectives, so I think we just settle for shocked. Imagine how shocked the uniform is going to be when we say she's a police officer? That's our element of surprise right there."

"It is, but then they'll want to be even more protective of her, Tash. That makes the job of killing her much more difficult. I think we should pretend we don't know her, and buy some time. Also, I have something in the glovebox that might do the trick, and not draw immediate attention." They looked at each other, torn by what action to take.

In the taxi, discussions took place as to what they should do when they arrived.

"I know this is nothing to do with me, but can I put forward an idea?" Rizwan said. "If you all go in there it's definitely going to draw attention. I reckon it would be better if some of you stay in the taxi with me."

"Good shout, bro. I reckon me and the kids wait here with Riz, and you go in and pretend to be concerned relatives. Obviously, I'd do it, but I think that would definitely raise suspicions," Tariq said. Riz laughed.

"Ok, yes. I think you're right. Do you two agree?" Cheryl said. She looked at Sarah and Will.

"Yes, let's do it," they said.

Cheryl, Sarah, and Will climbed out of the taxi. Tariq conversed with Riz in Urdu, so Robert and Lucy didn't understand what was being said.

"Look bruv, my dad is up to his neck in it. Shabeela has been kidnapped, and the guy that has her wants to find out where Sarah and Will's dad did his dodgy science experiments," Tariq said.

"What the hell, bruv. This is crazy. What have you got me wrapped up in?" Rizwan said.

"Riz, I hate to ask but I need your help, man. I think I know where the warehouse is, and I need you to confirm it for me."

"No way, Tariq. You go online and look up 'Frankenstein bounty hunters' or whatever this is, and leave me out of it." Rizwan was medium height with a slim build. He was considerably more streetwise than Tariq.

"What are you two saying? What language is that?" Robert said.

"We're talking in our language Robert. It's a respect thing and we're also talking about adult stuff, like girls," Tariq said as Riz nodded in agreement.

"Ugh. Girls," Robert said.

"Girls like Barbie?" Lucy said.

"No, not girls like Barbie. We're talking about Asian girls," Tariq said.

"Barbieinder," Rizwan said and chuckled to himself.

"Please, bruv, I thought you could ask Zams to help, as he's been in trouble for burglary, and you two are best mates," Tariq said.

"Zams owes me for some weed, so he might do it, but what am I going to tell him? How do you know where this warehouse is anyway?"

"Will was with me months ago when I went to get my car fixed at a garage on an industrial estate. We went for coffee, and whilst we were waiting, he made an excuse to go and make an urgent call. I thought it was odd, so I followed him without him knowing. I saw him enter one of the units there. Tell Zams the warehouse is a porn film location or something. Tell him it's Leidenstraum Productions."

"Ok, bruv. If it will help you get Shabeela back. Text me the address details, and however you spell Leidenstraum."

As Cheryl, Sarah, and Will approached the hospital, they saw Tanveer taken inside from an ambulance. He was accompanied by a police officer. They hid behind a wall so that he couldn't see them. They loitered near the front of the hospital before carefully manoeuvring through to the reception of the Accident and Emergency Department. They ensured they weren't spotted by Tanveer, who was somewhat helpfully escorted into a side room.

Cheryl asked the receptionist for the whereabouts of her husband, and having obtained the information, the three of them proceeded towards Ward number 101. They navigated the seemingly never-ending corridors like revellers in a maze; their anxiety was palpable.

As they turned the last corner, they saw a male and female enter the ward. They immediately recognised them from earlier, it was Herbert and Lyle. They stopped dead in their tracks.

"We need a plan before we go in there," Will said.

"You're right. If the three of us go in there, it's going to draw attention, and we don't know what those two coppers are up to," Sarah said.

"I agree. I'll go in and you stay here," Cheryl said.

"NO," Sarah and Will said.

"They've been in your house and they might have seen photos of you. I think it's better if they don't see you. You also don't know what Clare Stevens looks like. Thinking about it, I'm not sure how any of us are going to get in there," Sarah said.

"I've got an idea," Will said. His eyes widened as he watched an older male porter push a tall laundry trolley along the corridor towards them. "If you two approach him and distract him, I'll retrieve some uniforms from the trolley."

Sarah and Cheryl were hesitant but Will persisted. "Come on, this is our best chance. Approach him. Do it now."

Sarah and Cheryl reluctantly stepped in front of the porter's trolley. Cheryl asked him for directions to the maternity ward. The porter stopped, walked to the front of his trolley to speak to them both, and helpfully started giving them directions. Will walked past and sneaked behind the rear of the trolley. He made sure there was nobody in the vicinity who could witness what he was doing, and looked for items that would fit him. He did this as quickly, but as quietly as he could. As the porter concluded giving directions, Cheryl realised Will still hadn't found what he was looking for and tried to prolong the conversation.

"It's my friend from work's first child. It's so exciting, isn't it? Do you have children?" Cheryl said.

"Yes, it is. It's great news. I have three children. Two boys and a girl. They're grown up now of course. Anyway, I must get on."

Cheryl looked towards Will. He now had clothes in his hands, and nodded his head.

"Of course, I'm sorry to have troubled you. Thank you so much," Cheryl said.

Will moved away from the trolley and sat on a nearby bench. As the porter turned to return to the rear of the trolley, he hid the clothes from the porter's view. The porter looked at Will as he reached the rear of the trolley. Will smiled as the porter pushed the trolley along the corridor, none the wiser. Sarah and Cheryl both smiled at him, and said thank you as he walked past.

The three of them waited patiently for the porter to disappear into the distance. It felt like an eternity. They were so consumed by guilt they couldn't allow themselves to relax. Each of them thought the porter would discover what they'd done, would turn around at any moment, and shout 'THIEVES' at the top of his voice.

"I'm going to get changed," Will said. He scuttled along the corridor in the opposite direction to the porter and into a toilet.

Sarah and Cheryl breathed a heavy sigh of relief. They looked at each other and then at the now vacant bench. They sat down and stretched their arms and legs out to release tension.

As Will changed his clothes within the confines of a cubicle, he was overpowered by the latent smell of bleach masking other more pungent odours filling the air. As he placed his left arm into the jacket of the porter's uniform, his phone rang. "Aargh, why now?" he said.

Herbert and Lyle questioned the matron in her office about the respective conditions of John and DS Stevens. They pretended not to know the identity of the latter. The matron stated both were unconscious, and in serious but stable conditions, although it was hoped they would survive their injuries.

"Will you be finding out who this female is anytime soon?"

the matron said.

"We're making enquiries. I'm sure it won't be long," Herbert said with a knowing glance at Lyle.

In the cubicle, Will had awkwardly retrieved and answered his phone. It was Janice.

"Hi Will. Are you ok? I've not heard from you and Sarah. I've been worried sick about you both," Janice said.

Will placed the phone on the cistern on speaker, and continued to dress himself. "I'm sorry, Aunt Janice. It's all been a bit crazy what with the police and everything. We've not had chance to get in touch. We're doing ok, honestly," he said.

"I wanted to let you know, the funeral arrangements have been confirmed for Friday. Also, a Detective Chief Superintendent Johnson called me. He's in charge of the security apparently, and said they intend for you and Sarah to stay here with me on Thursday night. I can't understand why the police are so interested in your father's funeral."

"Johnson? Ok, we've not been told that, but we'll check. I'm sure it'll be worked out. I've got to go now. We love you, and we'll see you soon. Bye," Will said, promptly ending the call.

Will opened the cubicle door. He looked in the mirror, took a breath of anything but fresh air, nodded to himself, and proceeded towards Ward number one hundred and one. He stopped only to give his clothes to Sarah and Cheryl who wished him luck. His mind raced in a hundred different directions. He desperately hoped he wouldn't be identified as an imposter.

6

Chapter Six: Remorseless

A decade had passed since Will had last visited Oxford's main hospital. Ward number 228 was where he had seen his maternal grandmother for the final time. She'd suffered a massive stroke and was terribly weak. He vividly recalled standing by her bedside holding the Roland Rat doll she'd bought him a few years earlier, whilst Aunt Janice comforted a devastated Sarah. He adored that doll and took it everywhere with him. He was most definitely a self-confessed 'rat fan' as a young boy. Their grandmother had been instrumental in their early years following the death of their mother, particularly as their paternal grandmother had passed away two years before Sarah was born.

Will composed himself and stepped intrepidly through the doors to Ward number 101 as Herbert and Lyle were leaving the matron's office. Will turned away from them, anxious to avoid their gaze. He pretended to read a staff noticeboard as a bead of sweat emerged from his brow. Out of the corner of his eye, he saw Lyle look towards him. In his mind, Will told himself to remain calm as his heart rate pounded and the sweat beads multiplied. Lyle turned to speak to Herbert who hadn't noticed Will at all and then Herbert's phone rang.

"Who is it?" Lyle said.

"It's Johnson. I'd better see what he wants," Herbert said and answered the phone with "Yeah?"

"Why is he ringing her and not me?" Lyle said to himself under his breath and shook his head.

"Yeah? Yeah? That's no way to answer the phone to a superior officer," Johnson said.

Will stared ahead, the cogs in his brain whirred at the mention of Johnson. Aunt Janice had mentioned an officer named Johnson. Was this purely a coincidence?

"Sorry, sirrrr. How may I help you?" Herbert said.

"Tanveer Hussain is at the hospital. He is accompanied by officers. It has been deemed best he disappear permanently, but for now, he just needs to disappear. He's in Accident and Emergency so he's not going anywhere anytime soon. When he's finished you can tell uniform you're taking him to the station for interview but instead take him to... Well, you know where to take him to."

"Ok, got it, sir," Herbert said as the call ended abruptly. Lyle looked at Herbert impatiently. "After this, we've got to deal with Tanveer Hussain. He's here in the hospital." Lyle nodded.

Will's ears pricked up at the mention of Tanveer, but he'd become so lost in his own thoughts he was unaware the matron had noticed him from her office and was watching him as intently and suspiciously as a store security guard would a prospective shoplifter. She approached Will and asked if he was ok which startled him.

"Err yes. I'm fine," Will said with a look of guilt etched across his face.

The matron looked at Will sceptically. Fortunately, Herbert and Lyle were oblivious to the situation and were now heading further along the ward in the direction of the patients.

"Well, what are you doing here?" the matron said.

"I'm... I'm new. Yes, I'm new and they asked me to come here and collect rubbish."

"Really? It's a bit early for that. You, or a colleague would normally attend in about an hour to do that. You look quite young to be working here?"

"It's my first job out of school. Maybe it should have been in an hour. I must be mistaken. I'm sorry."

The matron looked at him and paused momentarily before giving him the benefit of the doubt. "Never mind. It's better to be early than late. They may have given you the wrong time as a prank, as it were. Come with me on my rounds."

"Thank you. I'd really appreciate that," Will said with a beaming smile. He was astonished his lie had worked but was unashamedly proud of his efforts.

He walked with the matron like an eager politician during a public engagement, asking pertinent questions whilst regularly looking in the direction of Herbert and Lyle.

Reynolds entered the ward and stood by the matron's office. A nurse approached her and asked if she could help.

"Hi, I'm DC Reynolds," she said showing her warrant card.

"Are you here to join your colleagues?" the nurse said.

"My colleagues?" Reynolds said with a bemused expression.

"Yes, two detectives have just been in the office with matron with regards to the gunshot victims. Matron is just doing her rounds if you'd like to wait or you're free to join your colleagues if you wish."

"Thank you. Thank you very much," Reynolds said as the nurse walked away to continue her duties.

The matron and Will were stood by the first bed on the left-hand side; the matron inspected the patient's charts thoroughly and explained what she was doing, but Will was distracted by the next but one bed along, which contained John, and was surrounded by an armed male guard as well as Herbert and Lyle. Will's attention was also drawn to the adjacent bed on the opposite side of the ward from where he was stood, which contained Clare Stevens and had an armed female guard. His scoping of the room drew the attention of the matron.

"Are you listening to me? What are you looking at?" the matron said.

"Yes, of course I am. I'm just taking in my surroundings. I'm not used to this. It's a bit of a shock, that's all."

"Sorry. I guess it's just business as usual for me. Come on, let's move along."

As they reached the next bed, Will could now eavesdrop upon the conversation between Lyle, Herbert, and the armed guard.

"Your lot failed with this one, didn't they?" Lyle said.

"We nullify the threat. Doesn't he look nullified enough to you?" the armed guard said.

"I thought nullified equated to dead. Maybe you lot need to get a bit more target practice in," Herbert said.

"Well, you can interview him now if you like. It'll be the same as if he wakes up: 'no comment,'" the armed guard said and sniggered.

Their unprofessional banter was abruptly halted by matron and Will's arrival. Will fidgeted nervously. Herbert and Lyle crossed the ward in the direction of Clare's bed, unaware Reynolds was watching from further up the corridor.

"I thought you said all armed officers were males," Herbert said.

"You'll have to talk to her about shoes and Sex and The City," Lyle said and shrugged.

Reynolds edged closer, strategically placing herself within earshot of them, but out of sight, she was stuck to the corridor wall, like Spider-Man climbing a building.

"We've got to try and identify this victim," Lyle said to the guard.

"Apparently, she arrived here in a taxi with another female. The female and the taxi driver left, taking her handbag with her," the guard said.

"Yes, she doesn't look like your average scumbag, does she?' Herbert said as she shuffled closer towards Clare and held her left hand tenderly.

Reynolds felt exposed in this situation and hampered by her inability to be able to see what was happening. Unbeknownst to her, she was being watched by Will, who was stood at John's bedside facing in her direction. His eyes darted around Ward number 101 like a kid in a toy shop; he looked at John, then matron, John's guard, Clare, Lyle, Herbert, Clare's guard and then Reynolds, who realised she was stood by the staffroom.

"Right. Let's cross to the other side of the ward," the matron said.

"Yes, ok," Will said.

As soon as the matron turned her back and with the guard's back facing himself and John, Will leaned in closely. "Hang on in there, John. Your family are safe. Cheryl, Robert, and Lucy love you," he said and squeezed John's hand. Will then obediently followed the matron and glanced right to see Reynolds entering the staffroom, which he observed contained a window with shutters looking down the ward, directly next to Clare's bed.

Herbert and Lyle continued to speak to the female guard, who was now stood up facing Clare, with Lyle to the guard's left and Herbert to her right. Will watched intently from the next but one bed and witnessed the flickering of a shutter and beady eyes peering through.

Reynolds watched Herbert and Lyle's behaviour and was confused, as, like her, they clearly knew the female in the bed was Clare Stevens.

The matron moved to the patient in the bed next to Clare's; Will followed her whilst desperately trying to capture everything, like an overexcited cameraman at a sporting event.

Herbert and Lyle's eyes locked. Lyle nodded. Herbert let go of Clare's hand and walked around the bed to form a barrier between the guard and Lyle.

"Check for marks, scars, and tattoos, Si. How long have you been an armed officer?" Herbert said as she turned to face the guard. This distracted the guard's attention and gave Lyle the opportunity to retrieve a pen case from his suit jacket pocket.

Will and Reynolds caught each other's eye as Lyle opened the pen case and took out a needle. Their pupils dilated with fear. Will walked as casually as he could to the right-hand side of the patient's bed and was now stood back-back with Lyle. Will glanced over his shoulder and saw Lyle preparing to inject Clare's wrist. He tried not to panic but was terrified. He noticed a jug full of water on the patient's table beside where he was stood. Almost instinctively, he flailed his right arm and knocked the jug off the table in the direction of Lyle. The jug and its contents flew into the head, neck and back of Lyle and onto the floor, causing Lyle to fall forward and the needle to propel out of his hand and under the bed out of reach. Lyle shouted out and the commotion drew everyone's attention to Will.

"I'm so sorry. I'm just incredibly clumsy," Will said.

"YOU IDIOT," Lyle said as he clambered to his feet and clenched his right fist. Herbert grabbed his left hand and Lyle realised all eyes were upon him.

"You really should be more careful working in a hospital, lad," he said.

"Yes, he should. I'm so sorry detective," the matron said staring sternly at Will. "Pick up the jug and clean this mess up. Then I think it's time you took the rubbish out, young man. Do you hear me? Come on detectives, let me take you to my office." The matron ushered Herbert and Lyle away and, as they walked past the staffroom, Reynolds again did her best Spider-Man impression, this time on the opposite side of the now familiar wall.

Will retrieved the jug and went to the staffroom to collect tissues to wipe the floor. He walked tentatively through the door. He and DC Reynolds looked at each other tensely.

"I'm Detective Constable Marcia Reynolds. Who are you?" she said flashing her warrant card.

"It's a long story and I'm not sure now's the right moment to discuss it, do you?"

"I'm a police officer. Do as you are told and answer the question."

"With all due respect, I've just prevented police officers from killing a police officer in front of other police officers, so why should I trust you? All I've seen is you skulking around suspiciously."

"Ok, as much as I hate to admit it you do make an undeniably good point, but I've no intention of harming anyone and I am a genuine police officer, unlike those two. I've identified something is not right and I'm skulking around as you put it because Chief Superintendent Johnson told me not to come here and therefore I need to be careful not to be seen."

"Oh, I see. Wait a minute. Johnson? Detective Chief Superintendent Johnson?' Will said as his eyes bulged wide and the colour drained from his face.

"What about him?" Reynolds said. She was perplexed by Will's reaction but the look on his face only added considerable weight to her own already growing fears.

"Nothing. My Aunt Janice mentioned him on the phone, that's all. I'd better clean that floor before matron comes back," Will said as he scrambled to change the subject and get away from Reynolds. He grabbed some tissues and headed for the door.

"STOP," Reynolds said with her voice subtly raised. Will turned to face her. "When you clean the floor, collect the needle from under the bed and bring it in here. Don't stab yourself with it whatever you do. After that, we're going to have a chat, do you understand?" Will nodded and left the room under Reynolds's watchful gaze.

"Aunt Janice," Reynolds mumbled to herself.

In the matron's office, Lyle dried himself off whilst the matron continued to apologise profusely, offering Herbert and Lyle refreshments.

"Very kind of you, but we're ok thanks, and really, there's no need to keep apologising," Herbert said.

As Lyle turned around, the matron noticed blood trickling down the back of his neck.

"You've got a nasty cut on your neck. I'll have one of my nurses tend to the wound." Before Lyle or Herbert could respond, the matron was already on her way out of the room.

"Tash, the needle went under the bed. You'll have to go and finish the job."

"How do you propose I do that exactly?"

"Say I've lost some keys or something and we think they might have come out of my pocket when I fell."

"Ok, I'll do it," Herbert said with a sigh.

Will cleaned the floor and carefully retrieved the needle with the delicacy of a bomb disposal officer cutting a wire. From a short distance away, he heard the matron beckon a nurse to her office and deliberately stayed under the bed like a naughty child trying to avoid further chastisement from a parental figure.

He watched the footsteps of the summoned nurse proceed in the direction of the matron's office and judged it was safe to come out of hiding. He firmly gripped the handle of the needle within the cover of the drenched tissues and smiled at the armed guard as he walked past her.

Will was relieved to see the back of the matron in the distance as she walked with the nurse, but as he was about to set foot in the staff room, he saw Herbert bump into them on her way out of the matron's office. The matron and nurse entered the office with the latter closing the door behind her. Herbert walked in Will's direction which caused him to panic and stand still.

"What are you doing? Get in here," Reynolds said.

Will did as he was instructed and gently closed the door behind him. He stood up straight like a soldier on parade with his back pressed up against the door. "The female officer is coming this way," Will said.

Reynolds darted to Will's position, pulled him away from the door and into the corner of the room where they huddled closely together. They remained so silent they heard every single anxious breath they took. The sound of footsteps grew louder; they braced themselves in anticipation of the door handle turning, but to their surprise, the footsteps proceeded past the door.

They both breathed a sigh of relief and, as the tension in his muscles relaxed, Will dropped the needle and tissues to the floor. Reynolds reacted instantly, picking the needle up and placing it carefully on the side.

"Search these draws and cupboards for a container to place

the needle in. I must preserve it as evidence," Reynolds said.

She walked towards the window where she carefully peeped through the shutters and saw Herbert about to get on her hands and knees by Clare's bed.

"I've found a plastic takeaway container," Will said.

Reynolds turned towards Will. "That will be fine, put it in that. We need to get out of here. Now," she said.

The armed officer stood over Herbert as she began scrambling under Clare's bed. "That porter cleaned under there just a few minutes ago. Maybe he found the keys you're looking for," she said.

Herbert shot up and banged her head off the underside of the bed in the process, much to the amusement of the guard. Herbert held her head and winced. From a seated position, she looked up to see the guard's reaction. "What are you grinning at? Make yourself useful and help me get up," Herbert said.

By now, Will and Reynolds were passing the matron's office about to depart Ward number 101, and nervously looked over their shoulders as they did so. Time descended into apparent slow motion; they stepped through the door and it closed behind them at the precise same moment the door of the matron's office was opened by Lyle and the closed door came into Herbert's view.

They were greeted by Sarah and Cheryl who were waiting

anxiously outside.

"Who's she?" Sarah said.

"The appropriate response to that would be the cat's mother, but the actual response is I'm the police so move it, and quickly," Reynolds said.

"Then I don't trust you," Sarah said, and stood rigid with her arms folded.

"We have to trust her. Well, for the moment at least," Will said.

"Thank you for your support," Reynolds said as she looked disdainfully at Will.

"I'm not going any... where," Sarah said. Her defiance was interrupted as Reynolds grabbed her firmly, placed her in an arm lock and tilted her head forward. Sarah shrieked and struggled for a few seconds as Reynolds marched her forward, before she eventually realised her resistance would prove futile. "Ok, ok. I'm coming with you, now let me go," Sarah said.

Reynolds released her grip but gave Sarah a firm push forward in the right direction as if to reaffirm her authority and ensure compliance.

"I spent two years on response going to pub brawls and domestics dealing with verbal and physical abuse, so don't think I'm going to tolerate your petulant, entitled attitude, do you hear me?"

Sarah stared angrily at Reynolds but sensibly didn't push her luck any further.

"I suggest we get to my car and we can all have a chat about things there," Reynolds said. Will, Sarah, and Cheryl nodded in agreement, but were all aware this was an instruction not a suggestion and their approval gave them a feeling of democratic choice when one didn't really exist.

Whilst this exchange was taking place, Herbert and Lyle had frantically checked every room of Ward number 101 and were now outside the ward, each looking left, right, up and down every turn, door, and corridor.

"He's vanished," Herbert said.

"HOW? He must be here somewhere," Lyle said as he furiously kicked the bench Sarah and Cheryl had earlier been sat at in frustration. "We need to find him and the needle," he said.

"Simon, I know we do, but this is a big hospital and we also need to deal with Tanveer Hussain. The porter or whoever he is, is going to have to wait. I guess Stevens gets a stay of execution for the time being."

"Ok Tash, we'll do it your way."

"It's not safe for us to sit here in my car and chat," Reynolds said. "We need to establish a common ground here, ok? I am a police officer, a decent one, regardless of whatever else is going on, and it is my duty to protect you. I think you're going to have to trust me and come with me to my flat where we can discuss this."

"I'm in agreement, but we need to get my children," Cheryl said.

Sarah looked at Cheryl, at Reynolds and then at Will. "I'll go with the majority vote," she said.

"Ok, your flat it is," Will said. "Cheryl's kids are in a taxi with my mate Tariq; his mate Riz is driving." Will paused and looked at Reynolds. "This trust thing between us. To work it obviously needs to be both ways, so it's probably best you don't ask too many questions about the taxi and Riz, ok?"

Reynolds looked at will awkwardly. "I'm a..."

"A police officer, I know. But you're also a person. A woman. A very strong, sexy beautiful woman," Will said slowly as he gazed lustfully at Reynolds and drifted into a world of his own.

"WILL, your raging hormones are so inappropriate," Sarah said.

"It's not raging hormones. It was her giving you a beating in the hospital that did it for me. She's quite a woman."

"Enough. I'll take it easy on the taxi driver. Just this once," Reynolds said as she winked playfully at Will. They then drove off in the direction of the taxi.

"Tanveer Hussain. We're looking for Tanveer Hussain," Lyle said, arrogantly flashing his warrant card at the receptionist of A&E.

The receptionist rolled her eyes and typed the details into the computer. "He's in treatment room number six," she said.

Herbert and Lyle approached the uniformed officer guarding the door. "You can go now, mate. The detectives will take over from here," Lyle said.

The officer knocked the door, and beckoned his colleague who was inside with Tanveer and a nurse treating him. Both uniformed officers left as Herbert and Lyle entered the treatment room.

"How are you, Mr Hussain?' Herbert said.

"I'm ok, thank you. All things considered. I'll be glad to get out of here."

"That's what you think," Lyle muttered under his breath.

THE DOCTOR'S HIDDEN PATIENTS

"What did you say?" Tanveer said.

"I said I'm sure you will," Lyle said and smirked.

"We are going to take you to the station and ask you a few questions. Your safety is our top priority," Herbert said with a menacing look in her eye.'

"Thank you very much, officers," Tanveer said, blissfully unaware of the peril of his situation.

7

Chapter Seven: Identify

As the evening progressed, the custody block filled with misguided souls who had found themselves on the wrong side of the law.

"One hundred and thirty-seven micrograms of alcohol per one hundred millilitres of breath he's blown on the machine, Sarge," the officer said.

"Almost four times the drink drive limit," the Sergeant said shaking his head. "It never ceases to amaze me that a person would consider driving a vehicle in such a state. No wonder he drove into that parked car."

"The car hit me, I'm tell tell... ing you the... truth," slurred a bleary-eyed male. He held onto the custody desk for support as his legs involuntarily swayed from side to side.

"The best of it is, Sarge, he has to drive for his job," the officer said.

"Well, he won't be driving to work in the morning," the Sergeant said.

The male reacted angrily to this, lifted his arms from the desk and attempted to throw a punch at the Custody Sergeant. His inebriated motor skills took him off balance and he collapsed in a heap on the cold, hard floor.

"Get him to a drunk cell with a low bench and search his pockets. Cell number six is free," the Sergeant said tutting.

With the desk now free, Rachel was escorted from her cell and brought to the custody desk by a detention officer.

"What is that smell?" Rachel said.

"It's the smell of a lengthy driving ban," the Sergeant said.

He duly informed Rachel there was currently insufficient evidence to charge her with any offences and she was to be released on police bail to return to the station in six weeks' time.

Rachel grinned smugly, collected her property, and departed the custody block. A stench of entitled arrogance filled the air. It was almost strong enough to mask the smell of alcohol and stale feet emanating from the remaining detainees wafting through the corridors of criminality.

Rachel inhaled the freedom of the warm Oxfordshire night air. Her moment of reflection was interrupted by the sound of a car horn beeping in the distance. Rachel looked to her right, and saw a taxi parked up with a hand waving at her through the window. She was intrigued, as she hadn't called anyone to say she was going to be released. She walked over to the taxi.

"Rachel?" the taxi driver said.

"Yes," Rachel said. Confusion etched across her brow.

"I've been sent to collect you."

"Really? I don't know how..." Rachel said and hesitated nervously, not knowing what to say, with her body language emitting a clear reluctance to accept the offer of a lift.

"I received a phone call asking me to collect a lady named Rachel and was given a description that matches you exactly. I've been told to take you to the Horse and Gallop pub."

Rachel smiled at the driver. The Horse and Gallop was a venue Rachel attended regularly when meeting criminal associates. This made her feel comfortable enough to accept the lift.

As the taxi pulled away, Detective Chief Superintendent Johnson watched through a window of the third floor of the police station. He made a phone call; a voice answered, Johnson said, "Rachel is on her way," and ended the call.

In a dirty, dusty, disused factory along the canal side, a man placed a phone in his pocket. He was dressed in an immaculately tailored navy-blue suit with a designer white cotton shirt and black silk tie. His balding head and rugged face were covered in so many lines it resembled a road map, villainy seeping through every pore of his body, a testimony to his life of crime and brutality.

A short distance from him, crying, scared, and shaking in a chair, with her hands tied behind her back and her hands and eyes covered with tape, sat Shabeela.

"Stop crying, little girl," he said. His croaky voice reverberated around every corner of the empty room, his vocal cords screamed from a lifetime of cigarette smoking, as if to parallel the echoes of the screams of the victims of his criminal activities.

Shabeela swallowed harshly and attempted to summon the strength to comply with the demands of her captor, as she didn't wish to exacerbate his anger further.

Accompanying the male and Shabeela in the room were Laura and one other male henchman.

"The Old Bill have let Rachel out and she's on her way. Be nice to see her, won't it?" he said as he stared intensely at Laura.

"Yes boss, it will," Laura said. She feigned a smile to mask how intimidated she felt.

It was quiz night at the Horse and Gallop pub. A handful of teams battled it out for the top prize of a gallon of beer. As a tricky question was asked about the capital of the island of St Lucia, a male approached the driver of the taxi which had pulled into the pub car park and paid the fare. Rachel recognised the male. She thanked the driver and climbed out of the vehicle.

"Are you buying me a gin and tonic as well?" she said to the male with a seductive wink.

"I'm afraid not. The boss wants to see you now," the male said.

Rachel looked at the pub and then at the male who shook his head. She got into a nearby car with the male, with another male already sat waiting in the driving seat. As they departed the pub car park, Herbert and Lyle departed the hospital car park with Tanveer. Both cars were now on their way to the same destination.

The sound of Laura's heels clomping along the factory floor started to grate on the easily irritated male. "Stop walking about and sit down," he said.

"Sorry, boss," she said with a quiver and immediately sat down at the nearest chair, like a competitive child in a game of pass the parcel when the music stops.

The creaking of a door could be heard. All eyes diverted in its direction. It was Rachel and the two males.

"Good evening, Rachel. I assume your stay at chez custody was a comfortable one," the boss said.

"I can't say it was the best day and a half I've ever had, but the fact it ended without any charges makes me feel somewhat better," she said.

"Jimmy messaged me to say you desperately wanted a gin and tonic. I stopped you from going into the Horse and Gallop so it's only right I bring the Horse and Gallop to you." The boss handed a glass of gin and tonic to a grateful Rachel who sipped the drink slowly and savoured every drop.

A stone's throw away, Herbert and Lyle grappled with a panicked Tanveer. "Please don't kill me, please don't kill me," he said sobbing hysterically as they forcefully dragged him from the vehicle.

"If you don't stop making so much noise, we'll kill you right here right now," Lyle said.

Herbert taped up Tanveer's mouth and they frogmarched him to the factory. They burst through the factory door, like unwanted gate crashers at a party.

Tanveer's fear turned to horror as he saw his daughter tied

up, bound, and gagged. His muffled screams could be heard through the tape encapsulating his mouth.

"Good evening, Tanveer. Lovely to see you. Give him a slap and tie him up will you, you two," the boss said to Herbert and Lyle.

The sound of her father's name made Shabeela rock in her chair and try to speak through her gag. The boss walked over to Shabeela.

"Daddy's here," he whispered in her ear sinisterly.

"I really enjoyed that," Rachel said as she digested the last of her gin and tonic.

"I'm glad you enjoyed it, really glad. Because it's the last gin and tonic you're ever going to have," he said staring viciously at her.

Realising her predicament, Rachel ran towards the door. The boss nodded and the henchman rugby tackled her to the floor, punching her hard in the face twice. The males who had driven her to the factory then assisted the male by tying her up with rope.

"I don't like failure, Rachel. Your arrest is indicative of failure," the boss said as if he were a judge summing up in court.

"But I didn't say anything. I wouldn't," Rachel said.

"Oh, I know you wouldn't. This isn't about failure of loyalty, Rachel, this is just about failure," he said walking slowly towards her which only served to prolong her fear. She looked up at him, her eyes begged for mercy. He knew this look well; he'd seen it in the eyes of so many men, women and children in his career. He crouched to her level, stroked her hair softly and kissed her on the cheek.

"Please, please," she said with a helpless whisper.

"The police know who you are now, they know all about you. They'll be all over your life. It's just a matter of time, and I'm afraid I can't have that. I'm sorry, Rachel, it breaks my heart to do this but we're going to have to terminate your employment, permanently."

"Don't kill me boss, please, please, please don't kill me."

He stood back up and walked away from her. He retrieved a handgun from the holster hidden under his suit jacket. He turned around and looked her dead in the eye. "I'm not going to kill you, Rachel. Laura's going to kill you."

Laura, who by now was herself shaking and in tears shook her head furiously at him. The boss placed the gun in her hand but she dropped it to the floor.

"Pick it up. PICK IT UP," he said and slapped her hard around the face. Laura fell to her knees and held her cheek for a few seconds. She picked up the gun and tentatively clambered back to her feet.

"I can't do it. I can't. She's my cousin, you can't," she said.

"I know that. But I need to know you're committed to this job. My cousin tried to rip me off back in eighty-seven. I had looked after him and paid him well. But greed got in the way and he wanted more. People always want more. In the end, it was the easiest kill I ever made and do you know why? Because I was so angry at him, I was seething. Other people rip you off, that's how the world is. But he was family and so it hurt me a lot more. We'd grown up together, climbed trees, played football. So angry was I, I didn't give him a nice death. I gave him a more unpleasant death than any of my enemies. I tortured him in ways that would make the devil himself cry. But I loved my aunt and uncle so much I made him write a letter saying he was going away and would never return, then chopped him into pieces and made sure he was never found. Once he'd written the goodbye note, I remember breaking every one of his fingers. I quite enjoyed that. Watching him write his last letter, like watching her drink her last gin and tonic. So, I need to see you shoot your cousin or I'm going to shoot you. Do you understand, Laura?"

Laura nodded. She looked Rachel in the eye and pointed the gun at her. She reached for the trigger but it was no good, she didn't have the courage to do it.

"She's never ripped me off. How can you expect me to do this, like you did to your cousin?" she said.

"Her failure could lead to you going to jail. Don't you think that once the police get into her life, they might then get to

THE DOCTOR'S HIDDEN PATIENTS

you? If she stays alive, she is a risk to you, a risk to all of us. I know it's tough but she has to die. Now shoot her," he said.

Laura directed her aim at Rachel's arm and then squeezed the trigger, the bullet grazed Rachel's shoulder causing her to yelp in pain.

"I'm so sorry, Rach. I'm so sorry," she said. This angered the boss. He slapped Laura even harder than before, took the gun from her hand and threw her to the floor.

"As I suspected, you don't have it in you. You're not up to this. Thinking about it, if they do get into her life, then they're going to get to you, and if John wakes up he can identify you, so actually you're as much of a risk as your cousin."

Laura's eyes widened with fear. She looked up at the boss, petrified, and before she had chance to plead for mercy, he shot her in the head at point blank range. "Laura, I'm sorry your services are no longer required," he said without the slightest hint of emotion or regret. Rachel screamed uncontrollably; the boss turned towards her and, without hesitation, shot her in the head.

"As you can see, I really don't like to be disappointed. For those of you in the room who are still breathing, let that be a lesson to you. Get them chopped up, and tomorrow they can be taken to Tony in North Wales and disposed of in the Irish Sea. Good evening detectives Herbert and Lyle, how lovely to see you. Grab yourselves a gin and tonic, there's plenty to go around, particularly now," he said with a sinister laugh.

"Now Tanveer, I think you want to save your daughter's life and, who knows, maybe your own if you're lucky. I've been in touch with your boy, and I think he might just be able to help." The boss took out a phone, typed a text message and hit send. "I've just sent Tariq a message. We shall wait and see what his response is. Herbert, hurry up with those drinks, will you? Dealing with staff disciplinary issues is ever such thirsty work."

Reynolds had bought her new-build flat as a home and an investment. She had been living with her parents, but it was time for her own independence and a space she could call her own. That space was now at a premium because of her need to accommodate half a dozen unexpected guests. Cosy wasn't the word.

She was keen to gather as much information as possible from Will, Sarah, Cheryl, and Tariq. Robert and Lucy were taken to a bedroom by Cheryl, who then joined Sarah and Will in the lounge.

"Where's Tariq?" Cheryl said.

"He's in the bathroom," Will said.

In the bathroom, a phone beeped in Tariq's pocket. He took it out, and the phone.

The Boss: "Your father is here now too. It's turning into a family reunion. Over to you Tariq."

He commenced urinating but became lost in thought, his aim drifted and he urinated over Marcia's tiled bathroom floor. Then the phone beeped to indicate the battery was low and his thoughts returned to the present moment. Tariq hastily cleared up the mess and joined the others in the lounge.

"Have you got a charger that would work with this phone, Marcia... sorry, Officer Reynolds?" Tariq said.

"Yes, I have and Marcia is fine. Has there been any contact?" Reynolds said. Her detective skills sensed urgency and panic in Tariq's request.

"No, it's just, well if they should make contact and the battery has gone flat..." Tariq's demeanour made Marcia suspicious.

"Perhaps I should keep hold of the phone?" Reynolds said.

Tariq looked Reynolds in the eye. "No, I think it's best I keep it as it was me that he spoke to, and it's my sister. Thanks though." Reynolds nodded and retrieved the charger. Tariq plugged the phone in.

"Right, who wants to go first?" Reynolds said. The others looked at each other in turn and then at Reynolds.

"I will," Sarah said, which broke the awkward silence. "Have you got a pen and paper?" she said to Reynolds with a smile. It was a clear attempt at breaking the ice following their earlier confrontation.

"I've compiled my fair share of witness statements, so yes I'm no stranger to a pen and paper," Reynolds said with a smile of her own that emitted genuine warmth.

"Please help me out guys if I miss anything. We, as in Will and I are the children of Dr Robert Leidenstraum, a leading scientist employed by the British government. Our father passed away on Saturday," Sarah's head fell forward slightly and Will placed a comforting arm on her shoulder, "and it has come to light he had been secretly making hybrid human-robots in a warehouse for many years. This information has been leaked and criminals are now seeking to find the warehouse and exploit our father's work, possibly on behalf of other governments. It looks like the leak is Tariq's dad, Tanveer, who is a scientist; Tanveer's manager is Cheryl's husband John. Following Cheryl, Robert, and Lucy's kidnap, John was forced by criminals to assist them in finding out the location of dad's warehouse in exchange for their safe return. We met up with a female called Rachel, who was apparently working with John, but she was arrested by the police and we were taken into police protection at a safehouse, well, apartment anyway. Will left the apartment and met up with Tariq. They saw Tanveer kidnapped from the Snooker Hall and taken to an address, which it turns out is where Cheryl, Robert and Lucy were being held hostage. John was shot by armed police after following DS Clare Stevens, seemingly with the intention of finding us, so that he could then find the warehouse. Clare Stevens collected me in a taxi from the apartment for my safety, having been shot by seemingly corrupt police officers who are probably working with the criminals. She risked her life for me; she's a hero. John and Clare are on the same ward where you met Will; the two officers who were there are the same ones I saw arrive at the apartment block in company with another officer, immediately prior to Clare collecting me, and who were at Cheryl's house when we went there earlier. Having taken Clare to hospital, I joined up with Will and Tariq outside the kidnap address where we forced entry, shot two men, beat Tariq's dad with a baseball bat and freed Cheryl, Robert, and Lucy."

"What's the betting the other officer at the apartment block was Chief Superintendent Johnson?" Will said. This drew baffled looks from all except Marcia, whose eyebrows raised. "Well, you did say to help you out if anything was missing," he said looking directly at his sister.

"Aunt Janice phoned me when I was changing into the porter's outfit. Our father's funeral is on Friday. She's received contact from a Detective Chief Superintendent Johnson who is in charge of security for it and advised he'd be arranging for Sarah and I to stay at Aunt Janice's on Thursday night. If this Johnson is corrupt, are we going to be kidnapped before the funeral or after or what?"

Marcia pondered briefly. "I need to get closer to Johnson, try and find out a bit more about what's going on with him in relation to all of this. For tonight, and for the safety of all of you, I suggest you stay here with me. I know it's not ideal for seven of us to be here in this flat but I don't think it's safe for any of you to go anywhere else. Tomorrow, we'll go to your house, Cheryl, so you and the kids can collect some clothes and personal items. Sarah, you and I are of similar build so I can lend you some of my clothes."

"What about me and Will? Do you expect us to wear your clothes as well?" Tariq said as he and Will laughed immaturely.

Marcia and Sarah rolled their eyes. "Well, you're both quite effeminate, it's only the poor fit that would give it away," Marcia said. Sarah laughed, whilst Cheryl raised a smile as the smirks were wiped off Will and Tariq's facial expressions.

"My brother has been staying with me. He's on holiday in Ibiza until next week. He still has some clothes here that should fit you two. He's very stylish. You're going to love them," she said. Will and Tariq looked at each other and shrugged.

As the occupants established plans for sleeping arrangements, Tariq took the opportunity to return to the charging phone. He ensured he wasn't watched as he quickly sent a reply to the earlier message which read:

"*I've got someone looking into the warehouse. Just give me a little time.*"

Ward number 101 was deathly silent, but the patients were thankfully still breathing. The occupant of one of the beds stirred, the fingers of one hand twitched and their eyes gradually opened. They attempted to move but grimaced in pain. This disturbed the guard at the end of the bed who turned around just as the patient closed their eyes.

8

Chapter Eight: Honourable

Wednesday 7th July, 1999. 4.55am.

The figure tiptoed daintily so as not to disturb the occupants of the flat, carefully opening the door which squeaked ever so slightly. Surely it wasn't loud enough to disturb the occupants, but then there was the sound of an almighty smash.

Marcia jumped out of bed and rushed into the kitchen to find Lucy surrounded by shards of broken glass.

"I'm sorry, I just wanted a glass of orange juice," Lucy said. She looked forlornly at Marcia.

"It's ok, sweetheart. Don't worry."

Cheryl entered the kitchen and berated Lucy which caused her to become very upset.

"It was an accident. It's just a broken glass. There's really no need to shout at her like that," Marcia said.

Cheryl calmed down and gave Lucy a comforting hug. "I'm so sorry for shouting, I'm so sorry."

"When can I see my daddy?" Lucy said.

Cheryl looked at Marcia and turned back to Lucy. "Soon Lucy, I promise."

They were joined in the kitchen by the others and they discussed the day ahead.

"I'll drive Cheryl and the children to their house, bring them back here and then I'll go to work. I think it's best you all stay here all day whilst I'm out. Don't go out anywhere or draw attention to yourselves." All reluctantly agreed with Marcia's plan.

The barrier to the Police Station car park was guarded by two uniformed officers. A bemused Marcia stopped and wound down the window of her vehicle.

"Good morning. I'm DC Marcia Reynolds. What's going on?"

"Increased security ahead of a VIP visit taking place later this morning. So, we need to check everyone coming in more thoroughly," an officer said.

"A visit from a VIP? I wasn't aware of that. Who is it?"

"It's on a need to know only basis, I can't disclose that information to you, mainly because I don't know who it is either," the officer said. Another officer made a note of the vehicle and raised the barrier to allow Marcia in.

As Marcia walked into the CID room, she could see Herbert and Lyle were with Johnson in his office. Discussions appeared heated.

"What is the plan for finishing Stevens off?" Lyle said.

"I'm working on the idea of seeing if we are able to coerce an armed officer to do it. I have it on good authority one of them who is due to be on the roster for hospital guarding is having an affair with his wife's cousin, who is a man," Johnson said. Herbert and Lyle looked at each other stunned. "He's only a couple of years from retirement. If this were to become public knowledge, he would face total ruin."

"What if Stevens wakes up before he gets the job done?" Herbert said.

"I'm afraid that's just a risk we're going to have to take."

"Well, if you'd done as you were supposed to..." Lyle said.

"Thank you, Simon. And if you'd not been thwarted by a junior porter last night, I suppose we wouldn't be in this position either."

Discussions were interrupted by a knock at the door. It was Marcia.

"Come in," Johnson said. Marcia entered.

"What do you want DC Reynolds? I'm busy." Herbert and Lyle looked at her angrily.

"Sorry sir. It's about this VIP visit?"

"And what about it?"

"I wondered if you needed any help. Is there anything that I could do to assist at all?" Herbert and Lyle sniggered.

"Sit at your desk, keep your mouth shut, smile and wave when the Minister walks in," Herbert said. She moved into Marcia's personal space and made her feel distinctly uncomfortable.

"Which Minister is that?" Marcia said. She stood firm and looked Herbert directly in the eyes.

"I'm afraid it's classified, Marcia. You shouldn't even know a Minister is visiting," Johnson said, and glared disapprovingly at Herbert. "Thank you for the offer of help but it won't be required. You can work with DS Patel today. Now, if that's all?"

Marcia contemplated asking why Herbert and Lyle were privy to the ministerial visit but thought better of it.

"Yes sir, that's all." Marcia left the office and closed the door behind her. She felt the retinas of Johnson, Herbert and Lyle penetrate the back of her neck as she did so.

"Typical, isn't it? It's a nice summer's day and we all have to be stuck inside. It couldn't have rained today, could it?" Cheryl said.

"Why can't we go to the park, mum?" Robert said.

"We just can't today. We need to stay here and wait for Marcia to return."

Tariq received a text message to his personal phone from Riz:

Riz: "Zams is going tonight."

"Who was that?" Will said.

"It's just Riz checking in," Tariq said. He then took out the other phone and, out of the line of sight of the others, messaged:

Tariq: "It's on for tonight."

He then quickly put both phones away as Will turned towards him.

"Are you ok, mate?" Will said.

"Yes, why do you ask?" Tariq said.

"Well, with everything going on. Your sister kidnapped and the fact your dad is—"

"I'm very worried about Shabeela. I've got to get my sister back safely. As for my dad, I'm just angry with him. I don't know what is going on with him. He's not been the same since mum left him and went to Pakistan. I really miss her. She held our family together." Tariq began to choke up and placed his right hand over his eyes, desperate for Will not to see him becoming tearful. Cheryl placed a maternal hand on Tariq's shoulder.

"I still can't believe your mum went to Pakistan leaving you and Shabeela here with your dad. Have you still not heard from her? How long has it been now?" Cheryl said.

'It's been eight months. I thought we'd have heard something from her by now. Dad has brushed her leaving under the carpet completely. He refuses to talk about it, which I find odd. I don't know if he's just embarrassed. I've thought about saving up and flying out to Pakistan to try and find her without telling him."

A convoy of swish cars swept into the car park of the police station which brought the attention of all staff to their nearest windows. Marcia peeked from behind DS Patel; her eyes parallel with his shoulder. A figure stepped out of the back of a sleek black saloon; his beautifully polished shoes gleaming in the sunlight.

"Who is it?" Marcia said, in far closer proximity to DS Patel's armpit than she would have preferred.

"I think that's the Minister for Security," DI Taylor said. "It's not often we receive this sort of attention."

"Maybe it's because we've seemingly turned into the O.K. Corral, guv," DS Patel said and laughed.

"You can laugh now, Sergeant but no good will come of this visit I promise you. We'll soon be under the microscope, scrutinised as to every little thing we're doing to reassure and protect the public and how we're going to solve the spiralling violence. That probably means my family holiday to Tenerife will be re-rostered which puts me in the doghouse with the wife and kids. Of course, the Security Minister will be under pressure to report back to the Prime Minister who'll then want pressure applied to the Chief Constable. You can guess the pattern of excrement rolling downhill from there," DI Taylor said.

"I'm surprised the Chief isn't here? There's only the Assistant Chief Constable with the Chief Superintendent," DS Patel said.

DI Taylor chuckled. "He's on holiday. Probably scrambling to get a flight back as we speak. Especially as the Deputy Chief Constable is currently recovering from surgery."

"So is the Minister coming to see us?" Marcia said. DI Taylor, DS Patel and others looked at her as if she was stupid.

"I think you're a bit naïve, Marcia. He's not here to see the rank and file. He's here to have a sausage roll and a scotch egg with the top brass in the main meeting room on the ground floor. He won't be getting a mark on those lovely shiny shoes traipsing up the stairs to see the CID office," DI Taylor said.

The Minister was escorted into the building and everyone retreated to their desks. Marcia knew she had to hear what was said at the meeting. But how? Marcia sat at her desk; her mind raced. Could she get close enough to the meeting room without alerting suspicion, she thought to herself. Her lips were dry and her pulse pounded. In a split second she acted decisively, climbed purposefully to her feet, and strode forward with courage and confidence.

As she reached the ground floor from the stairs, Marcia could see officers in the distance guarding the entry to the meeting room. She quickly darted into the ladies' toilets before anyone saw her. Marcia was desperate to establish a plan of action. She stopped momentarily and glanced at herself in the mirror, her reflection gave her the image of an outsider looking in at her actions. She felt a sense of pride that she was doing everything she could to serve her position with integrity despite the risk this invariably carried for her and her career.

Marcia looked up as if to seek reassurance from a higher power. It was in that moment she realised she could climb into the air duct running between the ground and first floor. She entered a cubicle, stood on the toilet seat, reached up and was able to remove a section of boarding. Marcia used every ounce of strength to push her frame through the gap, carefully moving the section back into place at the precise moment another officer walked into the toilets. Marcia felt more relieved than the unsuspecting person would soon be.

Eager to hear every single word of importance, Marcia manoeuvred herself along the unit in the direction of the meeting room like an army recruit tackling an assault course. Her timing proved to be as impeccable as Big Ben, an irony that surely wouldn't have been lost on the Security Minister seated a short distance below her, although the fact she was poised above him to hear him chime almost certainly would have been.

"The Prime Minister has been explicitly clear that we need to get a grip of this situation urgently, and certainly rather more quickly than has been the case so far. I shall be chairing a briefing with the intelligence agencies later this afternoon.

The Home Secretary is otherwise engaged so I've made the PM a firm promise that I'll be scrutinising the matter personally, and will be taking full responsibility for the outcome. I'll be very clear, gentlemen, if my head is on the chopping block you can consider that yours are also. Without sounding dramatic, careers are defined by moments such as these," the Minister said. His tone and fierce glance pierced through the immaculately pressed uniforms of the ACC and DCS Johnson.

"I certainly hope your Chief Constable is enjoying his holiday. I rather suspect he might find himself enjoying a much more permanent one soon. His absence of leadership in this situation hasn't escaped the attention of the Home Sec," he said, and grinned sarcastically. "Please tell me, what is the latest update?"

The Minister's personal assistant took out a notebook and pen, but as she did so the Minister placed a firm hand on her arm. "Oh no, Celia, they're the ones doing the writing. We will be leaving here with fully typed up briefing notes, won't we, gentlemen?" The ACC and DCS Johnson looked at each other and both nodded unconvincingly.

"Paul, I mean DCS Johnson is going to give an overview," the ACC said.

"Thank you, sir," DCS Johnson said. He stood up and walked confidently to the front of the room where he placed a briefing document on an overhead projector.

"Dr Robert Leidenstraum's funeral will be taking place on

Friday. It is our intention to deploy significant resource to this with the objective of ensuring it passes without incident and to protect the Leidenstraum family. Intelligence suggests this event carries the most risk to the family and Dr Leidenstraum's children, William, and Sarah in particular. We are anticipating hostile reconnaissance where their safety could be compromised by way of kidnap. It is a potentially volatile situation so we will have an increased covert armed presence in the vicinity of the church and strategically placed along the route there and back. The route will run from their aunt's house, a Janice Wilkins. Once the mission is complete, having given the Leidenstraums time to hold the wake and grieve for a short time afterwards, we plan to have Sarah and William Leidenstraum escort us to the warehouse where we will secure the site and process the site accordingly–"

"Thank you, Chief Superintendent," the Minister said. "But is this not a bit risky? Surely it would be safer to have the Leidenstraum children escort you to the warehouse before the funeral. Why don't you do that instead?"

DCS Johnson looked at the ACC for guidance. The ACC became flushed in the face and loosened his tie.

"We don't know where they are at the moment. We lost them yesterday," the ACC said.

"You've LOST them. Well, I suggest you FIND them. NOW, you imbecile." The ACC cowered in fear.

"With all due respect, Minister, they aren't going to miss their father's funeral," DCS Johnson said.

The Minister looked through him as if he wasn't there. "I don't recall asking to hear your opinion." The Minister looked at his personal assistant. "Celia, did I ask DCS Johnson to speak? I don't think I did, did I?"

"No, no Minister, you didn't."

"Assistant Chief Constable. Did I ask your subordinate to speak?" The ACC, whilst trying to avoid the Minister's gaze, shook his head furiously.

"Thank you, Assistant Chief Constable. Sorry, please allow me to correct myself. Thank you, former Assistant Chief Constable."

The room fell silent. Marcia was stunned into shock.

"Oh my god," she mouthed.

"Detective Chief Superintendent Johnson," the Minister said. DCS Johnson remained silent. "Sorry, please allow me to correct myself. Acting Assistant Chief Constable Johnson. You may enlighten me with your strategic acuity. Hold on a moment." The Minister looked at the ACC who continued to stare downwards. "I think you missed your cue to leave. Cheer up, it's a nice day outside. You can go and have a game of golf now or tend to your garden or something."

The ACC shuffled to his feet. "I've been a police officer for twenty-nine years. I have an impeccable record of public service. How dare you speak to me like that you−."

This statement brought the Minister to his feet. "I'd hold onto your tongue if you want to hold onto your pension, former Acting Chief Constable. Now get out."

The tension in the room was palpable, the ACC stared angrily at the Minister for what seemed like an eternity; the Minister's arrogance, contempt and outright goading provoked irrevocable fury in him. Out of the corner of the ACC's eye, Celia shook her head at him in an apparent last-ditch attempt to dissuade him from a costly outburst. Celia's intervention worked. The ACC picked up his hat, placed it on his head, gave a pitying look in the direction of Celia, one final angry look at the Minister, and as he walked out of the room, he sneered at Johnson.

"He shouldn't be angry with you Acting Assistant Chief Constable Johnson. He hasn't gripped this situation and has so little authority that you as a subordinate dared to challenge me, a Minister of the crown in his presence. You may continue with where you left off. I don't have all day. Something about the fact William and Sarah Leidenstraum won't miss their father's funeral."

Johnson was stunned. He paused for a moment. He composed himself and stood up perfectly straight. "Erm yes. It's Wednesday now and we've ensured that William and Sarah Leidenstraum are fully aware their father's funeral is scheduled for Friday. I instructed their aunt, Janice Wilkins to notify them by telephone and explain that we would be looking for them to stay with her tomorrow night. Wherever they are now, I fully expect they will go to their aunt's house tomorrow. I assure you we will continue trying to find them in the meantime and, if we locate them, then I will consider altering the plan."

"You have made a plausible argument, but I don't understand why we need the Leidenstraums to show us where their father's warehouse is. Why can't you find it without them?" the Minister said.

"We conducted an intricate search of the house but drew a blank. We found a safe which we removed from the premises but when it was broken into it was empty. I suspect whatever was in that safe is the information we need, and I strongly suspect William and Sarah Leidenstraum have possession of the contents of that safe."

"We'd better hope that nobody finds them or the contents of that safe before you do. That will be all," the Minister said.

"Yes, Minister," Johnson said. "Actually, there's just one more thing. What is going to happen to the Leidenstraums after Friday?"

The Minister shrugged. "They are a threat to national security and it is something that is on the itinerary for conversations I will be having this afternoon. I don't know what the answer is, but I don't think there's any conceivable outcome that involves them remaining free to carry on with their lives as normal. Now, if that's all?"

Johnson nodded obediently.

Marcia had heard every word and was now desperate to escape the claustrophobic confines of the air duct. She scurried back in the direction of the toilet; she was covered in dust and dirt, which she tried to brush away but to no avail. As Marcia carefully started to lift the section of the boarding above the cubicle it was unfortunately timed to view a person wiping away dirt, as it were. That person turned out to be none other than Natasha Herbert, and so this was a truly ironic stench.

Marcia patiently waited for her to leave and climbed down into the cubicle. She looked at herself in the mirror, proud to have preserved her integrity if not her dignity.

9

Chapter Nine: Perilous

On Friday 10th of February 1989, Paul Johnson married Sharon Dawson at a Registry Office in Cambridge. His final night of freedom had been a trip to the cinema to watch Die Hard. He envisaged running around a building in his vest barefoot, battling terrorists. He could most definitely see himself as Oxford's answer to John McClane. The weekend before had been his stag do in Blackpool. It had been a debauched affair. It was a good job Sharon had been none the wiser.

Sharon was a bubbly twenty-two-year-old, and twelve years his junior. Her family had begged her not to marry a divorced policeman with two young children. They'd said it would end in tears, and it had.

They'd met at the Rugby Club's annual gala night. Sharon was working there part-time as a barmaid to make some extra cash. Johnson had charmed her as she poured his sixth pint of Guinness of the evening. He had continued to charm barmaids, and policewomen, and any other female with a pulse throughout their marriage. She discovered one of his dalliances and forgave him. He promised to change; he didn't. The discovery of a second affair was the final nail in the coffin for their marriage, and she vowed to make him pay. She'd stayed true to that alright. She'd got him by the balls, and not in the pleasurable way that had contributed to his downfall.

Johnson summoned Herbert and Lyle to his office. He opened a folder and placed the contents on his desk.

"What did the Minister have to say?" Lyle said.

"He was so impressed with me he fired the ACC. So, you're looking at the new ACC," Johnson said with a wry grin.

Herbert and Lyle looked at each other and laughed.

"You're hilarious, Assistant Chief Constable," Herbert said.

"Thank you, Natasha. I'm pleased to see you're addressing my rank correctly already."

"You aren't kidding, are you?" Lyle said and frowned.

Johnson looked at them smugly.

"As the new Assistant Chief Constable, I've just received this. It's the case file from the team who searched the Leidenstraum address." Johnson took out two pieces of paper, they were A4 sized copies of photographs of William and Sarah Leidenstraum. "Do everything you can to find these two as soon as possible."

Lyle gasped. "That's the idiot porter from the hospital," he said.

"That is William Leidenstraum," Johnson said. "I don't think you'll find he works as a hospital porter."

"What? It's definitely him. Isn't it, Tash?"

Herbert looked closely at the page. "Yes, that's him."

"So, you had them in your grasp and they got away. Not so much Herbert and Lyle, more Laurel and Hardy."

Herbert and Lyle fumed. "What about Stevens?" Lyle said.

"I've just had confirmation it will be taken care of tonight. Hopefully, that won't end up being another fine mess you've gotten us into," Johnson said with a smirk.

"Fine mess you've gotten us into more like," Herbert said. "It's quite fitting you've been promoted to ACC, you're of the required level of competence and narcissism to fulfil the role adequately."

"Come on, Tash, let's go," Lyle said.

"Close the ACC's door on the way out you two." He whistled the Laurel and Hardy theme tune as they departed.

Sarah and Will were only a few years younger than Marcia. How could she explain to them the British government perceived them as an existential threat to national security. She'd not received the training for dealing with a situation like this.

"What on earth happened to you?" Cheryl said as Marcia entered the flat.

"What can I say. Police work is a dirty job but someone must do it, Cheryl."

"Will, Sarah, do you have the contents of your father's safe?" Marcia said.

"Yes, they're still in my bag. They've been in there since Sunday. Why?" Sarah said.

"Wait a minute, how do you know about our father's safe, and why are you covered in dirt and dust?" Will said.

Marcia hesitated as all eyes in the room gazed upon her. "This conversation isn't one for the children's ears. Sorry kids."

Robert and Lucy looked at Marcia with annoyance.

"This is so unfair," Robert said before skulking off towards a bedroom.

Lucy followed her brother, but stopped directly next to Marcia and looked up at her with squinted eyes. "Why are we always the ones getting discriminated against?" Lucy said. She stamped her foot in temper and crossed her arms.

"That's enough, you two," Cheryl said in a raised voice. She was keen to convey authority and conceal her embarrassment at her children's dissent.

"The reason I look like this is because I hid in an air vent at the station to listen to a meeting."

Will, Sarah, Cheryl, and Tariq all looked at each other bemused and then back towards Marcia.

"The Security Minister visited the station, and I managed to overhear his conversation with Johnson."

Marcia paused.

"What is it?" Sarah said.

"They seized your father's safe from the house because they wanted the contents of it to identify the location of the warehouse. They've guessed you two have it. The plan is for you to stay at your aunt's tomorrow night. They will have a significant covert police presence to secure your father's funeral and your safety. After the funeral, they intend to have the two of you show them where the warehouse is."

Marcia once again paused.

"And then what?" Will said.

Marcia looked wistfully at Sarah and Will. "I'm sorry, it doesn't look good for you two. The Minister alluded to the fact that, with the knowledge of your father's work, you are perceived to be a threat to national security. He has a meeting with the intelligence agencies this afternoon to discuss what will happen to you two after Friday. I didn't get a feeling there will be a good outcome for you."

"What do you mean by not a good outcome?" Cheryl said. Sarah and Will looked on anxiously.

"I don't know, and I really don't want to speculate or worry any of you, but I don't think there's any likelihood you will be able to return to your normal lives as if none of this happened. I'm not sure where that leaves your Aunt Janice either. I'm really sorry, but I didn't want to lie to you and obviously want to help if I can in any way at all."

"So, what do we do now?" Tariq said.

"I'm going to have to get changed and go back to work, but you all need to stay here, along with the contents of the safe. Then tomorrow, Sarah and Will will have to stay with their Aunt Janice's ahead of Friday's funeral. The rest of you are welcome to carry on staying here until Friday. We need to put a plan in place to be able to help Sarah and Will after the funeral, although I've absolutely no idea what we're going to be able to do." Marcia looked at Tariq. "What about you, still no contact from your sister's kidnappers?"

Tariq was caught unprepared and completely taken aback by

the question. "No, no. Nothing at all. They say no news is good news, right?" he said. His response and demeanour increased Marcia's suspicions.

"Maybe. It just seems a bit strange they've not been in touch yet. Don't you think?" Marcia said.

"I don't know. I've not been involved in something like this before. I mean, you're the police officer. What do you think?"

"Well, I've never dealt with a kidnap situation. I just thought maybe they'd have expressed some demands by now. Like you say, hopefully no news is good news." Marcia left the room to get changed. Tariq breathed a heavy sigh of relief.

Will, Sarah, and Cheryl were too shocked to notice Tariq's body language.

A blue Rover Metro was parked on an industrial estate late at night. Two young Asian men were sat in the driver and passenger seats.

"Zams, why have you asked me to bring you here?" the driver said. His name was Haroon. He was eighteen and not involved in criminality. He was short, overweight, unintelligent, impressionable, and easily influenced and led by others. Zams was the opposite of Haroon. He was tall, athletic build, handsome, bright, charismatic, streetwise, and becoming increasingly involved in criminality.

"I wish I could tell you, Haroon, but the less you know the better. I just need you to watch my back, bruv. If anything happens to me, then come, and help me or if you can't help me then let Riz know, ok?" Zams said.

"So, you're doing this for Riz?" Haroon said.

"I said the less you know the better but if something happens then yeah let him know, ok?" Zams took out a pre-rolled spliff of weed from his pocket and lit it up, unaware that a small bag of weed had fallen out of his pocket and under the seat as he did so.

"Zams, do you have to smoke that in my car bruv? You know I don't smoke it and my mum uses this car," Haroon said. He hastily wound his window down and waved his hands vigorously to clear the thick plume.

"I always have a smoke when I'm nervous, bruv. It relaxes me. You should have a smoke, it might chill you out a bit. You're far too stressed, Haroon. Now wait here."

Zams climbed out of the passenger seat, straightened his jacket, touched his collar, shrugged his shoulders, and puffed his chest out. He was determined to display confidence to Haroon and mask the fact he was apprehensive and scared. He saw eight units to his left and eight to his right. The unit nearest to him had 'number one' on the sign and on the next unit he could see 'number two.' He scanned his eyes along and saw there were eight in total to his left.

Haroon continued waving his arms. "That stuff stinks," he muttered to himself with a grimace and flared nostrils.

With adrenaline pumping, Zams walked pensively towards the final warehouse on his left. He reached the front of the unit, looked back towards Haroon in the car and approached the rear of the unit out of Haroon's view. He climbed a wall to be able to peek through a window of the warehouse and saw a group of males in discussion surrounded by cardboard boxes and pallets. As he surveyed the scene, Zams lost his footing and fell off the wall, his body grazed the warehouse on his way down, alerting the occupants inside.

As Zams tried to get to his feet, the rear door of the warehouse opened. "Don't move," a male voice said. Zams did as he was told.

A figure walked down the stairs towards Zams, who was too frightened to look. "Get up and move," the male said.

"I thought you said don't move?" Zams said.

"Don't get smart with me. Are you trying to be smart with me? Get up now."

Zams jumped to his feet and turned to see the male was pointing a gun at him, which made him shriek loudly. By now, Haroon was stood by his car to escape the lingering smell of Zams' joint and heard the squealing noise made by Zams.

"Zams," Haroon said, with a look of fear etched across his face. In a panic, he retreated to the safety of his car and immediately locked all the doors.

"Shut up," the male said. He grabbed Zams by the scruff of the neck, dragged him up the stairs and pushed him forcefully through the doorway of the warehouse and to the floor. The male stepped inside and closed the door behind him. The other four males present in the warehouse looked at Zams aggressively.

"Please don't hurt me," Zams said. His fears grew quickly as he realised the pallets and cardboard boxes were fully stocked with blocks of drugs.

A tall, stocky black male with short but not shaved black hair walked towards him. The male was wearing a tight-fitting t-shirt and Jeans. The smell of his aftershave was overpowering. Zams remained on the floor and tried to avoid the male's gaze as he winced at the acidic stench.

"Who the hell are you and what are you doing here?" the male said.

"My name is Zams–"

"Zams eh? Well, I didn't think you were going to say your name was Paul or Gary." The other males' present, two were white, one black and one mixed race, laughed at this remark. "But I don't think you were christened or whatever your equivalent is by the name of Zams were you? Is that some sort of street name or nickname?"

As Zams carefully contemplated his response, another male said: "I know what he'll be called soon, RT. Dead." He and the other males, except RT, laughed.

"Shut up you lot. I want to hear from Zams."

"My real name is Shoaib Zaman. Honestly it is. Zams is an abbreviation of my surname."

"Well, now we're getting somewhere. Shoaib Zaman, tell me what you're doing sneaking around outside my warehouse late at night. Who sent you?"

"Nobody. Nobody sent me," Zams said.

RT backhanded him across the face. "Don't lie to me. It'll be better for you if you don't lie to me."

The slap had hurt Zams, but he composed himself. "Ok. My mate Riz asked me to come here. He told me he'd heard that porn was getting filmed here." The males, including RT, burst into laughter.

"Is this a new business venture you've not told us about, RT?" the male who'd accosted Zams said.

"No, I think this Riz, or whoever Riz works, for has sent poor Zams here under false pretences." The male faced Zams. "I'll be respectful and call you by your nickname."

"Thanks," Zams said.

"Well, you're going to be dead soon, so I thought I'd be merciful enough to address you by the name you like."

"Please don't kill me. You don't have to kill me," Zams said.

"Someone sends you here to my warehouse to get your hands on my gear." The room erupted into laughter and even Zams managed to raise a smirk. "WHAT? Why are you all laughing?" RT said.

"RT, he said he'd come here looking for the shooting of a porn film and then you said he'd come here to get his hands on your gear. You've got to admit that's funny." RT cut a psychopathic look and the humour in the room evaporated faster than water in a desert.

In a fit of anger, RT again backslapped Zams, put his left hand tightly around his throat and moved so closely into his personal space, Zams could smell his stale tobacco infused breath. "I want you to tell me exactly who this Riz is and what he instructed you to do, right now," he said, as his eyes bulged and his mouth drooled. Zams nodded. He was terrified.

"Riz is a mate of mine from college. I've known him since we were little. We live on the same street, went to school together, go to the mosque together. He is a very low-level weed dealer and I buy off him sometimes. I owe him for an eighth, ok? He called me this morning and said that rather than pay him what I owe could I do him this favour instead. He said he'd heard they were making a porn film in a warehouse down here. Could I come and have a look and then report back to him exactly what I saw. I agreed to come this evening and he texted me the address."

"Have you got the phone on you?" RT said.

"Yes," Zams said. He took the phone out of his pocket and handed it over.

A petrified Haroon typed out a text message. He read it repeatedly before finally hitting send.

A phone beeped and a male looked at the phone. It was Riz.

Haroon: *"I'm on the industrial estate. I brought Zams here. I heard a scream from him and I haven't seen him since. What have you got him into, Riz?"*

Riz was shocked. He chose not to reply. Haroon held the

phone and looked at it incessantly in expectation of a reply from Riz. "Come on, Riz," he said repeatedly under his breath.

RT checked Zams' phone and found the text message from Riz.

"I'm afraid you've made a mistake, Zams," he said.

Zams looked up at him confused.

"This text message from Riz says to go to unit eight B. This is unit eight A. The one you wanted is in the opposite corner over there." This drew sniggers from others in the room.

Zams shook his head in disbelief at his mistake and the fact this had placed him in such peril. "I only saw the 'eight.' I never noticed the 'A.'

"Hang on. So, there could be a porn film in progress after all?" a male said.

"I think it's unlikely, but I think we should take a look at what is going on over there," RT said.

"Are you going to let me go now?" Zams said.

"I really wish I could, Zams, but you've seen too much, I'm afraid," RT said, with what appeared to be sincere regret.

Zams shook his head. "No, I won't say anything, I promise. You can trust me, RT." Zams became tearful.

"The fact you know my name is an issue as well. Look, I'm not a complete monster. I'll let you come over to unit eight B with us before we kill you." Zams held his head in his hands.

All five males walked with Zams over to unit 8B. Haroon watched on worriedly. He was sat in complete darkness in his car with the headlights off, and saw Zams look in his direction as if to plead for his help but he was powerless to intervene.

Haroon desperately pondered what to do. He decided to send another text message to Riz:

Haroon: "A group of males have taken Zams hostage at this warehouse. What the hell have you got him mixed up in? What do I do?"

This time Riz replied very quickly:

Riz: "I don't really know, bruv. Let me make some calls and get back to you innit."

Haroon read the message and shook his head. "Make some calls. I could make calls... to the police," he said to himself.

Riz immediately called Tariq. As Tariq's phone rang, all eyes averted towards him.

"Is it the kidnappers?" Marcia said.

"No, it's Riz. Hi Riz, how are you?" Tariq said.

"I've had a message from Zams' mate Haroon. He says Zams has been taken hostage by a group of males at this warehouse. What is going on Tariq? What do I do?" Riz said.

"That's a shame, Riz. I know you really liked that girl," Tariq said, desperate not to alert Marcia or the others to the truth of the conversation.

"What are you going on about? What am I supposed to tell Haroon?" Riz said.

"You should tell her that you're sorry and that you want to give things another chance. Maybe I can speak to someone to speak to her. I think I know some of her friends. That might help the situation. I know you're upset, mate. Let me get back to you. Ok, bye." Tariq ended the call before Riz could respond.

"Is everything ok?" Sarah said.

"Yeah. Riz is having girl trouble. He sounds pretty upset

about it. You know how it is. Well, I guess you'd know with boy trouble wouldn't you. Are you still seeing that jerk Will was telling me about? Simon, wasn't it?"

"Thanks a lot, Will," Sarah said, and looked angrily at her brother. Why are you discussing my private life with Tariq? Haven't you two got better things to talk about?" Sarah turned back to Tariq. "No Tariq, for your information I'm not seeing Simon anymore." She stormed out of the room in a huff.

This discussion had worked well for Tariq, as he had been able to take out the other phone whilst everyone was distracted. He sent the warehouse address to the kidnapper with the following message:

Tariq: "GROUP OF MALES THERE AND HAVE TAKEN A FRIEND OF MINE HOSTAGE. CAN YOU HELP? WHEN CAN I SEE MY SISTER? Txt Bk."

Tariq quickly received a reply.

The Boss: "Thanks. Yes. I'll be in touch."

Tariq's heart rate soared and he looked around the room with guilt emblazoned across his face. 'What have I done?' he thought to himself. He sent a text to Riz:

Tariq: "Help is on the way, tell Haroon to hang on."

Riz texted Haroon, who grew increasingly anxious for the safety of Zams. He read the message and gripped the steering wheel firmly.

10

Chapter Ten: Incomprehensible

'DELINQUENT YOUTH DIES BURGLING WAREHOUSE TO PAY DRUG DEBTS,' would be the headline on the newspaper noticeboard outside every shop in the city, Zams thought to himself. What a legacy of shame for his family. At least they wouldn't find out he was looking for a porn set, or would they?

Barry forced the lock on the front door of the warehouse. The five males and Zams cautiously entered and stared at the steel door.

"I know porn films are shot behind closed doors but this seems a bit excessive," Zams said.

"I don't think is going to be a porn film, RT. I think we should get out of here," a male said.

"Let's not be too hasty," RT said. "I want to see what's behind this door. Go and get the blowtorch."

Haroon watched as the male ran to and from the warehouses. The sight of the blowtorch on the male's return journey made Haroon petrified for Zams.

The boss called Johnson to let him know he'd mobilised re-sources, including Herbert and Lyle, to attend the warehouse as quickly as possible.

Sparks flew, as Zams, RT, and the others watched the male singe the door's locking mechanism. The searing heat caused it to melt, like butter being applied to a slice of toast. He opened the door.

RT held Zams by the scruff of the neck and moved him forward first. "Only fair you get to see the porn film, or whatever is going on in here first. Isn't it Zams? It's the very least we could do."

Zams nodded. He knew full well he had no choice but to do as he was told. He hoped for the sight of naked women but deep down he knew this was the last thing he was going to see. They proceeded slowly with weapons drawn, using Zams as a human shield. As they entered the dark room, RT switched on the lights.

RT stepped out from behind Zams and stood beside him to his left-hand side. All six males stood open mouthed, perplexed by what they were looking at.

"What was this mate Riz of yours sending you here for and more importantly, for who and why? I think I'd like to meet your mate Riz," RT said and glanced at Zams.

"Keep me alive and I'll make it happen I promise," Zams said as quick as a flash. RT chuckled and nodded at him as if to acknowledge his quick-witted riposte.

"Who are you?" a voice said from inside one of the containers.

Startled, RT looked in the direction of the voice. "I could ask you the same question, although I'd probably like to know what you are first?" he said. The question was met with silence. RT walked along and looked at each container. "None of you want to answer my question. Ok, that's fine." He turned around to face Zams and the others. "There's good news and bad news Zams. Which would you like first?"

Zams couldn't conceive there was any likelihood of good news but decided to proceed with optimism as his first option anyway. "Good news," he said.

"We're not going to kill you. Well, not yet anyway."

"Thanks. So, what's the bad news? You're going to kill me tomorrow?"

"Don't tempt me. We're taking you hostage instead."

"I don't want to sound facetious, but I think you'll find you've already taken me hostage."

"Well, I don't want to sound facetious either but we apprehended you breaking into our warehouse and we've brought you to the one you came here to see. I guess you could call it a citizen's arrest," RT said. He and the other males laughed. "Now we're taking you hostage."

"I can't believe I'm saying this, but I think I'd rather we go with the citizen's arrest and you turn me over to the police. My life chances will be better," Zams said.

"I don't know, Zams. I can maybe see a use for you in our organisation. You should look upon this as a career opportunity."

"If only the school career adviser could see me now. She'd be so proud," Zams said.

"You've got quite the sense of humour, Zams. I'm starting to like you. Barry, reverse the truck over here. We're going to empty this place."

"Why? What are we going to do with them?" Barry said.

"I'm not sure yet. I think they might be valuable somehow and I don't want to leave them here. Whoever asked this Riz to send Zams here knows more about this. You know me, I identify opportunities. I think there's potential in this. Let's get the truck over to Nathan's compound. They'll be safe there. Let's move. Don't just stand there Zams, you can help as well." All six males proceeded to clear out the warehouse.

Haroon could see the truck parked in front of the warehouse

but couldn't see what was going on. "Don't try and be a hero, Haroon," he said to himself. He ran his hands through his hair and looked up to the ceiling of his Metro for inspiration but none was forthcoming. He saw the rear of the truck close. The males then climbed into the front of the truck and two other vehicles. He couldn't see Zams.

As the convoy passed him, Haroon slumped into his seat and sat firmly still. A future as a surveillance officer seemed unlikely. He started the engine and revved his vehicle like a formula one driver on the starting grid. The wheels spun and a plume of smoke filled the air as he sped towards the warehouse and handbrake turned the car 180 degrees to face the other direction. He jumped out of the car and ran into the warehouse. Unbeknownst to him, a business card had fallen out of his pocket.

"ZAMS, ZAMS. Are you here?" he said. The warehouse was completely empty. He ran out, got into his vehicle, and floored it as fast as he could in pursuit of the convoy.

A few seconds later, Haroon left the estate at breakneck speed as a flurry of vehicles sped into the estate from the other direction. Herbert noticed Haroon's vehicle tearing away into the distance, quickly noting the registration plate details in her pocket notebook.

"What are you writing down?" Lyle said.

"That car speeding away. I don't know. Something just doesn't feel right, Si. I think that car might have just left the estate."

"You're overthinking it, Tash. It's probably a complete coincidence."

The three vehicles containing Lyle, Herbert, and several of the kidnapper's henchmen screeched to a halt in front of the warehouse. They all got out of their vehicles with guns drawn. One of the henchmen gesticulated at Herbert and Lyle to enter.

"Why should we go in?" Herbert said.

"Because you're the police," the male said. "I don't know what we pay our taxes for."

Embracing the machoism, Lyle moved forward at pace. "ARMED POLICE. GET YOUR HANDS UP OR I WILL SHOOT." He was closely followed by Herbert and then the henchmen. All walked into the empty warehouse.

"We're too late," Lyle said.

The henchman phoned the boss. "The place has been cleared. What do you want us to do?"

The boss was annoyed. "Have a scour around and see if you can find any clues and then leave it for this evening." The boss called Johnson.

"We were too late. I'll get to the bottom of what's happened but I want a promise from you. That you'll bring those Leidenstraum kids to me after their father's funeral."

"I'm not sure I can make you that promise," Johnson said. "Those kids are too hot to handle and the powers that be in this country have an interest."

"That's not good enough, Johnson. I wouldn't worry about your career if that's what you're thinking. You've well and truly crossed over into my world. If you think you're going to impress ministers and be able to progress your career by handing them kids over to the authorities you've got another thing coming."

"Don't threaten me. I've got more power than you realise and I'm not going to give in to the likes of you."

"Taking the moral high ground, are we? I'm a criminal, a vicious, nasty criminal, and I have been all my life. When you signed up as a police officer, you took an oath to protect and serve the community. I'm a lowlife, yes, but you, you're the lowest of the low. Be very careful who you make enemies of, Johnson. Don't let your arrogance and long-lost pride in that uniform of yours cloud your judgement. You might think you're safe and untouchable. Maybe you are more difficult to deal with, but what about those closest to you? Can you protect them from me? Are they safe? I'll let you think about that for a while." The boss ended the call and texted Tariq:

The Boss: "Your friend, his kidnappers and all the merchandise have gone. As you can't help me with that anymore, and as I assume you want to see your sister again with her head still attached to her body, the only thing you can do to help me now is to make sure those friends of yours find their way into my custody after their father's funeral. Do we understand each other?"

The phone bleeped in Tariq's pocket. He took the phone out and read the message. His eyes bulged. He looked at Sarah and Will. The betrayal was too much for him to take. He jumped to his feet. "I'm feeling very tired, guys, so I'm going to bed. See you in the morning."

"Are you ok, mate?" Will said.

'I'm fine, mate. Just tired from doing nothing today."

Marcia looked at Tariq but he did everything he could to avoid looking back at her or anyone else in the room. Maybe he was just scared for the welfare of his sister but his reaction reminded Marcia of guilt she'd seen in suspects she'd inter-viewed before when they were keen to cover up their lies.

One of the henchmen spotted the business card left behind by Haroon on the ground outside the warehouse. The henchman got down on one knee to take a closer look at the card which read: 'Simpson's Bicycle and Skateboard Shop, Haroon

(Retail Assistant),' with a mobile telephone number. He picked the card up and frowned.

"What's that?" Lyle said.

"I think it might be a clue," the henchman said.

"Since when did you become a detective?" Lyle said, swiping the card out of the henchman's hand, much to his annoyance.

"A business card for a retail assistant selling cycles and skateboards. Thanks, Poirot. I'll give this Haroon a call tomorrow and see if he can sell me some shin and elbow pads," Lyle said.

"Don't be so hasty, Simon," Herbert said, swiping the card out of his hand, much to his annoyance. "It was on the floor outside the warehouse, and I don't see a 'Simpson's Bicycle and Skateboard Shop' on this industrial estate. You always have been quick to ignore potential evidence and lines of enquiry."

The henchman grinned at Lyle. Herbert placed the card in her pocket.

"I'll let you chase up that lead tomorrow then, Miss Marple, shall I?" Lyle said as he tried to mask his embarrassment at Herbert's chiding of him.

Haroon sang at the top of his voice as he maintained his pursuit of the convoy. Zams had point blank refused to let him play his Spice Girls cassette earlier in the evening. Now that two had become one in the Metro, Haroon could do as he pleased.

As the convoy proceeded through a set of traffic lights, they changed to red. Haroon decided to jump the red light and narrowly avoided a collision with what transpired to be an unmarked police car. Haroon's pursuit was over. He slumped his head against the steering wheel in resignation.

"GET OUT OF THE CAR," the male officer, and driver, said.

Haroon climbed out of the vehicle and put his hands up. "Sorry officers," he said.

"TURN AROUND AND PLACE YOUR HANDS ON THE ROOF OF THE VEHICLE," the officer was clearly in no mood for Haroon's apology. "YOU'LL BE SORRY, ALRIGHT."

"Where were you going in such a hurry?" the female officer and passenger said.

"WHO CARES WHERE MICHAEL SCHUMACHER HERE WAS GOING IN SUCH A HURRY. HE NEARLY KILLED US. I BET HE HASN'T GOT A LICENCE OR INSURANCE," the male officer said as he glared at both his colleague and Haroon.

Tariq was alone in a bedroom panicking. He messaged Riz:

Tariq: *"Zams had gone by the time they got there. They were too late. Sorry."*

Riz read the message and misinterpreted it completely.

Riz: *"GONE? DO YOU MEAN HE'S DEAD? WHAT ABOUT HAROON?"*

Tariq read the message, shook his head, rolled his eyes, and puffed out his cheeks.

Tariq: *"NO, NOT DEAD. BY GONE, I MEAN THERE WAS NO SIGN OF HIM OR ANYONE ELSE. THEY'D LEFT. NO IDEA ABOUT HAROON."*

Riz: *"THEY'D BOTH BETTER BE OK SERIOUSLY. WHAT HAVE YOU DONE, BRUV?"*

Tariq buried his head in a pillow and screamed, using the pillow to drown out the sound from attracting the attention of his fellow flat dwellers.

Riz: *"WHERE ARE YOU HAROON? ARE YOU OK? WHAT ABOUT ZAMS?"*

The phone bleeped in Haroon's pocket as the male officer searched him. The officer took out the phone and read the message.

"Riz is worried about you Haroon and wants to know about Zams. Isn't that nice?" he said.

Haroon resisted the temptation to respond and risk antagonising the already riled officer further.

Riz: *"COME ON, HAROON. ANSWER ME. WHAT'S GOING ON, BRUV? I'M WORRIED."*

"Oh look, another message from Riz. He is very anxious about your whereabouts, isn't he?" the officer said.

"Can I just reply and put his mind at ease?" Haroon said.

The officer smiled at Haroon. "No, you can't," the officer said.

Whilst this exchange was taking place the female had placed her head into Haroon's car to have a look around and had detected the distinctive pungent odour of weed. She removed her head from the vehicle. "The car smells heavily of drugs," she said.

"Does it now?" the male officer said.

Haroon's phone then bleeped with another message:

Riz: "WHERE ARE YOU?"

"He was driving like a maniac the car smells of drugs and his mate Riz is desperate to know where he is. The plot thickens," the male officer said.

The female officer informed Haroon she would be searching his car for evidence of illicit substances.

"I've got some fruit pastilles in the glove compartment. You can have one if you like, but please don't have a green one. They're my favourite," Haroon said.

"She doesn't want your fruit pastilles. Under PACE, that's the Police and Criminal Evidence Act nineteen eighty-four, we don't search vehicles for fruit pastilles. You will have an opportunity to read all about PACE in your cell later," the male officer said, placing Haroon into handcuffs.

"Why are you handcuffing me? What do you mean I'll be in a cell? What on earth for? I was driving a bit fast and I'm sorry. I'm not a murderer," Haroon said.

"Driving a bit fast. That's putting it mildly. You're under arrest for dangerous driving. You do not have to say anything but it may harm your defence if you do not mention when questioned something which you later rely in court. Anything you do say may be given in evidence," the male officer said.

"I can't believe you're arresting me," Haroon said shaking his head.

"Is that your reply to the caution?" the male officer said.

"You're letting me off with a caution. Good. I've never been arrested before. I thought you could just warn me or give me a ticket."

"Don't get smart with me, Haroon," the male officer said. "I'm not giving you a caution. What I said to you was the caution which everyone receives when they're arrested. Your reply to that caution was; 'I can't believe you're arresting me,' which I'm about to make a note of in my pocket notebook. I just wanted to confirm that was your reply after caution."

Haroon looked at the officer terrified and nodded. "My mum is going to kill me. I can't believe I've been arrested."

"Well, you should have thought about that, shouldn't you?" the male officer said.

"I've found it," the female officer said.

"Found what," Haroon said with a puzzled look. "Is it my

Spice Girls badge, I've been looking for that everywhere, I love the Spice Girls."

"I've found a bag containing a substance believed to be cannabis. It was beneath the passenger seat," the female said smiling as she proudly held it aloft.

The male officer smirked at Haroon who looked confused. "So, you're a Spice Girls fan. Well, I imagine that you must WANNABE anywhere but here right now," the officer said chuckling to himself.

"Ohhh, Zams," Haroon said, as he realised the drugs must be his.

"Is that your name for it is it?" the officer said looking at Haroon, who looked back at him even more confused.

"In addition to your arrest under the Road Traffic Act nineteen eighty-eight, I'm now further arresting you under the Misuse of Drugs Act nineteen seventy-one for possession of cannabis. You do not have to say anything but it may harm your defence if you do not mention when questioned something which you later rely in court. Anything you do say may be given in evidence."

"Why are you saying that again? Do you like saying it?" Haroon said.

Both officers glared at Haroon. "I'm not going over this again," the male officer said retrieving his pocket notebook and pen. "I am writing that the P.I.C., that's you, by the way, replied after caution: 'Why are you saying that again? Do you like saying it?'."

"What is a P.I.C? I don't understand," Haroon said.

"It means in custody. Person in custody," the male officer said. "We need to get you to the station and we need to have this car thoroughly searched. I'm worried there are more drugs in this car, and Riz and goodness knows who else might come looking for you and the car." The officer turned to his colleague. "I'll request a transport vehicle for Haroon here. I'll drive our car back to the station and you drive this car back. It can be searched in the safety of the station car park."

Unable to reach Haroon, a panicked Riz called Zams' phone. Zams took the ringing phone out of his pocket. "It's Riz. Shall I answer it?"

"Give it here. I'll speak to him," RT said. "Hello Riz, how are you?" he said.

"Who is this. Where's Zams? Let me speak to Zams." RT held the phone to Zams's ear, nodded and raised his eyebrows.

"I'm ok Riz," Zams said. RT took the phone away from his ear as Riz continued to speak.

"I can't get hold of Haroon I don't know where he is."

"Haroon," RT said. "Who is Haroon? Is that who asked you to send Zams here to the warehouse with the robots?"

Riz was rendered speechless. His blood ran cold.

"What's that then Riz? Nothing to say? Well, I've something to say. I think you know a lot more about this matter than Zams here and you're going to tell me what I need to know. You will meet my associates and I on the first floor of the main car park on High St at nine thirty tomorrow morning. If you don't, Zams here, or should I say Shoaib Zaman is going to pay the price. It'll be wham bam goodnight Zam, if you catch my drift?"

"That sounds like you're going to have sex with him. I'm not risking my life to save Zams from that. No offence Zams, if you can hear me," Riz said.

RT held the phone away from his head, pointed at it, shrugged his shoulders, and shook his head. "I'm not going to have sex with him, Riz. I'm going to kill him, Riz."

"And what about me?" Riz said.

"I've no intention of having sex with you either. Let me just check with my associates. Are any of you interested in having sex with Riz tomorrow?" Everyone in the room looked perplexed by this comment. "That sound of silence is a no, Riz. You're really not our type, not even Barry's, and trust me he isn't choosy." All except Barry laughed at this.

"I meant will you kill me?" Riz said.

"No, we won't kill you, provided you do as we ask, which I promise won't involve anything sexual and you also tell me what you know and what I want to know."

"But what assurances do I have for me or for Zams?"

"You don't have any assurances. You must trust us. If you involve the police or any third parties, or I suspect something is not quite right in that car park tomorrow, Zams is dead. Do you understand?"

"Yes, I understand." RT ended the call. Riz threw the phone to the floor and put his head in his hands.

"Can I have my phone back now?" Zams said.

"No, I think it's best I keep it for now. You're going to be chained to the radiator in Nathan's office overnight. You won't be needing your phone," RT said.

"CHAINED TO A RADIATOR. WHAT, LIKE THOSE HOSTAGES WERE IN KUWAIT? LIKE, WHAT WAS HIS NAME, TERRY WAITE."

RT laughed. "No of course not. He was thousands of miles from home and kept prisoner for ages. You haven't even left the county, and Nathan's garage will be open for business tomorrow. You won't still be chained to the radiator in the morning when staff and customers arrive."

"You're going to chain me to it overnight though," Zams said.

"I'm afraid so, Zams. What can I say? Let this be a lesson to you. Lads of your age should be searching for porn on the internet, not in warehouses," RT said. Zams hung his head, resigned to his fate.

The thick wad of bank notes held together by an elastic band were separated and laid out on the desk ready to be counted, like a croupier would on a roulette table.

"Sarge, there's four hundred and eighty-pounds in twenty-pound notes; two hundred and fifty pounds in ten-pound notes; and ninety pounds in five-pound notes," the constable said as the Custody Sergeant recorded the detainee's property.

"That adds up to eight hundred and twenty pounds. Do you agree?" the Sergeant said to the detainee.

"Yeah, if you say so," the detainee said flippantly.

"Please sign this form to confirm we have retained eight-hundred and twenty pounds in cash, three mobile phones, a belt, a cigarette lighter, a gold-coloured sovereign ring, and a neck chain from you," the Sergeant said.

"I ain't signing nothing till my solicitor gets here," the detainee said.

"Very well, take him to cell nine please. Next guest please," the Sergeant said.

Haroon was presented to the custody Sergeant.

"And who have we here?" the Sergeant said.

"A Spice Girls fan who takes drugs and drives too fast Sarge," the escorting officer said.

"You'd have to make me take drugs to listen to the Spice Girls," the Sergeant said.

Everyone except Haroon laughed.

"They are the best band ever," Haroon said. "You will never hear anything quite like them again."

"Some might say that would be a good thing," the Sergeant said.

Haroon shook his head. Who were they to criticise the vocals of Geri, Emma, Victoria and the two Melanies? Haroon had been gutted when Geri left, and wasn't Mel B known as Mel G now?

"Sarge, I think this lad might have more drugs concealed about his person. Will you authorise a strip search?" the arresting officer said.

Haroon's eyes widened. "You want to see me naked? Why would you want to see me naked? Why would you do that?"

"We don't want to see you naked. It is a necessary procedure given the circumstances of the drugs concealed in your car," the Sergeant said.

"Necessary procedure. This is a police station not a hospital. How is it you need to see me with no clothes on. Is the female officer going to look at me naked as well?" Haroon said.

"No thank you," she said.

"That's good, I was getting worried about that."

"In order to preserve the dignity of detainees, strip searches of male suspects are conducted by male officers, and strip searches of female suspects are conducted by female officers," the Sergeant said.

At that moment, the arresting officer and another male officer placed latex gloves on in preparation for the search. This freaked out Haroon further.

"What are they putting gloves on for? Is one of them going to play with me you know what whilst the other one sticks his fingers–"

"Nobody will be playing with anything or sticking their fingers anywhere," the Sergeant said. "They are wearing gloves because they will have to search your underwear. Neither officer will be pulling, poking, prodding or otherwise inappropriately touching any part of your anatomy. It will be carried out discreetly and you will be asked to squat in such a way that anything you have plugged will find its way to the floor. If so, the officer will need gloves to retrieve it from the floor."

"All I did was drive too fast and nearly crash into the officers, for which I'm truly sorry. But now you want to go through my Superman pants and see me naked. Does that not seem a bit much to you?"

"I'm afraid it is wholly necessary," the Sergeant said.

"Well, can I please at least send a message or make a phone call to Riz. He's been messaging me ever since the officers stopped me."

"Sarge, we'll be looking for the Inspector to withhold that right at the moment," the arresting officer said.

"Ok. I'm afraid the officer will be seeking the authority of the Inspector to withhold that right," the Sergeant said.

"You're going to strip me naked and I'm not even allowed to tell anyone about it. It's because what you're doing is wrong, isn't it? When will I be allowed to make a call?"

"When our enquiries are complete," the arresting officer said.

"What enquiries?" Haroon said.

"Strip you naked, check out who you are, make some other enquiries, then we'll go and get something to eat, then catch up on paperwork and arrange for a full search of that car of yours in the morning. By the time you get interviewed tomorrow, I'll be tucked up in bed fast asleep."

A despondent Haroon resigned himself to his fate and was then escorted to a private room for his strip search to be conducted.

11

Chapter Eleven: Audacity

Forlorn faces were in plentiful supply in the Accident and Emergency Department of Oxford's main hospital, particularly those of the overworked staff. Most of the seats in the waiting room were occupied. A man wearing a red football shirt and black shorts hobbled away towards the exit with support from another man wearing a matching kit. His bandaged right ankle suggested he wouldn't need to wear the kit again for a while.

A distance away in Ward number 101, the occupant of one of the beds stirred. The fingers of one hand twitched and their eyes gradually opened, for the first time. They saw a guard sat facing away from them at the end of their bed.

On the other side of the ward, a guard stood up from by the patient they were guarding and stretched their arms out. It was the early hours of the morning and most patients were fast asleep. The nurses were in their rest room taking a break. The guard who had risen to their feet waved at the other guard to get their attention. They pointed up the ward and mouthed: "I'm off to stretch my legs and go to the toilet," and gave a thumbs up. The other guard nodded in acknowledgement.

A few seconds elapsed before the remaining guard stood and looked up to see the door to the ward closing behind their colleague. The guard took a sharp intake of breath and retrieved a small case from inside their pocket containing a needle. As the guard turned around, they were unaware a patient on the other side of the ward had awoken and was watching proceedings. The witness reached up and grabbed a hand towel from their side table. They placed the towel in their mouth to silence their painful screams as they attempted to get out of the bed.

The guard was shocked to see that Clare Stevens was awake. Clare looked at the guard and looked at the needle, she panicked and tried to move but was in agonising pain. The guard placed a hand over Clare's mouth and then reached with the other hand to jab her with the needle. Clare struggled which made it difficult for the guard but he then put his entire body weight over Clare which pressed on her wound and incapacitated her attempts to fight back. The guard regained control and as the needle was about to pierce the skin on Clare's left arm, the patient from the other side of the ward approached the guard from behind and smashed a vase of flowers over the guard's head. The guard involuntarily let go of the needle, slumped off the bed and onto the floor. Clare looked up. It was John. They looked at each other for a split second and nodded.

The guard stirred on the floor. John gritted his teeth into the towel and kicked the guard as hard as he could in the stomach. The exertion was too much for him and John fell on top of the guard. Clare was desperate to help John. Clare gritted her teeth and rolled out of the bed, wrapped up in the sheets, and on to the top of them both. The needle was now on the floor out of Clare's reach. The guard fought to move John and Clare from off the top of him. As he did so, Clare rolled off and the guard was able to pin John to the floor with his hands around his throat. John was powerless to stop him. Clare crawled along the floor; each movement invoked a grimace. She grabbed the needle and, in a burst of adrenaline-infused anger, she leapt up and plunged the needle into the guard's neck, like a basketball player hitting a slam dunk. The guard was almost instantaneously nullified. John gasped and coughed for breath which in turn left him in more pain.

"We need to get out of here quickly," Clare said, removing the guard's phone from his pocket and the gun from his holster. Clare and John helped each other get to their feet. Arm in arm they dragged themselves along the ward, leaving a trail of blood in their wake as they made it through the door of the ward and into the corridor, only to be confronted by the return of the other guard carrying a packet of cigarettes in one hand and a lighter in the other. He instinctively dropped them and reached for his gun but Clare persevered through the pain barrier, stood tall and pointed the gun at the officer.

"DON'T MAKE ME SHOOT YOU. I AM A POLICE OFFICER LIKE YOU. I DON'T WANT TO SHOOT YOU," Clare said.

The guard froze, his hand poised on the handle of his gun. John held Clare's waist as he cowered behind her. John's love of western films came to the forefront of his mind and this was one standoff he'd have preferred to be watching on a screen.

"You're not a police officer and you're not going to shoot me," the officer said as he swiftly pulled the gun from its holster, taking aim at precisely the same time as Clare clicked the trigger, unloading a bullet at his firing arm. The irony of Clare penetrating the officer's skin with a bullet as the other guard had tried to penetrate her skin with a needle just moments earlier was not lost on Clare.

The officer dropped his gun and fell to the floor. Unperturbed by having been shot, he reached for the weapon again. By this point, Clare's patience had worn so thin with him she shot him in the top of the thigh without an ounce of regret. Blood spurted out with such ferocity it spattered up to the ceiling and across the wall as sporadically as a toddler attempting to paint for the first time. The officer squealed in pain and rolled around the floor in excruciating agony. Clare hobbled over to the officer with gun still pointed.

"You're not going to kill him, are you?" John said.

"No, I'm not. I'm getting his gun so he doesn't get any ideas of following us."

John looked at Clare as if she'd took leave of her senses. "You've just nearly blown his nuts off. I don't think he's going to be following us anywhere, do you?" he said.

"YOU BITCH," the officer screamed at Clare as she picked up his gun. "YOU SHOT ME... TWICE. AAARGGGHHHH."

"If you'd listened to me, you wouldn't have been shot once, let alone twice," Clare said. "It could be worse, at least you're in the right place to get treatment. Oh, and if you call me a bitch again, police officer or not, I'll shoot you for a third and final time. Also, I'm gasping for a smoke so I'm taking your cigarettes and lighter."

Much to his surprise, Clare handed John the guard's gun. "I'm not sure I want to hold a gun again, perhaps you should keep both guns."

"We're fugitives now, John. I'd keep it if I were you. In fact, I insist." John reluctantly agreed. John and Clare made good their escape via the nearest fire exit and into the car park.

"Now what are we going to do?" John said.

"Firstly, I'm going to have a fag to deal with my nicotine withdrawal," Clare said placing a cigarette in her mouth from the pack she'd snaffled from the guard.

"Those things will kill you."

"John, we've both survived having been shot," Clare said and defiantly illuminated the smoke. "We need to get to the taxi rank and get out of here. We also need someone to help us but I'm not sure who I trust to call. I don't have any numbers either."

"Give me the phone, I know Cheryl's number off by heart."

Clare gave John a confused look. "Are you still out of it on morphine or something? They were kidnapped, remember. How is ringing Cheryl's phone going to help us?"

"No, a voice whispered to me the other night that they're ok. That helped me pull through, knowing my family are safe."

"What voice? Ok, I think you're definitely hallucinating from the morphine," Clare said. John furiously grabbed the phone out of Clare's hand and started typing out Cheryl's number.

"Ok, have it your way John but keep moving towards the taxi rank and stay down. We're not exactly inconspicuous in these hospital gowns, are we?" As Clare moved forward, John noticed that Clare's backside was exposed.

"You're not kidding. Couldn't you have at least worn under-wear?" John said.

"Stop looking, you pervert. I think you'll find you haven't got your Y-fronts or your boxer shorts on either. It's a good job it's a warm night, otherwise I think you'd be feeling the draught," Clare said.

The sound of a ringing phone caused the female and child occupants of Marcia's flat, who were all sharing Marcia's room, to awaken. Cheryl was first to stir as she was closest in proximity to the monotonous tone. She rubbed her eyes and looked at the screen. She didn't recognise the number but answered with a sleepy, "Hello?" The voice that greeted her left her convinced she was dreaming.

"Cheryl. Are you ok? The children, are they ok?" John said.

"John. Is that really you?"

"Yes. It's me. Please tell me you and the children are safe?"

"Yes John, we're ok," Cheryl said and cried.

"Is that daddy?" Lucy said. She jumped to her feet and ran into her mother's arms desperate to speak to her father.

"I LOVE YOU, DADDY," Lucy said.

"I love you too, sweetheart," John said as tears filled his eyes.

"When will we see you, daddy?" Lucy said.

"Soon, Lucy, I promise," he said choked up.

"John, pull yourself together," Clare said as she pointed a gun at a fearful taxi driver with tobacco smoke drifting into the air from the cigarette hanging from the corner of her mouth. The driver started his engine as if he was about to pull away.

This alerted John, who came back to the moment and realised he needed to support Clare, which he did by instinctively pointing his gun at the driver. The driver accepted he was cornered by two people who, though dressed in hospital nightgowns, were armed and dangerous. He placed his hands up in the air in surrender.

"Daddy, what's happening?" Lucy said. Robert watched on petrified and mouthed "dad" with a solitary tear. He noticed Sarah was looking at him and he wiped his eye, desperate to conceal his emotion.

"What the hell is going on?" Marcia said. The commotion had alerted Will and Tariq next door and they had now entered the room.

"John. Please talk to me, John. What is going on? You're scaring us," Cheryl said.

"Sorry Cheryl. I can't really talk right now. We're hijacking a taxi. At gunpoint."

"You're doing what. And who is 'we'?"

"It's ok. I'm with Clare Stevens. She's a detective. We just broke out of hospital."

"Clare Stevens," Cheryl said. She looked at the others in shock. All the other adults in unison said, "Clare Stevens."

Clare took a few desperate drags from the remainder of the

cigarette before dispensing with it and climbing into the taxi with John. Blood dripped onto the taxi floor.

"You're getting blood all over my taxi," the driver said with his hands still placed firmly in the air.

"At least it's not yours," Clare said as sirens could be heard approaching the hospital. "Now drive." The driver hesitated. Clare pointed the gun into the back of his head. "I SAID DRIVE," she said, which jolted him into action. The wheels of his vehicle span as he sped from the scene.

"Where are we going?" the driver said.

"I don't know yet. Hang on. John, can Cheryl pick us up?" Clare said.

"Pick us up. Pick us up from where?" John said.

Clare thought for a moment. "The front entrance of the park off Carnival St. Driver, take us there." The driver nodded.

"Cheryl, I don't know if you heard that. We need picking up from the front entrance of the park off Carnival St as soon as possible, and can you please bring some bandages?"

Marcia was next to Cheryl listening in on the call. "I'll go and get them and I've got a first aid kit in the car," Marcia said.

"Cheryl, who the hell was that?" John said, which drew Clare's attention. She leaned in close to John to hear Cheryl's response.

"It's Marcia Reynolds. She's a detective. We are with her. She's a police officer we can trust, John." Clare smiled and nodded at John.

"Ok, that's fine. I'll see you soon. I can't wait to see you. I love you," John said.

"I love you too John. Bye."

Clare held John's hand for moral support. For a brief moment and as the adrenaline trailed off, they breathed a joint sigh of relief.

"John, switch the phone off." Clare said.

"Why?"

"Just do it please. Trust me." John did as he was told.

The taxi arrived outside the park entrance. "Now what?" the driver said. Clare ripped the left arm off a beleaguered John's nightgown.

"What the hell are you doing?" John said.

"You'll see," Clare said and instructed the driver to hold out his hands. Clare proceeded to tie the torn garment around his wrists. She then ripped the left arm of her own nightgown. "Are you happy now?" she said to John. Clare placed it over the driver's eyes and tied it behind his head to act as a makeshift blindfold.

"I can't see," the driver said.

"That's the point," Clare said and rolled her eyes.

"I don't like it. You can't leave me here tied up and blindfolded. Anything could happen to me."

"These restraints are flimsy. Once we are gone you will be able to free yourself. Nothing is going to happen to you," Clare said.

"What is happening about payment?" the driver said.

"Where could you possibly think we are keeping the notes and coins?" John said.

Clare smiled. "You'll have to put it on your next fare," she said. At that moment, Marcia's car pulled up alongside the taxi. "We're off now. Count to one hundred and then break yourself free." John and Clare climbed out of the taxi and into the rear of Marcia's car.

"Thanks for this Marcia, I really appreciate it," Clare said as she placed her hand on Marcia's left shoulder. Marcia turned her head around, her eyes glimmered in tandem with her smile and she placed her hand warmly on top of Clare's.

"I'm just glad you're ok, Sarge." She handed her the first aid kit from the passenger seat, turned back to the front, and drove off at speed.

The sense of anticipation of those waiting inside Marcia's flat was palpable. Marcia placed the key into the lock and opened the front door. The living room door opened and the atmosphere erupted into one of perpetual joy and emotion. John fell tearfully to his knees.

"DADDY," Lucy said.

"DAD," Robert said.

Cheryl burst into tears and grabbed her face. She and the children ran lovingly into his welcoming arms. They embraced as a family, reunited after a terrifying ordeal.

"Don't hug him too tightly. I've only just rebandaged him," Clare said. This caused a ripple of laughter.

Sarah hugged Clare Stevens warmly and said: "We're so pleased to see you."

"Thank you. As a police officer it's not every day we deal with people who are pleased to see us is it, Marcia?" Marcia laughed and shook her head.

"We are pleased to see you and now you can thank me for saving your life," Will said.

"Ok, thanks. I look forward to hearing all about it," Clare said with a bemused look.

"That's the voice," John said as he looked up. "I didn't recognise it was your voice at the time, but you're the one that whispered to me in the hospital that my family were ok, weren't you?"

Will nodded proudly.

"Thank you. You're a hero," John said.

"Don't tell him that. We won't be able to fit his head in the room," Sarah said.

"You're just jealous because you wish you were a hero, sis."

"I am genuinely very proud of you, Will. I'm not sure it makes up for everything else over the last seventeen years but it's a start, and I do love you." Will smiled at his sister.

"I'm proud of you as well, sis." He paused. "I love you too." They smiled at each other with genuine warmth, respect, and admiration.

Throughout the exchanges, Tariq felt uneasy as he harboured an overwhelming sense of not only his own guilt, but also that of his father. He was grateful that his father's involvement had been withheld from John for now, but the situation was becoming too much for him to handle and his body language was telling.

Following a few refreshments, the room gradually began to clear as calm was restored and everyone sought much needed rest, until it was just Clare and Marcia left sat on the sofa.

"I think we'd better bring ourselves up to speed on everything, Constable," Clare said.

"Yes, Sarge, I think we should," Marcia said as she gazed obediently at Clare. They moved closer together, their eyes closed and they kissed tenderly on the lips for a few seconds. Their eyes opened and as their lips parted, they both smiled with their eyes fixated on each other.

"I didn't know you were–" Clare said before Marcia placed her left forefinger on Clare's lips. Marcia moved in and kissed Clare passionately which was instantly reciprocated.

"I've wanted to do this since the day I joined CID, Sarge," Marcia said.

"As have I. Now shut up and kiss me again." They continued to kiss for a few minutes before Clare pulled her lips away. "As fun as this is, Constable, I don't want us to get too carried away. Well not yet anyway."

"I'm more than willing to get carried away, Sarge," Marcia said with a glint in her eye.

"Patience is a virtue, Constable. Perhaps we can start by calling each other by our names instead of our work titles when we're off duty, Marcia. I don't want us to be caught in a compromising situation with the house guests here."

"I find the risk of a guest or guests disturbing us quite exciting, Clare. It adds to the thrill of it and it is my flat after all."

"Yes, but you wouldn't say that if one of the children were to walk in," Clare said as she gave Marcia one last kiss on the lips. "Now, tell me what's happened and then I'll tell you what I know."

Having updated each other and digested the information they sat in stunned silence.

"I can't believe Johnson shot you. He is evil," Marcia said.

"The fact it was him hurts more than the bullet itself. I'm devastated. And we need to do something about Tariq. I agree with your suspicions; I got some bad vibes from him in here tonight and not just because of his sister's kidnap and what's happened with his dad. We are going to have to establish a strong plan of action but I don't know about you I need some sleep first. It has been a lot of excitement for one day," Clare said.

"Are you sure you don't want a little more excitement? I'm pretty sure the children and the other adults are asleep by now," Marcia said as she looked at Clare submissively and bit her lip seductively.

"I could be tempted. You'll have to bring the first aid kit over here though."

Marcia looked puzzled. "What do we need the first aid kit for?"

"If anyone walks in, we will be able to explain you're simply changing my bandage," Clare said as she licked her lips flirtatiously. They both smiled at each other knowingly as Marcia stood up to retrieve the first aid kit.

12

Chapter Twelve: Authoritative

Thursday 8ᵗʰ July, 1999. 6.30am.

The early morning temperature signalled the start of another glorious summer's day. Two men in greasy overalls stood alongside a uniformed Police Officer looking at a car.

"You got us out of bed early for this?" one of the technicians said.

"Time is of the essence, and for what it's worth, I think you'll be sweating buckets if you try to do this later in the day," the officer said.

"He's right, Jim," the other technician said. "They've said it'll be twenty-eight degrees by lunchtime."

"It'll be twenty-eight degrees when I'm in Mallorca next week drinking an ice cold cerveza," Jim said. "I can't wait to get on that plane. Andy, get me the wrench. We'll make a start."

DCs Herbert and Lyle arrived in the police station car park in separate vehicles, parked next to each other and exchanged pleasantries as they stepped out of their vehicles. As they walked towards the building, they noticed a blue Metro was in the process of being dismantled.

"A blue Metro," Herbert said.

"What's significant about that?" Lyle said.

"The car from last night that sped out of the industrial estate. It was a blue Metro," Herbert said retrieving her pocket notebook from her bag. "I think it's the same vehicle. It is. It's the same one."

Herbert and Lyle approached the technicians and uniformed officer.

"What's happening here?" Herbert said.

"What does it look like? We're dismantling a car," one of the technician's said shaking his head. "Perhaps you can make yourself useful and put the kettle on," he said.

Herbert seethed at the sexist remark but maintained her composure and turned to face the officer. "Constable, who is in custody connected to this vehicle?" she said.

"Some young Asian lad. I think his name is Harpoon or something like that. I'm going to be interviewing him."

"Haroon," Herbert said.

"What?" the officer said

"The lad's name. Is it Haroon?"

"Yes, I think that's it. If there's nothing from this search, I'm going to interview him for possession of cannabis and dangerous driving. He's got no previous convictions. I don't think he's even been arrested before."

"I think this is going to be a matter for CID, Constable. If you can tidy up the handover package, we'll take it off your hands and you can get back out on the beat," Lyle said and nodded at Herbert, who was mouthing the words 'business card' at him whilst wielding a condescending expression which he wilfully ignored.

"Why would CID want this?" the officer said.

"This car is linked to a burglary that is of interest to us. We'll need to further arrest Haroon for that and interview him so it makes sense if we deal with it all," Herbert said.

"You'll get no complaints from me. It saves me the paper-work," the officer said with a smile.

Herbert scowled at the technician and without turning her head away from him said: "Constable, can you make sure this grease monkey civilian does a very thorough search. I want the search to be so thorough there is a chance he might find a personality or evidence of something particularly miniscule, like his brain or even his penis. And if we find out he has taken a break for so much as a glass of water let alone a cup of tea or coffee before he's finished, you can kiss goodbye to that CID attachment you asked for, do you understand?"

"You can't talk to me like that, you jumped up little bitch," the technician said.

Herbert smirked, walked over towards him, and grabbed his crotch area fiercely. He fell to his knees in agony as she whispered in his ear: "I'll speak to you as you spoke to me. It's important to treat people as they treat you. Now stop squirming and strip this car," she said squeezing even more tightly which made his eyes water.

"Tash, I think that's enough. Any more and he'll have to explain to his wife why his balls are bluer than this Metro tonight," Lyle said and laughed.

"I think he's enjoying it, Si," she said, as she finally released her vice like grip. "Now who is the little bitch," she said through gritted teeth as the technician writhed in pain. Herbert and Lyle then proceeded nonchalantly towards the building.

"LYLE, HERBERT. My office NOW," Johnson bellowed as they entered the CID room.

They trudged into Johnson's office as the rest of the CID room looked on. Johnson slammed the door behind them.

"What is so special about them two? They're always in the gaffer's office," DS Patel said.

"They're just lackeys for the gaffer," DI Taylor said. "They probably think he'll support them with the promotion board."

"He's Acting ACC now so I suppose he's well worth grovelling up to. He didn't support me in going for promotion to Inspector though, did he? The racist," DS Patel said.

"That's not because he's racist. He just doesn't like you. In fact, none of us do," DI Taylor said chuckling. Other officers laughed, including an ironic laugh from Patel himself.

"Thanks for that, gaffer. A real boost for my confidence, that is."

"You're welcome. Besides, you've got more to do to develop as a Sergeant before you become an Inspector."

"Have I? Like what?"

"You've not been in the custody block. You'll be in their faster than you can say 'Sir, you're a racist' if you're not careful," DI Taylor said.

"Speaking of lackeys for the gaffer, I haven't seen Clare Stevens for a few days. Where is she?" DS Patel said.

"Maybe she's on annual leave," DI Taylor said.

"I don't think she ever takes leave. She loves the job too much," DS Patel said.

"We've got big problems," Johnson said furiously. Herbert and Lyle were confused by Johnson's demonstrable anger.

"We're working on it, gaffer. I think we've had a potential break on the way in," Herbert said.

"That is the least of our worries," Johnson said. "Clare Stevens and John Paterson murdered a police officer last night, the one that was meant to kill Clare, and they shot and seriously wounded another." Herbert and Lyle gasped. "You can gasp. They then took a taxi driver hostage and made him drop them off outside a park where they were picked up by another vehicle. Now, we don't know where they are, and the whole thing is a circus. The media are all over the hospital. Everyone is involved including the Police Complaints Oversight Unit. With the resources the PCOU will throw at it and the pressure from above, it's only a matter of time before they establish the identity of Clare Stevens." Johnson held his head in his hands, his face a perfect picture of worry and insomnia. Herbert and Lyle looked at each other bemusedly.

"You're Acting ACC now so surely you've got more opportunity to access information and influence this than before,"

Lyle said. Johnson looked at him sternly.

"To a degree yes. I've got a briefing to attend with the Chief Constable and the PCOU at nine before the Chief addresses the media. We'll also have to deal with the inevitable parliamentary pressures, bearing in mind the Chief is on rocky ground as it is. The PCOU will run a tight ship on this, so even as Acting ACC it may not be as easy as you think."

"If the Chief is on rocky ground as you say, maybe you should throw a few more stones in the mix and get him moved on," Herbert said.

"Then you can be Acting Chief and you'll be in the driving seat," Lyle said.

"Do you two really think me throwing the Chief under the bus means I'll become Acting Chief? They'd simply draft in a Chief, a Deputy Chief and an Assistant Chief from neighbouring forces. That would make things even more difficult. Honestly, the PCOU will be difficult to navigate. I need to keep the Chief in place to give me half a chance of staying even remotely in the know. That brings me to the next thing we need to do," Johnson said as he looked anxiously at Herbert and Lyle.

"By we, I take it you mean us," Herbert said.

Johnson glanced at Herbert angrily but chose not to respond to her insolent comment.

"The truth about Clare Stevens getting shot, killing a police officer, and shooting another. It must be concealed. A tireless, hardworking, dedicated detective like Clare with an exemplary record isn't going to make much sense to the public, the media, and more importantly the PCOU is it, if you catch my drift? I think you know what to do."

"Yes, we know what to do. But as Tash said before we've had a potential break on the other matter and we need to deal with that first."

"What could possibly be more important than the matter at hand?" Johnson said. "Time is of the essence. It's probably a few hours before the PCOU will have Clare Stevens as the most wanted woman in the UK."

"There's a lad called Haroon in custody. He's connected to the industrial estate last night. Uniform intended to interview him. He's never been in trouble with the police; we think he's a weak link. With a bit of gentle cajoling, we think we can get him to tell us what he knows," Herbert said.

"Ok. Do it. Get whatever you can out of this lad and then deal with the other matter as a priority. Keep me updated."

A calendar of nude models hung proudly on a nail in the wall of the office in Nathan's garage. Looking at 'Miss July' whilst chained up in a motor-oil-stained office was as close as Zams was going to get to the set of a porn film. He couldn't even see what the rest of the year looked like, which was disappointing, not that Miss July wasn't good enough company. Zams was just grateful he was alive, and journalists weren't writing about his embarrassing demise, at least for the time being.

The shutters to the garage opened and ended the silence of his self-pity. He was greeted by an overly cheerful RT.

"Good morning Zams, sorry I mean Mohammed. Let me unchain you."

"Why did you call me Mohammed?" Zams said looking at RT quizzically.

"Because that's the name on your new passports," RT said.

"New passports. What do I need a new passport for? What do I need a passport for full stop? And what do you mean passports?"

"You're going to the Netherlands today using your British passport and you'll be coming back using your Dutch passport. Isn't that exciting?"

"I'm going where?" Zams said with an expression of abject horror.

"You're going to the Netherlands. You know Holland. Flat country in Europe. They are known as the cloggies."

"Yes, I've heard of it, but why would I be going there, and what's the deal with all the passports?"

"I have a job for you to do. But don't worry, your mate Riz will be joining you. They have great drugs there, Zams, which you can smoke legally in cafes and everything. I don't want you thinking it'll be all work and no play."

"I can smoke drugs here, thanks. I don't think I want to go to Holland or the Netherlands and I don't think Riz will either. What job would it be doing anyway?"

"Well, put it this way you won't be picking tulips, and you don't have a choice, the two of you are going."

"Can I have my phone back now? My family are going to be worried about me," Zams said.

"No, I'm afraid not. Not until you come back from Holland anyway. You and Riz can have some new phones. Clean phones. But you're right they are going to be worried, so I'm just going to message them from your phone and let them know you're with Riz. When I get Riz's phone, I'll message his family to say he's with you. The two of you are going to have such an adventure, you really should be thanking me."

"I am Pakistani. I was at risk of getting sent overseas when I didn't want to be to do things that I don't want to do without the help of some black guy I've just met."

"What difference does it make that I'm black? RT said.

"In the context of getting kidnapped and sent to Holland, nothing. I wouldn't feel any better about it if you were white, put it that way, but I think I'm perfectly entitled to refer to you as the black kidnapping psycho."

"There is really no need to continue to bring race into it, Zams. You could have just left it at kidnapping psycho. Don't propagate negative racial stereotyping like the white oppressors do."

"You're one to talk about oppression. No white man ever chained me to a radiator and tried to send me to Holland. You're going to pay for what you're doing. You mark my words."

Marcia was making herself a coffee in the kitchen as Clare swept in, grabbed her lovingly around the waist and gave her a kiss.

"Careful, Clare, one of the others could walk in at any minute."

"It's just a hug and a gentle kiss on the lips. Nothing compared with what they'd have walked in on last night," Clare said with a knowing wink.

The others started to emerge from their slumber and joined Marcia and Clare in the kitchen and lounge areas, except for the children.

John looked awkwardly at Tariq as he tried to formulate the words in his mind that he wanted to convey to him. "Tariq, Cheryl has brought me up to speed on things as it were and I just wanted to say, well, I just want to say I have no hard feelings towards you because of your father's actions. Cheryl and I are fully supportive of you and will do anything to help you bring Shabeela home safely."

"Thank you, John. I really appreciate that. My father's actions make me feel totally ashamed. I can't believe he'd be involved in something like this and can't believe he'd do this to someone who has been such a good friend and colleague to him for so many years. I'm so very, very sorry," Tariq said as he struggled to look John in the eye.

"I'm shocked too, Tariq, but your father's behaviour has grown ever more erratic over the last year. Having the affair with Amanda from work and trying to—"

"AFFAIR. WHAT AFFAIR?" Tariq said as Cheryl nudged her husband and cut him an angry look.

"Oh, I'm sorry, Tariq. I didn't realise, I thought you knew. I would never have—"

"Amanda. Who is Amanda? When was this?" The room fell silent. "Talk to me John, please."

"Ok. Amanda worked in accounts. She was married, no kids

but I don't think her husband was ever home. He was a sales rep, travelling all over the country. Your father paid her quite a bit of attention and they became good friends," John paused briefly. "Fairly soon after rumours started to circulate that they were more than just friends and your father became obsessed with her. About eight or nine months ago he tried to convince her to leave her husband –."

"Eight or nine months ago. Wait. What, that's when my mum disappeared to Pakistan. Did she find out?"

"I don't know if she found out about it, but the timing would certainly make sense."

"What happened to this Amanda?" Tariq said.

"She left a couple of months later and got a job somewhere else. I think it was a combination of your father's persistence and the embarrassment of the whole thing with colleagues. As far as I know she's not in contact with your father anymore."

"I don't know who he is anymore. Look at what he's done. Keeping secrets and lying. He's destroyed everything."

John placed a hand on Tariq's shoulder as his whole body sunk in resignation.

"Keeping secrets and lying. It's a family trait, isn't it?" Clare said.

"What are you implying?" Cheryl said.

"I'm not sure Tariq here is quite as innocent as he's making out. I think he may be as adept at lying and keeping secrets as his dad. The apple doesn't fall far from the tree, after all," Clare said.

"What do you mean?" Tariq said trying to plead his innocence, but his face was etched with guilt.

"What is going on? What has he done?" Will said.

"We're about to find out," Marcia said. Will, Sarah, John, and Cheryl all looked at each other confused. Clare and Marcia walked over towards Tariq and John withdrew his comforting hand from Tariq's shoulder.

"You may not have noticed, but mine and Marcia's officer radars have been going into overload where Tariq is concerned. His body language, his overprotectiveness towards that criminal's phone, his insistence he hasn't heard from the kidnappers. We strongly suspect he's lying. You're lying aren't you Tariq, aren't you?" Clare said. She stared at him intensely as his eyes darted around the room and he wanted the world to swallow him up.

"Tell them they're wrong, Tariq," Will said. "They are wrong, aren't they?" Tariq couldn't look his friend in the eye.

"Hand over the phone, Tariq," Marcia said. "Hand it over, now."

"Don't make things any harder than they have to be, Tariq,"

Clare said. Tariq did nothing in response to their instructions. His mind raced as he desperately tried to think of something he could do. In his blind panic, he decided to make a run for it but was rugby tackled to the floor and restrained by Marcia, as Clare took possession of his phones.

"I'm sorry, I'm sorry," Tariq said. "I didn't know what to do. Please don't hate me."

"What have you done?" Cheryl said. Tariq remained silent and looked at the floor. Marcia retained control over him as Clare started to read the messages on his phones.

"Oh my god. He's helping the kidnappers," Clare said.

"HE'S WHAT?" Will said and ran aggressively towards Tariq but was held back by John.

"How could you? What on earth have you done, Tariq?" Will said. He was aghast at his friend's betrayal. He began to calm, sat down with his head in his hands and refused to look at Tariq.

"I had no choice, ok. They have my sister and they're threatening to kill her. I didn't know what to do. They have my dad too now, not that he's a priority given everything he's done." Tariq became emotional. "I swear I never intended to hurt any of you. I'll do anything. Please help me. Help me to get my sister back."

"Why should we trust you or help you get Shabeela back?"

Sarah said.

"Hold on a minute. Tariq may have made some poor choices under duress but an innocent young girl's life is at stake. Neither Shabeela nor Tariq should suffer any more than they already have done for the actions of their father," Cheryl said.

"You're not going to try and run off again or do anything silly are you?" Marcia said to Tariq. Pinned to the floor all he could do was shake his head slightly to convey compliance. Marcia slowly released her grip.

"Clare and I are police officers. We don't have a choice. We took an oath to preserve life and so we are duty bound to take all steps to help Tariq's sister and even his father. I think we've more chance of helping them whilst protecting you all and us by working together as a team. For what it's worth, I think Tariq is sorry. I don't think he wanted to betray, hurt or upset any of you."

"I didn't. I—"

"Shut up. I'm talking and I'm trying to help you. Are we all agreed that we move forward together, work together, trust each other, and don't keep things from each other. Well, are we?"

13

Chapter Thirteen: Manipulative

Haroon lay in the foetal position on the hard bench of the uninviting cell with just a blanket for a pillow. He'd not had a good night's sleep. The man in the cell next to him was quiet now, but the noise he'd made last night was excruciating. For what felt like hours, Haroon had heard him pounding the cell hatch like a boxer training with a punch bag.

The walls of his cell were inscribed with an array of messages, some more explicit than others. 'JB WOZ ERE', 'FK THE POLICE', 'TANYAS A SLAG'. Haroon had no desire to be here, let alone proudly etch it into the wall like JB had. He just wanted to go home and listen to the Spice Girls.

"Good morning, Sarge. How are you?" Lyle said cheerily as he swaggered into the custody block in company with Herbert.

"I'm ok thank you. How can I help you?" the Sergeant said. With beady-eyes, a gruff tobacco charred voice and weathered face of fury, he remained firmly rooted in his seat as he turned the page of his newspaper, mildly irritated by the disturbance of his morning read.

"We are going to be interviewing this lad Haroon," Herbert said.

"For a bit of cannabis and careless driving? I thought CID would be far too preoccupied to trouble themselves with such triviality," the Sergeant said, before swiftly turning his attention back to the newspaper.

"We're planning to further arrest him for burglary so it makes sense we interview him for the lot. We'll arrest him in interview for that, Sarge," Lyle said.

"Burglary," the Sergeant said as he stood to his feet and put his paper down. "This lad has got no previous and now you're arresting him for burglary?" the lines on his face scrunched up perplexed by this development.

"We think he's maybe got caught up with the wrong crowd, Sarge. I think we can steer him back on the right path," Herbert said.

"Well, you'll have to wait for his legal representation to arrive. I'll give the law firm a call now," the Sergeant said as he picked up the phone handset. Herbert and Lyle puffed out their cheeks and rolled their eyes at each other.

"Steady on there, Sarge. What cell is this lad in?" Lyle said.

"He's in cell four but you know the rules. If the lad wants legal representation, he gets legal representation."

"Of course, Sarge," Herbert said. "Lyle just wants to have a chat with Haroon and tell him we'll be interviewing him and put his mind at ease. How about I make you a coffee and we have a chat. The last I heard you were having your kitchen extended. How is that going?"

"Milk, two sugars please. Between my wife and the builders, frankly I'd rather be dealing with the horrible scrotes in here instead."

Herbert laughed and continued to engage the Sarge in conversation as Lyle purposefully pounded the corridor to cell four, desperately trying to avoid inhaling oxygen infused with stale alcohol, sweaty feet, and body odour so pungent it could turn cheese.

Lyle opened the cell hatch and observed a tired and scared Haroon. "Good morning, Haroon, I'm Detective Constable Simon Lyle. I'll be interviewing you this morning."

"Will it be long, sir? I just want to get out of here," Haroon said meekly as he cowered on the corner of his cell bench.

"My colleague Tash and I are ready to interview you right now. The trouble is you want a legal rep, don't you? Traffic is bad at this time of day and the Sarge has got to call the law firm. I'm not going to lie to you, Haroon, it could take a while. I reckon you could be out of here in the hour otherwise. Still, what can we do, Haroon? We'll just have to wait until they get here."

"Out in the hour? If I can be out of here within the hour, what do I need a lawyer for? Cancel the lawyer. I'll be interviewed now."

"It sounds good to me, Haroon. You'll just have to sign some paperwork with the Inspector to say you no longer want legal representation. When the Inspector asks, just say you want to get out of here and you've done nothing wrong. You asked for a lawyer last night because you were afraid but you've slept on it and don't need one. Do not say I told you to say that ok?" Lyle said with a wink and smile.

"Yes sir. I won't say anything, I promise. Thank you, sir."

"Sarge, he doesn't want a legal rep anymore, can you call the Inspector?" Lyle said, as he abruptly interrupted the Sarge and Herbert's chat about the cost of plasterers and his disagreement with his wife's choice of lilac tiles, much to the annoyance of the Sarge.

"The Sarge is having an issue with his wife's choice of lilac tiles Si," Herbert said to placate the Sarge's ire.

"Lilac tiles? Sounds awful, Sarge, you should get rid," Lyle said.

"Get rid?"

"Yes, of your wife, and the tiles, and in that order," Lyle said sniggering to himself.

The Sarge grunted and walked to the phone. "You'd better not have applied undue pressure to that boy not to have legal representation," he said staring suspiciously at Lyle.

"Absolutely not, Sarge. That would be a breach of the codes of practice and bring into disrepute the integrity, ethics, and values of the profession which I hold so very dear to my heart."

The Inspector attended the custody block and duly confirmed with Haroon he no longer required legal representation and had not succumbed to duress.

"Book us into interview room number two please, Sarge," Lyle said.

"Yes, Constable, I will," he said.

"Haroon, I'm arresting you for burglary. You do not have to say anything but it may harm your defence if you do not mention when questioned something which you later rely in court. Anything you do say may be given in evidence," Herbert said.

"What are you talking about? Right, I want a lawyer right now. I'm being framed. This is crazy," Haroon said.

"SHUT UP," Lyle said. He leaned over the desk and clenched

his fist a short distance from the face of a petrified Haroon.

"I told you that you'd be out of here within the hour and you will, provided you give us the information we want. We will make sure you'll be bailed to return to the station in a few weeks and the most you'll end up with out of this is a speeding ticket. But you comply fully or else, do you understand?" Lyle said.

Haroon nodded frantically.

"What were you doing at the industrial estate last night? I saw your car leave there," Herbert said.

"Aren't you supposed to switch the tape recording on for the interview?" Haroon said.

"All in good time. Now answer my question." Haroon shuffled in his seat reluctantly.

"I took my mate Zams there. He asked me to drive him but wouldn't tell me what he was doing. All I know is he was asked to go there by his friend Riz. He was nervous and he smoked a joint in my car, he must have accidentally dropped some in the car and that's what the policewoman found. He went to one of the units and I heard a scream. A short time later I saw him taken by a group of males to another unit. I contacted Riz and he said he'd make some calls. He came back to me to say help was on its way." Herbert and Lyle frowned at each other at this point. "They put stuff into a truck but I couldn't see what and they drove off with Zams," Haroon continued.

"When I was stopped by the police, I was in pursuit of them. I wanted to see where they were taking Zams."

"Excellent Haroon. Now when Tash switches the tape on you say you took Zams to the industrial estate but you had no idea he was going to break into a unit. He smoked cannabis in your car but you didn't and you didn't know he'd left cannabis in your car. When you realised that he was committing burglary you panicked and drove off at speed because you wanted nothing to do with it and in your panic, you admit you were driving too fast and you're very sorry you nearly hit the police car." Haroon nodded.

The interview was conducted and at its conclusion at the very second Herbert stopped the tape, Haroon said: "I've done what you asked. Can I go now?"

"Patience is a virtue, Haroon, it really is," Lyle said with a grin.

"The interview is over but you're not going anywhere until you tell us exactly what we want to know," Herbert said as she and Lyle switched their good cop bad cop roles.

"I've told you everything I know," Haroon pleaded and waved his arms in frustration.

"Calm down, Haroon, or the next time I clench my fist you'll be on the receiving end of it. We need full names and addresses of Zams and Riz and we need their phone numbers, which you have in your phone here at the station."

"I'm not a grass. My life won't be worth living if I grass."

"We don't care, Haroon. We've got enough to charge you with conspiracy to commit burglary, possession of drugs and dangerous driving. You wouldn't believe how many outstanding burglaries and robberies we will connect you to. We'll have you charged and remanded to go before the next court with a recommendation that you're sent to prison awaiting trial. You think grassing on Zams and Riz is bad, how do you think you'll get on in prison? You're weak, Haroon, and that weakness will be exploited in prison. You'll be assaulted and violated daily, and I mean violated," Herbert said with her teeth gritted aggressively like a bulldog staring down its prey.

"What kind of police are you? I haven't committed any burglaries or robberies. I should have had a lawyer," Haroon said shaking his head in despair.

"That was your choice, Haroon. We are police you should fear. In fact, you should be more scared of us than Zams or Riz," Lyle said as he worked in tandem as bad cop bad cop with Herbert to pile the pressure on a terrified Haroon.

"They don't have to know it's you that grassed. We can protect you, Haroon, we really can. You'll be doing the right thing in helping the police," Herbert said softly as the duos manipulation of Haroon continued unabated.

"I'll do what you want, just let me go," Haroon said.

"That's the correct decision, Haroon, it really is. I'm glad you have come around to our way of thinking. Let's get this wrapped up and you can get out of here. Si, do you want to update the Sarge whilst Haroon gives me the details?"

"Yes, Tash," Lyle said. He clapped his hands together and took to his feet. "He can give us the phone numbers when we give him his property back. I'll also give you my contact number, Haroon. That way, if anything should come up that we need to be aware of then you can give me a call." Haroon nodded.

"Full and frank admission was it then, Constable?" the Sergeant said with a strong degree of scepticism in his voice, as Lyle burst confidently out of the interview room.

"No, it was a full and frank denial. Interview concluded at zero nine zero two hours. For the record, he was further arrested for burglary at zero eight forty-two hours."

"Constable, for the record you're going to have to do a bit better than that. What are the circumstances of this burglary? What did he say about the dangerous driving?" the Sergeant said, unable to disguise his contempt for Lyle.

"You never did make it to CID, did you Sarge? Although from what I hear it wasn't for the lack of trying. The world loves a trier, don't they, Sarge?" Lyle said.

"I beg your pardon. What has my career path got to do with this?" he said. His eyes squinted as if he were looking directly into sunlight.

"Nothing. It's an observation, Sarge, and that is what makes me a detective, a good detective, even if I do say so myself. The PIC was arrested for a burglary at a warehouse last night where several high value items were stolen. The PIC's vehicle was witnessed in the vicinity of the industrial estate at the relevant time and a business card of the cycle shop where the PIC works was found outside the burgled warehouse."

"That's hardly evidence of him being involved in the burglary. What are these high value items that were taken?" the Sergeant said.

"A full inventory is not yet available Sarge but I'm sure you'd accept it would be remiss of us not to interview a subject who was arrested driving at speed late at night in an area where a burglary had taken place. As it is, he has named a possible offender for the burglary as well as a likely orchestrator. The offender is the same male he maintains is responsible for the cannabis found in his car. He's sorry he was speeding and bitterly regrets the fact he nearly hit the police car. We will be endeavouring to arrest the outstanding offenders as a priority so we would like to bail the PIC to return to the station in four weeks, Sarge."

"No, you can bail him for the burglary and charge him for possession of cannabis. We'll drop the dangerous driving to driving without due care and attention and you can charge with him that as well," the Sergeant said. "What is that, Constable, you don't want to do a file for court for minor drugs and driving offences? Is that beneath you, detective? Well, that is not my problem." Lyle licked his wounds and took a deep breath.

"Sarge, he's going to be an informant for us. He's got no previous. He isn't responsible for the drugs or the burglary. I don't care about a court file because I'm not doing one. He's getting bailed and if you don't like it, well I'd hate for your wife to find out you've been taking down PC Morris's particulars. Let's keep the lilac tiles as the biggest problem in your marriage shall we, Sarge?" Lyle said.

The Sarge seethed as his face glowed redder than a tomato. "Your time will come, Lyle, I promise you." Lyle merely sniggered in response as Herbert and Haroon exited the interview room and approached the desk.

"You're going to be bailed to return to this station in a few weeks, Haroon," the Sergeant said.

"Thank you, Sarge. I am so glad we are on the same page with this," Lyle said.

As the clock ticked around to nine thirty, Riz nervously opened the grazed graffiti covered door to the first floor of the car park. He stepped pensively out into a wall of concrete, filled with an array of the pride and joys of the many commuters and shoppers that had parked there that morning.

In a millisecond, Riz's world was plunged into darkness. He was tackled from behind and an onion sack placed over his head. He heard the screech of tyres as he was bundled mercilessly inside the back of a van.

"Good morning, Riz," RT said. "What a pleasure to meet you."

"Who are you? Where are you taking me? Where's Zams?" Riz said. His pleas muffled by the shallot-less facial covering. RT snatched the bag from over the head of a restrained Riz and saw tears in Riz's eyes.

"No need to cry, Riz, Zams is over there." RT pointed at a figure tied up in the opposite corner of the van, lying in the foetal position, also with an onion sack covering the head.

"I'm not crying. It is the onions. Couldn't you have at least washed these bags? How do I know that's Zams? It could be anyone."

RT lifted the bag covering Zams as if he were unveiling a prize on a game show. Zams's eyes and mouth were covered in tape; his desperate utterings silenced.

"It's good to see you, Zams. I'm so sorry I got you into this mess. I'll put this right," Riz said in Urdu.

RT punched Riz hard in the stomach which winded him

significantly. "You speak in English. This is Oxford not the Ganges. It's disrespectful."

"Disrespectful. You've kidnapped us and you're talking to me about respect. Isn't that a bit hypocritical?" Riz said whilst coughing up phlegm and trying to catch his breath."

"Big words, Riz. Big words. Now, how about you tell me what you know about these robots," RT said.

"Why should I tell you anything? You're not going to let me and Zams go regardless."

"I'm a very reasonable man, Riz. I'll even take on board your feedback about ensuring Barry buys some washing powder to clean items before we next kidnap someone. I promise you and Zams will have a future, provided you tell me everything you know about the robots. I think that is a fair offer. Now, if you don't agree with that offer then I'm afraid you are going to endure pain and suffering like you wouldn't believe. Barry loves the Spice Girls; I'll have him play their album to you on repeat whilst you are tied up in his flat."

"I'm not having these pair in my—"

"Shut up, Barry. I'm talking. And if I want to tie them up in your flat I will. If I want to tie you up in your flat I will. To torture you I'd switch the Spice Girls off." RT turned back to face Riz. "What's it going to be, Riz?" RT said.

"Ok. I guess I'm going to have to trust you. I'll tell you what I know. Not that it's a lot."

Zams wriggled and shook his head furiously which drew a concerned look from Riz.

"Get that onion sack back on his head and control him, will you?" RT said. "Go on, Riz. Tell me what you know."

Riz reluctantly conveyed his knowledge to RT and his cronies.

"It's quite a fascinating story. Isn't it, lads?" RT said.

"I wish I wasn't aware of it," Riz said. "Are you going to let us go now?"

"Not just yet—"

"You promised—"

"Don't interrupt me Riz. The devil is in the detail. I didn't say I was going to let you go. I said I would promise you and Zams a future and I will."

"You're full of—"

"I'd watch your mouth if I was you. That promise of a future can be saved for just Zams, you know?" RT stared menacingly at Riz who desperately averted his gaze. "Anyway, I have great news for you, Riz," RT said as his scowl turned to a smile. "For your impressive loyalty to the safety of your friend and your greatly appreciated honesty, I'm going to reward you."

"Really. How?"

"Do you like the programme 'Stars in Their Eyes'?" RT said. "You know, the one presented by Matthew Kelly. Where the contestants say, 'Tonight Matthew I'm going to be…' and then they come out transformed as a pop star."

"I, err, don't watch that, no," Riz said with a bemused look, which was matched by RT's henchmen.

"Well, tonight Riz you're going to be Akram," RT said taking some passports from out of his pocket.

"What?"

"You and Zams are going to Holland to do some work for me. Tonight, Matthew, Zams is going to be Mohammed, you are going to be Akram and you are both going to be in Amsterdam."

"Tonight, I'm going to be Riz at home in Oxford, England, you crazy psycho."

RT laughed maniacally.

"I hate to go all Judith Chalmers on you, Riz, sorry I mean Akram. But I wish you were here and here is Amsterdam."

"Don't call me Akram, and here is Oxford, and that's where I'm staying."

"Dig your heels in all you like, but you're going to do as I say or I'll take your stubbornness out on your family and Zams's family. I won't even promise to wash the onion sacks. I suggest you do me and them a favour and take a nice city break. You'll love it." RT banged the van hard with the outside of his right fist and said; "Driver. Next stop. Airport."

14

Chapter Fourteen: Control

When he was six years old, he'd told his family he would be Prime Minister one day. His family supported his youthful ambition with the benefits of a private education. A well-funded education provided him with the comprehensive learning a comprehensive school would not have done. He'd aspired to be Winston Churchill, and, in his mind, that is what he now was. He lay back in his exquisite, claret-coloured chair and closed his eyes. The beeping of the desk on his phone quickly reminded him that the job he'd aspired to and achieved didn't give you much time to yourself.

"The Security Minister is here to see you," the Prime Minister's Principal Private Secretary said.

"Please send him in, Henry," the Prime Minister said.

"Thank you so much for agreeing to see me in person this morning, Prime Minister," the Security Minister said.

"It's no trouble at all. Would you like a cup of tea or coffee?" the Prime Minister said.

"No, thank you. I'm cutting down. On a bit of a health kick at the moment."

The Prime Minister poured himself a cup of coffee. "Ok. What is the latest update on this sensitive matter in Oxford? You seemed rather concerned during our call last night."

"Well, yes, Prime Minister. I wanted to talk to you in person as I think it's reaching a crescendo, and it will soon be time for you to make a rather difficult decision."

"You don't have to tell me. As Prime Minister every decision is difficult, believe me. It is simply impossible to do right by everyone. Please continue."

"As you are aware, following my visit to Oxford yesterday I was briefed by the Security Services. "Well..." the Security Minister stuttered and then hesitated.

"Go on," the Prime Minister said.

"Well, there's no positive solution for the Leidenstraum children or their aunt if you catch my drift."

"No positive solution?"

"I'm afraid not. I hate to–"

"May I ask? Do you aspire to be in my chair one day? Be Prime Minister of this great country?"

"No. Well, I don't know Prime Minister. I am ambitious yes, but—"

"Your response tells me you can never be Prime Minister, and I'll tell you why. As Prime Minister you must make decisions that cost lives, both seen and unseen by the public. I'm not saying you have to turn into a heartless unemotional vacuum, but you do have to be incredibly decisive. If you sit and contemplate the potential human misery a decision you make could result in, well you'd never make a decision at all."

"Prime Minister, I note you speak about it in the third person. Is that to disassociate yourself from the decisions you've made which you regret?"

"It's not for you to question how I live with my decisions. I was merely explaining how I and others in my position must make difficult decisions, often truly impossible decisions. The Leidenstraums is it? Well, they and the aunt will have to be taken care of. The security services will have the difficult job of planning and executing it of course. I simply authorise it. Consider it authorised."

"As clinical as that? You wouldn't consider any other options? They must lose their lives."

"Listen to yourself. What other options do you really think there are? You're focusing on the human side of it. When you see it on the television, hear it on the radio, read it in the newspaper, it will be three people who tragically died today of carbon monoxide poisoning, were in a head on collision with a tree, were crushed in a building collapse, and you will not give it a second thought. It's a sad fact that three lives lost to preserve national security is an extremely small price to pay. Life is precious, but it must end, sometimes earlier than it would or should have."

The Security Minister was stunned into silence.

"The most important thing is that we have those robots. Preventing their falling into the hands of a rogue state is the main thing. The cleaning up around it, well that is a secondary consideration," the Prime Minister said.

"Y-y-yes, Prime Minister. Of course. You are right."

"I know I am right. I really do not require your affirmation on that. Although there is one small matter we have not discussed."

"What's that Prime Minister?"

"The initial investigation into Dr Leidenstraum's activities?"

"Yes, what about it?"

"You oversaw that. Had access to all the confidential material."

"Yes, Prime Minister. Under the instruction of yourself, the Home Secretary, and the Foreign Secretary, I provided ministerial oversight. Why?"

"In your role as Security Minister you have visited some hostile nation states and met some of the world's most despicable despots, haven't you?"

"Yes," the Security Minister said as he became increasingly perplexed by the Prime Minister's questions.

"You are the traitor. Here you are pretending to care about what happens to the Leidenstraums, knowing full well you are responsible for their plight. You disgust me."

"What? No. Prime Minister how could you possibly accuse me of something so preposterous. I would never betray—"

"For money. You have sold your soul and compromised the security of this country for money."

"I've done no such thing. These allegations are unfounded and beyond hurtful. Why would you accuse me of such things?"

"Evidence. That's why. We have evidence. Your Swiss bank account. Money moved all around the world into it. How can you possibly explain the receipt of six figure sums from Iran, Kazakhstan, Uzbekistan? The letter from the Colombian Ministry offering you political asylum. Your Turkish passport. The photograph of you with Saddam

Hussein's third in command. Given the cocaine in your office and the rendezvous with the rent boys, maybe you were blackmailed or made an offer you couldn't refuse but that's no excuse."

"Someone is setting me up. I've done none of the things you are talking about. I will prove my innocence."

"Do you think you'll get a chance?" The Prime Minister said with a scowl.

The peril of his situation started to dawn on the Security Minister.

"Please. Prime Minister. I'm an innocent man. It is innocent until proven guilty in this country."

"Not when it is so deeply damaging to the country. Innocent or guilty, and sadly I believe it is the latter, you could never have a trial. The damage to the country. I wouldn't have a hope of winning the next election. Mine and my family's futures ruined. Save your concerns for the Leidenstraums for yourself. I told you a few moments ago about how decisive you must be as Prime Minister and that life is precious but it must end, sometimes earlier than it would or should have."

"No. Prime Minister you can't do this. You can't."

"I would like to thank you for the service you have given this country and sorry it must end. You will be given a painless death. Nothing embarrassing will be released that hurts your family. I promise you that." The Prime Minister then pressed a button under his desk.

The Security Minister was enraged and leaned forward to strike the Prime Minister but was tackled from behind by two men who had entered the room through a secret internal door. The Prime Minister watched passively as the Security Minister was nullified.

"He really should have had a tea or coffee. I suppose I'd better finish writing his obituary." He looked up at the two men expectantly. "Not with him lying there. Get rid of him."

The Security Minister was unceremoniously dragged along the carpet and through the secret door. The Prime Minister telephoned his secretary. "Can you please push my next appointment back ten minutes? I just need to finish writing something. Thank you."

Marcia enjoyed relaxing in her lounge with a glass, or two, of chilled Chardonnay watching 'Friends' after a tough day. She loved inviting friends around for a gossip and a giggle. It was her solace from the world, but today the atmosphere was more tense than a courtroom awaiting the verdict of the jury.

"You expect us to trust him?" Will said to Marcia and Clare, as he looked pensively at Tariq.

"I'm sorry, bro," Tariq said. He stood up and paced the room. "I didn't want to double-cross any of you in the first place. You can trust me. I want to get my sister back and I want you guys to be safe as well."

"We can trust him," Marcia said, which drew some raised eyebrows in the room. "Without us, he isn't going to get his sister back. There's no way he can trust her kidnapper, but he can trust us." Marcia turned to face Tariq. "Well, do you trust Shabeela's kidnapper?"

Tariq shook his head and was about to speak when Robert and Lucy entered the room shouting.

"Clare, you're on TV. You need to see this," Robert said.

Marcia quickly switched on the television in the lounge.

"We can now go live to our crime correspondent, James, for more on this breaking news story," the TV reporter said.

"Oh my god. That's my photo," Clare said.

"Thank you, Amanda," James said.

"Oh my god. That's my home," Clare said.

"You join me outside the home of Detective Sergeant Clare Stevens. Oxfordshire Police have confirmed in the last half an hour that she is wanted for the murder of the yet unnamed police officer who was killed at Oxford's main hospital in the early hours of this morning. Whilst information is limited, we understand Clare Stevens was a patient at the hospital receiving treatment for a gunshot wound. It's not known how Clare Stevens came to be the victim of a shooting, but we understand a few undisclosed items recovered from her address behind me are indicative of the serving officer's involvement in organised crime. It is also understood she left the hospital in company with a male named as John Paterson, who himself had been shot by armed police following an incident in a car park yesterday. Police have issued this photo of him which you should now see on your screen. They have urged the public not to approach either suspect as they are understandably considered highly dangerous and instead encourage people to report any sightings immediately by calling 999. Neighbours here are in a state of shock with most describing the officer as friendly. Many here have said they were completely unaware Clare Stevens was even a police officer."

The room fell silent but for Lucy and Robert who both started crying and were comforted by their mother.

"James. I am sorry, we are going to have to cut your broadcast short as we have some other breaking news coming through. Downing Street have just announced the Security Minister has been found dead in his office. We are awaiting further details but the Prime Minister has released the following brief statement: 'I am shocked and saddened to hear of the untimely passing of a truly outstanding colleague. It is of course too early to speculate on the cause of his death, but my thoughts and prayers are with his family and friends at this difficult time.'

"The Security Minister is the one that came to the station," Marcia said. "This is highly suspicious."

"I'd say so, particularly considering he'd promoted Johnson, who'd shot Clare," Sarah said.

"Never mind the Security Minister. I have just been named as a murder suspect and evidence has clearly been planted in my home."

"It's not much better for me either," John said.

The conversation was interrupted by a call to Marcia's work phone.

Marcia instructed everyone in the room to be quiet. "Hello, DC Reynolds speaking," Marcia said.

"Hi Marcia. It's DI Taylor here."

"Good afternoon, sir, how can I help?"

"I know you're on late shift this afternoon but I need you to come to the station earlier."

"Yes sir, of course. Is everything ok?"

"You haven't heard then?"

"Heard what sir?"

"Clare Stevens is wanted for the murder of a police officer. It's a complete media circus down here. We're under a lot of pressure to track her down as soon as possible, along with an accomplice of hers and anyone else who could be involved."

"Sir, I'm really shocked. I wouldn't have thought DS Stevens could be involved in such a thing."

"No, it's taken all of us by surprise. Just be mindful of all the journalists and reporters when you come to work. If approached, don't say anything."

"Of course, sir. I understand. I'll see you shortly."

"Thanks, Marcia." The call then ended.

"I've got to go into work early to help look for the people who are in this room. This is going to be a bit odd," Marcia said.

"Do you think you can keep your cool?" Clare said.

"I'm going to have to. If nothing else, it gives me an inside view of what is happening. Can you all stay here and remain calm?"

"We don't have a lot of choice," John said.

Zams and RT heard the thrust of the engines of commercial airliners in the airspace above them as the van entered the airport and parked.

"We're here," RT said. "I'm excited, and I'm not the one going on holiday?"

"What are we going to do when we get to Holland?" Riz said. The tone in his voice conveyed he'd resigned himself to his involuntary excursion.

"You'll be collected from the airport by a Dutch friend of mine called Johannes. He'll look after you, ensure you have a great time, and when it's time to go to work he will take you there."

"How can you trust that we'll even go?" Riz said.

"You're not going alone. Barry is going with you. He will be your chaperone."

"You'll do exactly as I say," Barry said. "Or else."

"Barry is right. You must be one hundred percent compliant. Even the slightest hint that you two aren't playing ball and you will be penalised. Harshly," RT said.

"When will we be flying back?" Riz said.

"Who said you will be flying back?" RT said.

"What? I assumed this would be a short trip?"

"You shouldn't make assumptions, Riz, although I can con-firm it is going to be a short trip. It's just that you might not be flying back. You may be returning using other transport, but all will become clear in due course. Please just enjoy your all expenses paid city break and stop worrying."

The roads surrounding the police station were choked up with cars, vans, and news trucks straddling the pavement. Swathes of men and women stood on the pavement chatting whilst surrounded by equipment and satellites. They practiced reading from scripts; held microphones; reporters had their hair and make-up attended to.

You don't see this on the news, Marcia thought whilst gently manoeuvring her vehicle through a tight gap to reach the police station car park. She showed her ID to a uniformed officer who raised the barrier and let her through. Once parked, she was greeted by more uniformed officers who escorted her to a room inside the station.

"What is going on?" Marcia said.

"Good afternoon DC Reynolds, I'm DI Ian Jarvis from the London Police Confidential Unit. Due to the conflict of interest, we are working with the Police Complaints Oversight Unit to lead the investigation into Clare Stevens. It is not appropriate for this matter to be investigated by Oxfordshire.

As a matter of course we need to interview everyone who worked with her."

"Oh, I see," Marcia said. She tried to remain calm but her heart rate soared and her pupils dilated.

"Are you ok? You seem a bit on edge," DI Jarvis said.

"Yes fine. It's just a lot to take in. I can't quite believe it. DI Taylor never mentioned this when he called me."

"Standard procedure, I'm afraid. I was there when DI Taylor made the call. Look, provided you cooperate and we are happy with your answers, you should be able to resume work as normal. We are almost finished with our enquiries in the CID office and we have interviewed several of your colleagues already. Please take a seat. DS Sarah Radcliffe and I will be interviewing you shortly."

Marcia sat down and tried to maintain her composure. She was certain from DI Jarvis's reaction that her face was etched with guilt.

DI Jarvis left the room to find DS Radcliffe, who was stood with Johnson. "Sarah, are you ready for this interview now?" DI Jarvis said.

"I am sir, but there's a problem," DS Radcliffe said. "ACC Johnson seems reluctant to recall DCs Natasha Herbert and Simon Lyle to the station."

"Sergeant, I find this insinuation wholly disrespectful. Aside from the shocking and appalling situation we find ourselves in with regards to Clare Stevens, I am a senior ranking officer who must make operational decisions in the interests of public protection and solving crime."

"Sir, we respect that, we really do," DI Jarvis said. "However, it would be particularly helpful if you could call them and ask them to attend the station now. If you require urgent support with something, I'm sure we can find resources to assist you."

"Very well. I will call them." Johnson proceeded to call Lyle. "Hi Simon, it is Acting ACC Johnson here. I need you and DC Herbert to return to the station as a priority."

"But we're tracking these phones of Riz and Zams. They are at the airport," Lyle said.

"I know but those enquiries will have to wait, I am afraid. This is more important."

"Are you free to speak right now?" Lyle said.

"No, I'm not able to explain why you're more urgently needed here. You just are and that is a lawful order."

"Do we need to get cleaned up, forensically speaking, before we come back?"

"Yes, you absolutely must. I'm very sorry, I know how hard you've both worked on this investigation. I have trust, faith, and confidence you will be able to effectively pick it back up from where you leave it. Thanks Simon." Johnson feigned to end the call but left it running so Lyle could hear.

"Do you normally direct enquiries so closely with your DCs, sir?" DI Jarvis said.

"I don't know how you do things in London, DI Jarvis, but here we operate much more as a close-knit team, irrespective of rank."

"Outside of your current unfortunate circumstances, I don't suppose Oxfordshire has the level of crime to contend with that we do in London, does it sir?"

"I imagine not, Inspector. Although, so busy are you, I note the Police Complaints Oversight Unit have drafted you in here very quickly. Very quickly indeed."

"Well sir, I'd like to reassure you that the very best officers have been chosen to come here to deal with these troubling matters of police corruption."

Johnson then ended the call.

"Turn around Tash, we've got to get back," Lyle said. "And stop off at a unisex clothes shop on the way back." Herbert looked at him blankly. "Just trust me," Lyle said.

"DC Reynolds, before we start the interview, I need my colleague here to carry out some forensic swabs," DS Radcliffe said as she entered the room with a male crime scene investigator in a full forensic suit. "Is that ok?"

"Is this really necessary?" Marcia said.

"I'm afraid so. You seem a bit concerned. It's nothing to worry about," the male said. His words muffled by his face mask."

"The forensic results will dictate whether or not the officer has anything to worry about," DS Radcliffe said. "You really don't seem comfortable with this, DC Reynolds. I wonder why that is?"

"Well, if you must know. I had nightmares when I saw the film ET with all the people in the forensic suits," Marcia said and forced a smile. DS Radcliffe's facial expression remained stern and wary.

"I've come to work and now I'm sat in a room getting swabbed. I'm going to be interviewed. Surely, I'm entitled to be a bit apprehensive."

"Of course. Although apprehension can of course be indicative of guilt rather than just nerves," DS Radcliffe said.

"What are you looking for with these forensic swabs anyway?" Marcia said, in an attempt to divert the conversation away from her emotions.

"Anything that could connect you to Clare Stevens and/or

her offences. Fibres on your clothes or gunpowder residue on your hands, for example," DS Radcliffe said, as she stared closely into Marcia's eyes like a poker player trying to intimidate an opponent.

Marcia swallowed hard as she realised how much close contact she'd had with Clare, recalling how she had touched Clare's hand in the car when she had picked Clare and John up from the taxi, let alone other more intimate contact. "Can I have a glass of water please? My mouth is dry."

"You can wait until the swabs are complete. Water will be available when DI Jarvis and I interview you."

Clare Stevens had wanted to explore a life outside of Scotland and she'd wanted to be a Police Officer. At the age of twenty-one, her dream came true. It hadn't been easy. The rumours about her sexuality had made her the butt of jokes from male colleagues, but she was determined it wouldn't interfere with the job she loved. The job had turned into an incredibly rewarding career. Yet now, a mad scientist making robots, not that she'd call him that in front of Sarah and Will, had somehow brought all that crashing to the ground. The force had taught her patience, leadership, and planning. A plan of action was required.

Clare switched on the phone she and Marcia had retrieved

from Tariq. "I'm going to text your father and sister's kidnapper," she said.

"Why did you switch that phone off anyway?" Tariq said.

"I'm a detective. Trust me. These devices are as good as having a tracker under someone's skin."

"I think my phone is still on," Cheryl said worriedly.

"Then switch it off and keep it off. All of you, make sure your phones are off. The last thing we need is the police turning up here looking for us," Clare said as she started sending a text.

"What are you writing to the kidnapper?" Sarah said.

"I'm explaining how Tariq here is going to be in the funeral car and will do whatever is required to help deliver you two to him during the cortege's route from the church."

"This is our father's funeral and it's going to be a complete charade," Sarah said.

"The service will be genuine, sis. Our love for him is genuine. Our anger with him right now is simply for the position we find ourselves in, the position he has put us in," Will said.

"I'm sorry. I know how difficult tomorrow is going to be. I didn't mean to be so insensitive," Clare said. "It's just, things have got to be put in motion for tomorrow to try and protect us all as best as we can."

"I know," Sarah said. "It's just a lot to deal with."

"As soon as Marcia gets back, we'll get you two and Tariq over to your Aunt Janice's. It will give you an opportunity to grieve, at least for a short while."

Clare hit send on the text message and switched the phone off.

A phone beeped loudly and vibrated on a table in the kitchen of a plush residence. A man led a woman into the kitchen and removed her restraints. She was pale, weak, and her eyes were sullen. He picked the phone up from the side and sat down at a table.

"Make me dinner. I want steak. Medium rare with oven cooked chips and garden peas. Go on, get on with it. I'll have a beer from the fridge whilst you're going that way," he said.

The lady knew by now that complaint was futile and would only lead to further pain.

"I've got a message here with some plans for tomorrow. This is good news," the male said. "Very good news."

The lady walked over to where the male was sat, with a can of beer and a glass in her hand. She placed them on the table and turned to walk away.

"Don't walk away. Pour it. Pour my beer for me. When are you going to learn?" he said.

"I'm sorry, sir," the lady said and did as she was told.

"Never mind. Do you know who this message is from? It's from Tariq, your son."

Her eyes lit up at the mention of his name.

15

Chapter Fifteen: Suspicion

Frequent flyers probably never think about airports any more than train dwellers think about railway stations, but Riz and Zams were not frequent flyers. They were in awe as they walked through Schiphol Airport.

"This place is huge," Zams said.

"You can transit anywhere in the world from here, but don't get any ideas about flying to Karachi or anything like that," Barry said.

"We won't, Barry. We'd simply settle for a return flight to the UK," Riz said.

In the distance, they saw a tall, muscular dark-haired male holding a sign saying "Oxford."

"That man has a sign that has "Oxford" written on it. What a strange coincidence," Zams said.

"It's not a coincidence," Barry said.

As they got closer, the male extended his right hand whilst holding the sign in his left.

"Hi, you two must be Riz and Zams. My name is Johannes," the male said in a soft Dutch accent.

Riz and Zams both looked at him warily.

"I thought you'd prefer me to greet you by your real names, rather than the names in your passports," the male said with a cheeky grin. "Now come on, it looks odd if you don't shake my hand when I've come to collect you from the airport."

His attempt at easing the tension worked as in turn both Zams and Riz shook his hand, followed by Barry.

"Good to see you again, Baz," Johannes said.

"You too, Johannes," Barry said.

"So Riz, Zams, is this your first trip to Holland?" Johannes said.

"Yes, it is," Zams said. "I must say, Johannes, your English is good."

"So is yours, Zams," Johannes said and laughed.

Zams looked baffled.

273

"He's making a joke at our expense. Because we're Pakistani," Riz said to Zams in Urdu.

"My Urdu is as good as my English and is as good as my Dutch," Johannes said in Urdu and laughed again.

Riz and Zams were a combination of stunned and impressed by Johannes's multi-lingual ability.

They were walked to the airport car park and taken to a parked taxi, where stood a striking, tall, blonde female in an air stewardess uniform with flared nostrils, and her arms impatiently folded.

"Hey Riz, wasn't she on our flight?" Zams said.

"Yes, she served me a hot chocolate," Riz said.

"A hot chocolate. You are so rock and roll, Riz," Johannes said. "Her name is Dafne. She works for me, as well as the airline. Do you have the cash to pay for these passengers to take this taxi journey, Dafne?"

"Yes Johannes, I do," Dafne said in a strong Dutch accent. "Do you want the money now?"

"No Dafne, it can wait until we get our guests to the destination. As long as you have the money."

"What is going on?" Zams said.

"Shut up. It's none of your concern," Barry said.

"There's no need for that, Barry. It's fine for him to ask questions," Johannes said. "I have a financial arrangement with RT for your visit. It was safer for Dafne to bring the cash over from the UK instead of any of you. Don't be fooled by the taxi. I can afford a better vehicle but it makes me less conspicuous if I drive around in this."

"We won't ask more questions, Johannes," Riz said. Riz looked at Zams and firmly shook his head.

DI Jarvis sat down and looked across the table at Marcia with his steely brown eyes. "Detective Constable Reynolds. Tell me about how well you know Clare Stevens?" DI Jarvis said.

"B-b-barely at... barely at all really. To be honest with you."

"Well, are you being honest with me? That is the question, isn't it?"

"Of course. Why on earth wouldn't you think I'm being honest with you?"

"Well, the Acting ACC has informed us that earlier this week Clare Stevens asked to work with you. Tell us about that?" DS Radcliffe said.

"I'm a new detective and I think DS Stevens was going to show me the ropes, as an experienced detective."

"How very noble of her," DI Jarvis said. "You've got to look at it from our point of view Marcia, if it's ok to call you Marcia. DS Stevens is corrupt—"

"No, she is not. And no, you can call me Detective Constable Reynolds. Sir."

"You're very protective of Clare Stevens, aren't you Detective Constable Reynolds?" DS Radcliffe said.

"Sarge, I'm finding it hard to believe a highly experienced, dedicated and successful detective like Detective Sergeant Clare Stevens, and I will continue to call her that, despite your best efforts to find her guilty and strip that from her, is linked to organised crime."

"Assisting an offender is a very serious matter," DI Jarvis said. "Assisting an offender who is a police officer, well that's misconduct in public office. I do hope your defence of Clare Stevens is just that of a concerned colleague and not evidence that you're helping her, or John Paterson, or anyone else for that matter."

"I have done nothing wrong. You are aware the Acting ACC refused Clare's offer to supervise me? He appointed DCs Herbert and Lyle instead. Of course, you must already know that. What have they got to say for themselves? Well, I'm waiting. I don't wish to appear insubordinate but perhaps you need to do some more investigating and stop making assumptions."

DI Jarvis and DS Radcliffe turned to face each other and then back towards Marcia.

"You watch your tone," DI Jarvis said. "We will be speaking to Herbert and Lyle and we are conducting a thorough investigation."

"Can I go now?" Marcia said.

"You're very keen to get away, aren't you?" DS Radcliffe said.

"I have work to do. Is that so suspicious?"

"On an ordinary day, no. But today is no ordinary day," DI Jarvis said. "I think we are done for now. So, yes you are authorised to go about your business."

"Thank you. What about the forensic results?" Marcia said.

"I didn't think you'd done anything wrong," DS Radcliffe said.

"I haven't."

"Then why are you asking about the forensic results?"

"It's just a question."

"All forensic swabs are undergoing fast-tracking," DI Jarvis said. "We anticipate we will have most of the results by tomorrow afternoon. You already know the outcome though, Constable, so you won't be waiting on our call, will you? Have a nice day."

Marcia stood up and opened the door. She saw the door at the end of the corridor open, through which walked Herbert and Lyle. The sight of which made Marcia burst into a fit of laughter.

"What are you laughing at?" DS Radcliffe said.

"These two. Look at them," Marcia said.

Lyle was stood in three quarter length Khaki shorts, white socks, and sandals. His top half adorned with a white vest and an unbuttoned Hawaii shirt, sunglasses and a Panama hat. Herbert was in a low-cut knee length floral dress with white trainers, sunglasses, and a baseball cap.

"Who are they?" DI Jarvis said.

"Sir, may I introduce you to Detective Constables Simon Lyle and Natasha Herbert," Marcia said.

At that moment, Johnson stepped into the corridor, and was so baffled by the sight of Herbert and Lyle, he was rendered speechless.

"Acting ACC Johnson, why are these officers dressed like

this?" DI Jarvis said.

"We have been undercover. Who are you?" Lyle said.

"Undercover. Yes. Excellent," Johnson said. "They have been working undercover."

"Well, I look forward to hearing all about a covert investigation in Oxfordshire that has you dressed as extras from Magnum PI. I am DI Jarvis."

"It is covert DI Jarvis, so I'm afraid you will not be present for the debriefing," Johnson said. "Come on, Simon, Natasha, let's go for a chat."

"Oh no you don't, sir," DI Jarvis said. "This debrief is going to have to wait. I am interviewing them first. You can hear about how they infiltrated filming of a pop music video or whatever this is later."

Fixing cars was Nathan's passion, admin was not. However, if he didn't place the order for the tyres, brake pads, and the carburettors, he wasn't going to be able to continue to maintain a profitable business. Those component parts were vital to the smooth running of his profitable, cash rich, legitimate business, which in turn was a vital component of the smooth running of laundering money.

As Nathan added fifteen car batteries to his parts order, Brett Sadler walked into the office. Nathan looked like he had seen a ghost.

"How did you get out? Where are the others?" Have they escaped too?" Nathan said panicked. He stood up and looked towards the compound but it was secure.

Brett was perplexed by Nathan's reaction. "I'm Brett Sadler, I'm going to be working here over the summer."

"Working here. Who said you will?" Nathan said.

"You did. My dad asked you. He said you'd said yes. I'm really looking forward to it."

"Your dad?"

"Yes. My dad is Dave Sadler."

At that moment Dave Sadler climbed out from underneath a car and wiped his greasy hands on his overalls. He looked up and saw his son was in the office and waved.

"There he is," Brett said and waved back at his father.

"Oh, that Dave Sadler. You should have said," Nathan said.

Brett continued to be perplexed by Nathan's behaviour. His dad then walked into the office.

"You've met my son then," Dave said.

"Yes. He's going to be working here over the summer," Nathan said.

"We're really grateful to you for giving Brett the opportunity. He loves cars. I think you'd be keen to become a mechanic when you leave school, wouldn't you?"

"I want to be an engineer, dad."

"I know you do, but maybe after the summer you might want to follow in your dad's footsteps and become a mechanic."

Brett turned towards Nathan. "I'm really grateful to you for giving me the opportunity. I will work hard, but I really do want to be an engineer."

Dave shrugged his shoulders and shook his head. "Nathan doesn't want to hear about your pipe dream ideas. Thanks again, Nathan. Wait for me if you want, Brett. I'll be finished soon. Before I forget, it's still ok for me to have tomorrow off, isn't it?"

"Tomorrow?" Nathan said as he stared intently at Brett.

"Yes, it's the funeral of our next-door neighbour."

"I'm sorry to hear that, Dave. Hope it goes well. What happened to your neighbour?"

"Dr Leidenstraum died of a heart attack. I was never that fond of him myself. My wife and Brett liked him. I feel sorry for his children Sarah and Will–"

"Dr Leidenstraum," Nathan said with eyebrows raised.

"Yes, you know him?" Dave said.

"N-n-no. Never heard of him. It's just an unusual name, isn't it?" Nathan said.

"Yes. It's German. Anyway, I'll be back in on Saturday."

"You seem quite upset, Brett," Nathan said.

"Robert, Dr Leidenstraum. He was a nice man. I'm sad he's gone."

"I'll tell you what. Give me the details of the church service for tomorrow and I'll have flowers sent over. It's the least I could do," Nathan said.

"That's not necessary. You didn't know him," Dave said and looked uncomfortable with the offer.

"I insist, Dave, really, I insist. Give me the details, please."

"Ok, if you're sure. I'll write them down for you. Have you got some scrap paper I can use?"

"What's in that building over there?" Brett said as he looked out of a window across the compound.

"Mind your own business, son," Dave said. "Sorry, Nathan. Too nosy for his own good that one."

"No, not at all Dave. It's a fair question. I rent out storage space; use some of the space for buying and selling goods, I keep tools and mechanical parts in there. I promise you, Brett, you wouldn't believe your eyes if you saw what was in there."

"Can I go in and have a look?" Brett said.

"Brett, that's enough," Dave said.

"I'm afraid your dad's right on this occasion Brett. There's some precious cargo in there and the man renting it out would be very upset with me if I was to show anyone. Part of the payment I receive is to ensure it's kept safe and secure and away from prying eyes."

Brett nodded and said nothing further but his intrigue deepened as a shiver passed over his body, that served only to draw him closer to the secrets that lay a short distance away.

Tucked away at the back of the building within Nathan's compound, the figures in the pods were becoming as increasingly exasperated as they were weakened by their peril.

"What has happened to Dr Leidenstraum and what is going to happen to us?" one said.

"We are going to die. That is what is going to happen," another said.

"Dr Leidenstraum will find us and Dr Leidenstraum will save us. We must not give up hope," the one that was a clone of Brett Sadler said.

The Prime Minister was skim reading briefings ahead of several forthcoming engagements. A visit to a factory in Hartlepool followed by a flight to Italy. So much travel and so many handshakes. It was exhausting. A knock at the door disrupted his visions of the succulent pasta and delicious red wine he would be consuming, in Italy rather than Hartlepool.

"Come in," the Prime Minister said.

"You wanted to see me, Prime Minister," the Home Secretary said.

"Yes. I want an update on the Oxfordshire situation. We also need to discuss the Security Minister situation."

"Frightful business, sir, frightful business. With the Security Minister in particular," the Home Secretary said.

"What are you saying? That you think I have done the wrong thing?" the Prime Minister said.

"Not at all. You did the right thing. I'm talking about his betrayal. It just goes to show you can't ever truly trust anyone. Anyway, I understand it has been confirmed the Security Minister committed suicide by hanging himself in his office. There is no danger of the truth getting out on that one. All taken care of as discussed. The suicide note should be sufficient but I will speak to the press—"

"Speak to the press? Are you mad?"

"Please do not worry Prime Minister. I am going to say how he had been under a lot of pressure and commit that we as a government recognise the importance of mental health. I am going to advise anyone who is feeling low should reach out for help. We need to show compassion. I will say that you have asked me to speak on your behalf and that you will be raising the provision of mental health services in parliament as an urgent priority."

"Very well. And Oxfordshire?"

"We will ensure all matters related to the Leidenstraums are dealt with, Prime Minister."

"And what about this business with a corrupt police officer killing another police officer. I hope that isn't going to inadvertently scupper our plans or throw some unforeseen spanner in the works."

"We have deployed plenty of resources to Oxfordshire to take care of that matter. I've no doubt she will be apprehended soon. If anything, Prime Minister, the corrupt policewoman will hopefully serve as a helpful distraction as we deal with tidying up the Leidenstraum situation. The media and public will be so aghast by her, especially as a female, that it will detract entirely from the other matter altogether."

"Hi Nathan, what's up?" RT said as he answered the phone whilst sat at his desk in unit 8A "What? Slow down Nathan you aren't making sense. Real life human replica of one of the robots. What the... The Leidenstraum funeral details. You've got a plan. Calm down Nathan, take a breath will you. Ok, I'm listening." RT listened intently. "Oh, nice one Nathan, nice one. This is the opportunity we've been waiting for. I like it. Me, no I'll wait a short distance away as back-up. Give me a shout if you need. If not, drop me a text when it's done and I'll meet you at the compound. You see, I told you we did the right thing in taking them robots. I'm just sorting some admin out in the warehouse. Word from the flats is that Goodness Gracious Me are settling in just fine. I'm buzzing Nathan. Buzzing. Top work. Ok, see you tomorrow."

RT placed the phone on the desk and reclined in his chair with his hands behind his head. "Yes," he said to himself with a beaming grin. "Yes."

Dr Leidenstraum had almost certainly envisaged a future receiving accolades and global recognition the day he first put pen to paper in 1983. Instead, his meddling had left his children hiding in the flat of a Police Officer with their future in jeopardy. Sarah had delayed sifting through her father's journals for long enough. It was time to satisfy her curiosity once and for all.

"What are you doing?" Clare said.

"I'm trying to kill the boredom of us all waiting around in this flat, but I also want to find out more about a man I thought I knew that I clearly didn't," Sarah said.

"Are you ready for this, sis? You don't know what you might find in there."

"Will, I don't think it's possible it can get much more shocking than it already is, so yes, I'm more than ready," Sarah said.

Sarah turned the pages and digested the information as the others watched on in collective anticipation.

Clare switched on the phone that had been used to send a text message to the kidnapper.

"What are you doing?" Cheryl said. "I thought you told us to keep the phones off."

"We do, but I need to quickly check to see if the kidnapper has acknowledged the message yet. It's a risk I'm going to have to take unfortunately." The phone beeped. "It's the kidnapper. He is grateful, Tariq. He has asked if you can remain in contact with him throughout the journey." Clare then switched the phone back off.

"OH MY GOD," "I don't believe it. I don't believe it," Sarah said and put her hand over her mouth.

"What? What's the matter?" Will said. The look in his sister's eyes terrified him.

Sarah didn't respond so Will snatched the journal from her hands. She looked away from her brother with her head facing down to the floor.

"What? No. No way," Will said and threw the journal at the wall in a fit of anger.

"Hey, hey, what's going on?" Clare said.

"It's Brett, our neighbour. He's... he's our brother," Sarah said without looking up.

"Our brother, and in my father's own words he is much more of the son he had hoped for than me," Will said. He walked out of the room and slammed the door behind him.

"Shall I go and talk to him?" John said.

"No, I'd give him chance to cool down," Clare said.

"This must have come as such a shock. I'm so sorry you've found out like this," Cheryl said as she placed a comforting arm around Sarah.

"It is, but it's worse than this," Sarah said.

"Worse. In what way?" Cheryl said.

Sarah looked up at Cheryl and at each of the others in turn. "One of my father's robots is a clone of Brett." The room fell deafly silent. Sarah stood up and shuffled out of the room. She found her brother lying on a bed in the foetal position crying hysterically. She nestled up behind him and held him tenderly and lovingly in her arms.

The touching moment was interrupted by the sound of the front door opening and closing as Marcia bounded into the property and through the door into the lounge.

"Where are they? We've got to get them to their aunt's," Marcia said as she frantically scoured the property before finding them in the bedroom. "We've got to go."

"What's wrong?" Clare said as she entered the room. "Please give them a few minutes Marcia. I'll explain in the other room," she said and escorted Marcia out.

A short while later Sarah and Will walked into the lounge. "You said we need to go," Sarah said.

"Yes, as soon as possible," Marcia said. "They're interrogating everyone at the station as a potential suspect in the hunt for Clare. I could be wrong but I felt like they were on to me. My fear is they'll put me under surveillance so the sooner I get you two out of here the better."

"How do you know you weren't followed here?" Tariq said.

"I was very careful. They were still conducting interviews at the station so I think they'll weigh it all up at the conclusion of that. That's why I figured it was best not to wait."

"It sounds sensible to me," Clare said. "Best to drop them a short distance from their aunt's so nobody sees you."

"And everyone is ready for tomorrow?" Marcia said. Sarah and Will looked at Marcia forlornly. "Well, you know what I mean?" All eyes looked at Tariq.

"I won't let any of you down. I promise," Tariq said.

DI Jarvis was a wily character. A keen amateur dramatist and seasoned chess player; he was the perfect mould for a senior investigating officer in charge of covert investigations for the London Police Confidential Unit. He relished the challenge of getting under the skin of his targets and outmanoeuvring those who thought they were smarter than him, especially those in positions of power. Jarvis nonchalantly entered

Johnson's office.

"Don't you know how to knock?" Johnson said.

"Sorry, sir. But I must speak to you urgently," Jarvis said. "I need to understand the plans for tomorrow's funeral and ensure the full precautions are taken."

"That is none of your concern. You carry on the search for Clare Stevens and let us handle the funeral. Too many cooks and all that."

"Well, that's just it. Clare worked on the Leidenstraum case. I think there's a chance she could make an appearance and risk the security of the event," Jarvis said.

"That has already been considered as part of the operational planning and resourcing. We'll be sure to give you a shout if we see her. Although, she'll already be in custody by then of course."

"You seem quite relaxed about tomorrow, sir."

"What's wrong with that? Surely, it's better than taking an alarmist attitude. Have you finished with Herbert and Lyle?" Johnson said diverting the conversation.

"Yes, sir. For now. Why?"

"Because I need them to get back to work. That's why. Now, is that all?"

"Yes, sir."

"Good. Then close the door on your way out will you, Inspector Jarvis." Jarvis nodded and did as he was instructed.

No sooner had Jarvis left when DI Taylor knocked Johnson's door.

"Yes, come in. It's like Grand Central Station in here today," Johnson said shaking his head.

"Sir, we've just had a call from the surveillance at Janice Wilkins's address. William and Sarah Leidenstraum have just turned up there in company with an Asian lad."

"Thank you very much, DI Taylor. This is great news. Keep me updated."

Janice lived in a terraced house in a quiet cul-de-sac. The house was clean and tidy but, if it was placed on the market, an Estate Agent would likely describe it as requiring modernisation. The arrival of Sarah and William on her doorstep was a sight for Janice to behold. She couldn't contain her joy.

"Come here and give your aunt a big hug," Janice said as she hugged them both tightly. "And who is this?" she said whilst looking at Tariq.

"This is our friend Tariq. He is coming to the funeral tomorrow as moral support. We thought he could stay here tonight," Sarah said.

"Yes, of course. Lovely to meet you, Tariq."

The long hours and high stress of Johnson's career had not been conducive with a healthy lifestyle. And that was long before Sharon's smug Solicitor had ignited his path to corruption. His struggles to resist fish and chips on late shifts had certainly contributed to the increased girth around his midsection. He would lose weight one day, but for now he dipped the final delicious chip in ketchup and savoured it. He relaxed back in his office chair and made a telephone call.

"Good evening, Johnson, I do hope you have good news for me," the boss said.

"The Leidenstraums have turned up at their aunt's house as expected. I'd say that's good news, wouldn't you? Everything is good for tomorrow. I hope your crew are up to it," Johnson said.

"My crew are up to it alright. You just make sure you do your part. And how are things coming along with the other matter?" the boss said.

"We had a minor setback but we'll be back on track shortly. Now, tomorrow. The Leidenstraums and their aunt will be well taken care of, won't they?"

"They will be in receipt of my very best care package. Three for the price of one."

The call ended as Herbert and Lyle arrived in Johnson's office looking excitable.

"What is it?" Johnson said.

"You're not going to believe the location of the phones now," Lyle said.

"Go on."

"The industrial estate where the robots were taken from," Herbert said.

"What? Are you sure? There's definitely no mistake?"

"No mistake," Herbert said.

"Why are you still stood here then? Go on. Get moving." Herbert and Lyle hastily left Johnson's office.

In convoy, three vehicles turned into the industrial estate which was now eerily quiet as evening approached. They parked a considerable distance away from unit 8B. The occupants of the vehicles, ten in total including Herbert and Lyle, were on edge as they spread out and proceeded nervously with weapons drawn.

RT was sat on the toilet, reading a men's magazine, whilst outside everyone took up their various positions and a flurry of panicked hand signals and angry looks were exchanged. At that moment, RT flushed the toilet and the attention of every one of the would-be mercenaries was drawn to unit 8A.

Lyle waved to the two people nearest to it and held his earlobe inferring they should listen. He then held up a mobile phone, made a call and placed the handset to his ear. It was ringing; he received two sets of thumbs up. He pointed in the direction of unit 8A, and nodded. RT made his way back to his desk where a phone was ringing.

"Hello," RT said as he answered the phone.

"Hello, where's Riz?" Lyle said as the sound echoed.

"He's not here at the moment," RT said as the echo worsened.

The phone went dead. "No, but I'm here," Lyle said as RT frantically turned around to find a gun pointed at him. RT placed his hands in the air, shuffled backwards and rested his backside on the edge of the desk.

"Who are you?" RT said.

"I might ask you the same question," Lyle said as several of the others, including Herbert, entered the room, also with guns drawn.

RT swallowed hard. "I asked first and you're in my warehouse pointing guns at me."

"It's the police," Herbert said.

"Speak for yourself," one of the henchmen said. "You two are police, well sort of, but the rest of us most definitely aren't."

RT looked confused. "Who are you and what do you want?" he said.

"You're under arrest," Lyle said, as he flashed his warrant card.

"For what?" RT said.

"Kidnap of two Asian lads. Oh, and some robots," Lyle said.

"I don't know what you're talking about. I think you've made a mistake," RT said. "Close the door behind you and we'll forget all about it."

"Why have you got the phones of Riz and Zams?" Herbert said.

"They're working for me. They've just left them here. They'll be back soon. And as for robots, I don't know what you're talking about. There certainly aren't any here."

"No, although it looks like there's plenty of other stuff here that I can arrest you for," Lyle said.

Another henchman entered. "I thought I recognised that voice. You're RT. We were in prison together some years ago," he said.

"Yes, you look familiar," RT said.

"Save the reunion for some other time," Herbert said.

"It begs the question what he's doing here with a warehouse full of gear," the henchman said."

"Why? Do you want to be a detective or something?" Lyle said.

"Shut up," the henchman said. "He's a long way from his usual patch in Essex. We've had an issue lately with inferior gear flooding the area and selling at a cheaper price than ours. The boss will be pleased with this discovery."

"You've got it all wrong. This is just storage. The heat's on in Chelmsford now and we needed somewhere out of the area to work from. This is nothing more than a distribution centre for operations in Essex."

"You are lying. Why on earth would you come to Oxford of all places. You are a dead man, RT, and this gear's ours now."

"Ok calm down," Lyle said. "You can't kill him. We need to find out what he has done with the robots."

A bead of sweat appeared on RT's forehead. He swiftly reached for his gun which was behind a box on his desk, unaware another person was outside the warehouse with a sniper rifle sighted on his chest. In an instant RT was shot, and fell backwards across the desk and into his chair.

"CEASE FIRE," Lyle said. "IDIOT. YOU IDIOT," he said as he turned around. "NOBODY TOLD YOU TO SHOOT."

The sniper walked in calmly and said: "He reached for his gun and I shot him."

"Well for your sake, I hope he's just wounded," Lyle said.

"Si," Herbert said.

"What?"

"He's dead. Look at him." Everybody looked at RT. "Rambo here shot him in the heart," Herbert said.

"Now what are we going to do," Lyle said.

"We're going to empty the place of all this gear," the hench-man said.

"And how does that help us find the robots?"

"It doesn't, but it means my kids will have a good Christmas. I suppose we'll have to find another way of tracking down the robots, won't we?"

Herbert and Lyle looked at each other despairingly. As the henchmen began emptying the warehouse, they both looked at RT. Blood continued to pour out of his chest like a waterfall.

16

Chapter Sixteen: Memory

Friday 9th July, 1999. 8.50am

If you were looking for a word to describe Aunt Janice's lounge
it would be chintzy. The floral, emerald-coloured curtains
matched her cotton upholstered sofa and chair. The salmon-
coloured wallpaper was sandwiched between a dado rail and
coving. A wooden mantelpiece crammed with quirky trinkets
surrounded the fireplace. The photographs on the wall were
mainly of Sarah and Will, but there were a few of Janice and
some of their mother. A George Michael CD played in the
background on low volume. Sarah and Will had bought the
CD Player as a birthday present for their aunt.

Will, Sarah, and Tariq were sat in silence in the lounge when
Janice entered carrying an array of hangers with various items
of clothing.

"I went to the trouble of hiring some suits and dresses for you.
I wasn't sure of the sizes exactly so I guessed and selected two

different outfits in different sizes for you to try on." Janice looked at Tariq. "Obviously I wasn't expecting you. You'll have to take the one Will doesn't, although I'm not sure it's going to be a particularly good fit." Will, Sarah, and Janice looked Tariq up and down.

"What are you all looking at me for? I'm sure I will squeeze into it somehow."

"Well, yes dear I'm sure, but–"

"But what?"

"I paid a deposit and if you burst a button or split the trousers–"

"Then he'll pay for it, Aunt Janice. Won't you Tariq?" Will said.

"Yes. I will. I promise."

"Ok. Well may I suggest you don't have much for breakfast. Give yourself the best chance of squeezing into the clothes," Janice said.

Tariq looked down and held his stomach whilst breathing in.

"You won't be able to hold your breath all day, Tariq," Sarah said.

"No. You'll do yourself a mischief. Or give yourself indigestion or something," Janice said. "I'll get you some water. Should help you to debloat before you need to put the clothes on."

"Thanks," Tariq said.

"Why, will you be putting some laxatives in it?" Will said.

"That's not nice, Will. It's just a bit of puppy fat," Janice said.

"I wouldn't compare him to a puppy, Aunt Janice. Puppies are cute and adorable, after all," Will said.

"He's quite cute and adorable," Janice said and grabbed Tariq's cheeks playfully. Janice then left the room, closely followed by Sarah and Will, whilst a self-conscious Tariq hurriedly attempted some sit ups.

Haroon's mother didn't care that the DVLA had assessed her son and deemed him safe to be on the road. If she was in the car with him, she would be the one driving.

"Haroon. This car has never been the same since your run-in with the police," his mum said as the Metro barely chugged along the dual carriageway. Other drivers impatiently beeped and overtook at the earliest opportunity.

"I know, mum. I'm sorry. I'll take it back to the police," Haroon said sat in the passenger seat.

"You'll do no such thing. We're going to get it sorted out today. At a garage."

"Ok, mum. If you turn left at the lights, I think there's a garage not far along that road on the right-hand side."

Haroon's mum followed her son's directions, and pulled into the garage. It was Nathan's garage.

"How can I help you?" Nathan said as Haroon and his mum climbed out of the car.

Haroon looked at Nathan and then looked away trying to work out where he recognised him from. He looked at him again and had a flashback in his mind to when Zams was kidnapped. Haroon had the stark realisation he was stood with one of the kidnappers.

"We've a problem with the car," Haroon's mum said.

"Forget it, Mum. Get back in the car. We should go somewhere else," Haroon said.

Nathan looked at Haroon sharply. "You don't need to go anywhere else. This is a reputable garage I run here."

"I didn't mean anything by it," Haroon said backpedalling. "It's just–"

"It's just nothing, Haroon. The man is going to look at the car and you can be quiet. This is your fault, after all. Stupid, stupid boy."

"What did he do?" Nathan said to Haroon's mum.

"It's a bit embarrassing. I don't want to talk about it. He's an idiot."

"I understand," Nathan said. "But anything that'll help me understand the problem will help me get it fixed for you."

"Let me just say the car has been worked on recently," Haroon's mum said sheepishly.

"I'm happy to take a look, but I really think you should take it up with whoever has worked on it. You don't want to be paying twice. Was it someone local? I probably know them and can have a word."

"It was the police. I was wrongly arrested on suspicion of dealing drugs and they stripped the car."

"Haroon, shut up," his mother said.

"I don't want to get caught up in anything illegal," Nathan said with such convincing sincerity Haroon could scarcely believe his ears.

"It was a mistake, sir, we aren't involved in anything illegal, I promise you," Haroon's mum said.

"Ok. I believe you," Nathan said. "I can't have my garage caught up in anything that isn't strictly legitimate."

Again, Haroon was astonished by Nathan's performance.

"Unfortunately, I've got a mechanic off today and I've got some business to attend to myself shortly. Can you leave the vehicle here overnight? I possibly may need to keep it here until Monday."

"That's fine. We will leave it with you. We can get the bus, can't we Haroon?"

"Yes, mum," Haroon said as he glared at Nathan.

"I just need some details from you if you can follow me into the office," Nathan said. Haroon's mum followed Nathan whilst Haroon took out his phone and looked for Lyle's number.

Haroon pontificated over whether to make the call, and as he was about to tap the call button he heard: "Come on Haroon. We need to go and get this bus. You can send a text or whatever it is you're doing later."

"Yes, mum," he said and reluctantly put the phone away in his pocket.

Will, Sarah, and Janice were dressed and ready for the funeral. They congregated in the lounge.

"You both look so smart. Your father would be very proud. And your mother of course." Janice's sentiment made Sarah and Will feel awkward. "So, are you going to tell me why the police are guarding your father's funeral?" Janice said, which increased the awkwardness a notch further.

"Something to do with dad's work. That's all we know. Isn't that right, sis?"

"Yes, Will's right. Something to do with dad's work."

"I wasn't born yesterday you two, so I'd kindly ask you stop treating me as such. I've a right to know."

At that moment, Tariq walked into the room dressed in his funeral attire which was excruciatingly tight.

"I can barely breathe and I look completely ridiculous," Tariq said.

"Not as ridiculous as you'd look if we had you wear the spare dress," Will said.

"I don't wish to be rude, but don't you think it's rather disrespectful to have him attend your father's funeral dressed like this?" Janice said.

"Aunt Janice. You were asking about the police's interest in the funeral—" Sarah said.

"He's undercover," Will said.

"Undercover," Janice said.

"Yes, the police have insisted," Sarah said.

"The police have insisted on a badly dressed young Asian man attending your father's funeral undercover. What a strange idea."

"It's true. I am PC Hussain," Tariq said.

"Well, PC Hussain, perhaps you can explain why such a strong police presence is required for my brother-in-law's funeral?"

"I'm afraid that is top secret. I'm sorry, I can't speak any further on the subject."

Janice sat down and looked at Sarah's bag. "I've been meaning to ask you, Sarah. What is in that bag?"

"Some of dad's journals."

"Would you like me to put them away for you until we get back?"

"No thank you, Aunt Janice. I'm taking them with me."

"Whatever for, dear?"

"To help me feel close to him when we say goodbye. I think they are important."

Janice gave Sarah a hug. "That's a lovely sentiment dear, it really is."

"What are you doing Haroon? Put that phone away," Haroon's mum said as they walked from the bus stop into the Supermarket car park.

"I really need to make a call, mum."

"You really need to show some more respect. I've had to get the bus here because of you. There was nothing wrong with that car before. You can speak to whoever later. For now, you're going to help me find a trolley, help me in the store and then you will carry the bags back. In fact, give me the phone."

"But mum."

"But mum nothing. Give it to me now." Haroon reluctantly gave his mum the phone. "You can have it back later."

A hearse and funeral car pulled up outside Janice's house. Two uniformed police officers spoke to the chief mourner who knocked the front door.

"We're ready to go," the chief mourner said as Janice opened the door.

"Ok, we'll be out in a second." Janice said. She left the door open, walked into the lounge and hugged Sarah and Will. She looked at Tariq. "I don't see why I shouldn't give you a hug as well. Come here, officer," she said and held him tightly.

"Mrs Wilkins," Tariq said.

"Yes dear, and please call me Janice."

"Please let me go. I really can't breathe with you hugging me in this tight suit."

"Sorry, dear," she said and walked out of the room towards the front door. As she walked through the front door she stopped and addressed the uniformed officers. "You really should have found some nice clothes that fit PC Hussain properly," she said and walked off to the car shaking her head. The officers looked at each other bemused.

"Who is PC Hussain?" one of the officers whispered.

The other officer shrugged and said: "I'd put it down to grief. She's probably a tad overwhelmed."

Will, Sarah, and finally Tariq walked through the door, with the latter closing the door behind him. The officers stared at him.

"I need to go on a diet. This would have fit me a couple of months ago," he said as he held his breath in and walked uncomfortably to the car.

The funeral director walked behind a police motorcyclist in front of the cortege, followed by the funeral car, a marked police car, an unmarked police car and another motorcyclist, with the police helicopter flying overhead. As they reached the junction with the main road, the chief mourner climbed into the cortege vehicle and the procession made off at speed towards the church.

At various points along the route, the occupants of the funeral car were staggered to find junctions blocked off by marked police cars to allow them through red lights. As they turned into the road of the church, they could see the pavement and road littered with a mix of police, civilians, and their respective vehicles.

Marcia was parked up in a side street looking through binoculars when she was startled by a tap at her driver's side window. It was a uniformed police officer who instructed her to wind her window down.

"What are you doing?" the officer said.

Marcia flashed her warrant card. "I'm a police officer. I'm watching the funeral," she said.

"I don't have you on my itinerary," the officer said and duly inspected her badge fervently.

"I've been deployed by Chief Superintendent Johnson as an additional resource. There are a few of us dotted about. It helps to shore up the security of the operation."

"Ok, Detective Constable Reynolds. Thank you. You can wind your window back up." The officer then walked away.

The bells tolled at the house of God, summoning the final return of a man who had dedicated many years to playing God himself. Mourners waited patiently for the funeral cortege to arrive; it was a warm day to be dressed in black. Dave Sadler felt sweat rolling down his spine like a tear would roll down your cheek. Not that he'd be crying any tears for Robert Leidenstraum.

"Isn't that the Sadler family over there?" Janice said as their car approached the church entrance.

Sarah and Will looked out to see Alice, Dave, and Brett Sadler stood by the gate entrance to the church's driveway. Sarah and Will looked at each other, neither said a word.

"Two of your shirt buttons have burst open, PC Hussain. I

can see your belly," Janice said. Everyone looked at Tariq, including the driver of the car.

A mortified Tariq tried desperately to do the button up but it was impossible to do whilst he remained seated.

The vehicle turned into the driveway; Sarah and Will could barely look at the Sadler family.

"It's odd that they wouldn't look at us, don't you think?" Dave Sadler said.

"Goodness knows what they must be going through, Dave. Their father has died, the police have been at their house all week and they've been nowhere to be seen. There are more police here than there are mourners. What on earth is going on?" Alice Sadler said.

"I don't know, Alice. There must be a good reason for it. Although I didn't think there were this many police officers in Oxfordshire. I imagine our council tax will be going up to pay for all this," Dave said as Alice puffed her cheeks out at him.

"Why is Tariq in the funeral car and why is he wearing clothes that don't fit? I could see his—" Brett said.

"Thank you, Brett. That's quite enough," Dave said.

"Belly button. I was going to say I could see his belly button."

Dave gave him a scathing look.

The police motorcyclist at the rear of the cavalcade stopped and turned around to face the mourners at the gate. "You may all follow me," he said. The mourners did as they were instructed and walked behind the motorcyclist along the driveway.

Will, Sarah, Janice, and Tariq had climbed out of the car and were stood by the church entrance.

"Breathe in harder," Janice said as she attempted to button Tariq's shirt. "Honestly PC Hussain, I will be having words with your superiors about this."

"Tariq, please call me Tariq."

"There. I've done it. Just keep on breathing in, PC Tariq, particularly when you sit down in the church. I don't suppose you've been in a church before. Strange the police chose you for this assignment, really," Janice said.

"It is my duty to protect and serve all members of the community," Tariq said as he looked uncomfortably at Sarah and Will.

As the mourners neared the church, Sarah and Will both scowled at Alice. Will, Brett, Tariq, and a reluctant Dave joined the drivers of the funeral cars as pallbearers for Dr Leidenstraum's coffin.

They entered the church to the sound of the hymn, 'All Things Bright and Beautiful.' The irony of the lyrics was not lost on Will, Sarah, and Tariq.

Everyone took to their seats and the service commenced. Part way through the service, Sarah and William were invited to speak. Sarah stood up; Will held her hand.

"Are you sure you want to do this?" Will said to Sarah.

"Yes, I think it's important. I'll be fine."

Sarah addressed the room. "Thank you for coming here today. I know you will all have concerns about the police presence but I'd like you to put that to one side for now. I want us to take a moment to remember my father as the kind, funny, intelligent soul that he was and reflect on the moments in our lives with him that we cherished most dearly." Tears filled Sarah's eyes as Will and Janice looked on bursting with pride.

"I have always and will always love him. Nothing can ever truly change that. His mistakes prove he was human and I hope and pray he finds forgiveness in the Lord. Thank you." She bowed her head and walked back to her seat. Sat either side of her, Will and Janice held a hand each. A minute's silence was held to conclude the ceremony.

As the minute elapsed, in the nearby city centre a convoy of motorbikes, four by fours, and high-powered vehicles arrived. As the final second of the minute ticked past, a male in full motorcycle leathers and helmet turned into High St and stopped his motorbike in the middle of the road. Cars beeped their horns at him. He took out a handgun from inside his jacket and pointed it towards the drivers nearest to him before firing it into the air as if to indicate the start of a race. Chaos quickly unfolded at the same time as the mourners poured out of the church. Armed masked men terrorised shoppers and staff as they robbed and looted shops and banks at will.

"We need to go now," a plain clothes police officer said to Will, Sarah, Janice, and Tariq who compliantly climbed into the funeral car and departed from the church grounds as they had arrived. As they turned out of sight, a call came across the police radios:

"WITH THE EXCEPTION OF AIR SUPPORT, ALL UNITS ARE TO PROCEED TO THE CITY CENTRE NOW. ARMED INCI-DENT IN PROGRESS. THAT INCLUDES THE UNITS COVERING THE FUNERAL. THIS INSTRUCTION IS AUTHORISED BY ACC JOHNSON."

The vehicles in the convoy with the funeral car and the vehicles around the church all sped off towards the city centre, apart from the helicopter which remained with the funeral car. Marcia drove off in the direction of the funeral convoy and was stunned to see the lone funeral car in the distance, with just two cars and a van in front of her. She turned on her police radio to hear the commotion taken place in the city centre. 'Decoy,' she said to herself.

"What do I do now?" the funeral car driver said.

"Drive back to Mrs Wilkins's house," Tariq said. "But for safety, take a different route. Travel along Barks Field Rd."

"As part of Clare and Marcia's plan, are you going to let Shabeela's kidnapper know our location?" Will whispered to Tariq.

Tariq nodded. Will whispered the information to Sarah to ensure Aunt Janice was none the wiser.

Tariq then messaged the boss:

Tariq: "BARKS FIELD RD."

The male in full motorcycle leathers and helmet on the High St fired his gun into the air twice and sped off erratically. This signalled the end of the attack on the city centre as the armed masked men retreated to their respective vehicles with their ill-gotten gains.

"IT'S A WARZONE DOWN HERE," an officer arriving in the city centre bellowed across the radio. "WE NEED AIR SUPPORT NOW." His plea was suddenly interrupted by the sound of gunfire. "WE'RE UNDER ATTACK," he said as bullets pelted his vehicle like hail stones bouncing off a conservatory roof. The tyres of the police vehicle were deflated by the merciless assault.

"LET'S GO," one of the gunmen shouted as he jumped into one

of several vehicles that fled the scene sporadically in different directions.

The boss phoned Herbert. "Got it," Herbert said and ended the call. "Barks Field Rd, Si, let's go." Lyle nodded and they sped off.

"AIR SUPPORT TO CITY CENTRE. NOW AUTHORISED BY ACC JOHNSON," was announced across the police radio.

"It's too late now," an officer said as he climbed out of his bullet ridden car and surveyed the carnage of the High St in sheer disbelief.

The helicopter pilot did as he was instructed and headed towards the city centre, leaving the funeral car unprotected.

Nathan was sat in his recovery truck at the garage when his mobile phone rang.

"Hello," Nathan said.

"We are in pursuit of the funeral car. All the police, including the chopper have abandoned it," a male said.

"Excellent. Where are you? How close are you to the car?"

"We're on Vale Rd. We couldn't be closer. Our car is directly behind it and we are directly behind the car in a van. Now turning right onto the main Kempton Rd."

"Ok, I'm making my way towards you now. Keep me posted."

The helicopter arrived overhead the city centre. "We're too late," the co-pilot said to the pilot. "They've gone."

"Yes, and concerningly the funeral car has been left alone. This feels like a set-up," the pilot said as he looked worriedly at the co-pilot.

"Nathan, we're now taking a left off Kempton Rd into Barks Field Rd," the male in the van said.

"That's perfect. I'm on Vine St which leads into Barks Field Rd from the opposite side to where you are."

"Excellent. See you shortly."

Tariq texted the boss.

Tariq: "We're now stopping at the traffic lights at the junction with Mill House Rd."

The boss phoned Herbert. "They're at the lights at the junction with Mill House Rd," he said.

"We're on Mill House Rd. Si, floor it so we make the green light," Herbert said.

Lyle accelerated hard. "COME ON," he said gesticulating

wildly at the flow of traffic ahead of him dawdling towards the junction. The lights turned to amber as both cars directly in front waited for a break in oncoming traffic to turn right onto Barks Field Rd. The break came and as the lights changed from amber to red, the cars in front proceeded to turn right slowly. Lyle impatiently beeped his horn to encourage the manoeuvre to be performed more swiftly as he crossed the light on red.

"There it is," Herbert said as she looked to her left and observed the funeral car was the first car waiting at the lights.

"Brilliant. They'll be directly behind us," Lyle said.

"Did you catch that?" Herbert said to the boss.

"You're directly in front of them, did I hear that right?" the boss said.

"Yes."

"Well done. Keep me updated," the boss said and ended the call.

Nathan turned from Vine St into Barks Field Rd and was now travelling towards Herbert and Lyle and the funeral car on the opposite side of the road.

Herbert made a call. "We're heading south on Barks Field Rd. We're directly in front of them and they're just crossing the junction with Mill House Rd; the one with the Red Lion pub on the corner," she said.

"We'll be with you shortly. We're on Barks Field Rd heading south towards that junction," a voice said.

Haroon traipsed a few paces behind his mother. His hands and shoulders ached under the strain of having carried a few heavy supermarket shopping bags from the bus stop. He placed the bags down and stretched his weary arms out as he summoned the strength to complete the final steps of his journey.

"That's it, Haroon, you're almost there," Haroon's mum said in Urdu as she put the key into the front door of their house. "Hurry up, Haroon. Useless boy. There are items I urgently need to put in the fridge freezer," she again said in Urdu.

"Yes, mum," Haroon responded forlornly. He picked the bags back up and carried them through the doorway with the relief of an athlete completing an energy sapping race.

"Can I please have my phone back now, mum?"

"You and this phone. It's as if young people can't live without them," she said in Urdu, shook her head and tutted loudly.

"Please, mum. I really need to make a call."

"Fine. Please yourself. Here you go," she said as she handed him the phone.

Haroon went upstairs to his bedroom and scrolled through the phone's directory to find Lyle's number. He paused for a brief second and then pressed the call button.

"Why now?" Lyle said as the phone rang in his pocket. He scrambled to take the phone out from his trouser pocket and passed it to Herbert. "You answer it," he said.

"I'm not your secretary," Herbert said.

"Please, Tash?" Lyle said.

"Fine. As you asked so nicely. Hello, Simon Lyle's phone, Natasha Herbert speaking how can I help you?"

"Herbert. From my interview at the police station."

"What? Yes. Who is this?"

"It's Haroon."

"What do you want Haroon?" Herbert and Lyle looked at each other with dismissive expressions.

"Detective Lyle said if I had any more information then I should call him."

"And, do you have more information?"

"Yes, one of Zams's kidnappers is fixing my mum's car. You should really pay for that, for the damage you did searching it–"

"Get on with it, Haroon. The kidnapper, who is it?" Lyle stared at Herbert with a furrowed brow.

"He's from Nathan's garage. I recognised him when we took the car there this morning."

"Thank you, Haroon. Is that all?"

"Yes, that's all I know. What are you going to do?"

"We'll look into it. Thank you for letting us know. Goodbye." Herbert then ended the call.

"What was that about a kidnapper?" Lyle said.

"He reckons one of Zams's kidnappers is from Nathan's garage. You know, the repair place."

"I know the one. TASH, LOOK OUT," Lyle said as a truck swerved across from the other side of the road in front of them. Lyle slammed his foot hard on the brakes as he and Herbert both screamed.

17

Chapter Seventeen: Evolve

Barks Field Rd was a busy, two-mile-long single carriageway with detached houses set back from the road on either side. A retired couple were working to maintain their pristine garden. The female was on her knees tending to her azaleas. She wore bright yellow marigolds. Her husband pushed an electric lawnmower through their sizeable lawn. He was wearing a light-blue t-shirt which was drenched in sweat. His face was tomato red from a combination of sun exposure and exertion.

The tyres screeched and rubber moulded into the tarmac as Herbert and Lyle's vehicle came to a stop within inches of the side of the truck. They both jolted forward and backwards in their seats, like thrill seekers on a rollercoaster. Their momentary relief was shattered as the funeral vehicle travelling behind ploughed into them, forcing their bodies into another involuntary jolt, and their vehicle into the truck.

"Are you ok, Tash?" Lyle said, holding his neck, and then his leg. He winced in pain.

"Just about... I think," Herbert said, with her face scrunched up in pain. She turned to face Lyle and then turned her head back to the front.

"Si. Oh my god. Look."

"What?"

"The truck. It's—"

"NATHAN'S GARAGE," Lyle said, as he gazed wide-eyed at the brightly painted letters that were almost pressed against his windscreen.

In the vehicle behind, the occupants were taking stock of what had happened.

"Is everyone ok?" Will said.

"Some of my shirt buttons have popped, but other than that I'm fine," Tariq said.

"Aunt Janice. Aunt Janice. Are you ok?" Sarah said. She was unresponsive.

"Will, I can't wake her," Sarah said.

"Aunt Janice," Will said, as he looked over to see the blank gaze of his aunt's dilated pupils. Instinctively he knew. He put his hand across his mouth.

"NO, NO, NO, YOU CAN'T. AUNT JANICE," Sarah said holding her aunt desperately in her arms.

Nathan approached the front of Herbert and Lyle's vehicle.

"I'm so sorry," he said holding his hands up in the air.

Herbert opened the passenger door and climbed out slowly. "You should be sorry. What on earth do you think you were doing?" she said flashing her warrant card. Lyle opened his car door and summoned the strength to attempt to climb out through the pain; he lifted his feet out of the vehicle and onto the road.

Armed men got out of the car and van directly behind the funeral car, cruelly interrupting the emotion of the situation unfolding inside. Herbert and Lyle both turned to see what was happening.

"I'm very sorry, officer," Nathan said. "I'm very sorry I have no choice but to do this."

Herbert turned back around as Nathan pulled out a handgun from his oil-stained overalls and shot her in the neck. Herbert fell to the ground in a heap as blood squirted out like a fence being spray painted. Nathan swivelled and pointed the weapon in the direction of Lyle who hastily pulled his legs back into the footwell of the vehicle and ducked for cover on to the passenger seat as a bullet penetrated his windscreen and lodged in the headrest of his seat. He was horrified as he glanced into the eyes of a dying Herbert through the gap in the open passenger side door.

Marcia watched events unfolding in front of her and froze in shock. At that moment, a speeding vehicle braked harshly and pulled directly alongside Marcia's car and the car in front of her, which was behind the armed men's van. Armed men jumped out and a firefight broke out.

The sound of the hail of bullets filled the air along with the stench of gunpowder, as innocent parties screamed despairingly and tried to shelter from the carnage. The retired couple retreated to the safety of their house in the nick of time. They would survive; the lawnmower and the azaleas would not. The bursts of gunfire were interspersed with agonising screams as one after another, men from each side clutched their bodies in pain as they became the latest gunshot victim of the bloody battle.

Nathan retreated to the relative safety of his truck and anxiously phoned RT for assistance, unaware his calls would ultimately be in vain. His panic deepened further with each unanswered call as bullets riddled his truck.

"RT, WHERE ARE YOU?" he said.

"He's where you're about to go," Lyle said as he approached the driver's side of the truck. Nathan turned, gun in hand, to face Lyle as Lyle launched into him and plunged a knife vociferously into his groin area. Nathan squealed and let go of the gun. Lyle headbutted Nathan on the nose, pulled the knife out and then pushed it forcefully back into the open wound.

He turned the blade the way Nathan would have turned a tyre wrench at his garage, punching Nathan relentlessly about the head and upper body with his other hand as he did so. Lyle retrieved Nathan's gun from the footwell and pointed it at him.

"A bullet's too good for you," Lyle said as Nathan whimpered helplessly. Lyle pistol-whipped him time and time again, until he was completely unrecognisable. Nathan's blood spattered over Lyle's face and clothes throughout the relentless assault. Lyle stopped mid pistol-whip as he saw through the passenger window of the truck a bullet put into the head of the last ally that remained from the boss's crime group, by one of two injured but still alive and armed enemies. Lyle yanked the knife from Nathan's groin and plunged it firmly into his chest. He took Nathan's keys from out of the truck's ignition and got out of the truck with Nathan's gun in his hand.

"You're coming with us," a male said as he pointed a firearm at the window of the funeral car. Will, Sarah and Tariq cowered inside.

"No, they're not," Lyle said and shot him in the chest, before shooting the remaining male in the leg as he dived for cover. The male wounded in the leg crawled haplessly along the floor towards a weapon in the distance. Lyle stalked him like a lion following a gazelle in the Serengeti. As the male's hand reached the handle, Lyle kicked the weapon from his grasp and then kicked the male onto his back before ruthlessly executing him with a bullet through the centre of his forehead.

As sirens could be heard approaching, Lyle opened the rear door of the funeral car and said: "It's time to go." They were all in such a state of shock that nobody uttered a single word in response. Lyle closed the door and then opened the driver's door. The driver, who had visibly been hit by a stray bullet, slumped out of the seat and onto the ground. He was dead. Lyle casually rolled him out of the way and climbed into the driver's seat of the funeral car. He reversed back from the rear bumper of his own vehicle and sped off, driving around the rear of the truck and back onto the right side of the road. A stunned Marcia proceeded to follow cautiously.

Alice entered the dining room, sat down, and began crying. Dave entered the kitchen and began clattering cupboard doors and clanging cutlery impatiently. Brett was solemn and retreated to his bedroom; he always retreated to his bedroom when the atmosphere turned sour at home. Not that the sanctity of his bedroom had ever stopped Dave from beating him, when he'd finished beating his mother. He'd tried to take a kitchen knife to Dave when he'd passed out in a drunken stupor on the sofa one Saturday night, but his Mum had stopped him. She'd begged him not to do it and prised the knife out of his hand. Brett was a powder keg. It was just a matter of time.

"What's wrong?" Alice said.

"Nothing," Dave said. "Do you want a cup of tea or not?"

"Why are you being like this? I don't understand."

"Why? I'll tell you why Alice. I think you're more upset today than you would be if it were me in that casket. That's why."

"How could you say such a thing?"

"I've always had my suspicions about you and him. Is the boy even mine?" Alice could barely look Dave in the eye. "You can look away. It's true, isn't it? He doesn't even look like me. And what with his fancy plans it wouldn't surprise me. Showing me up in front of my boss. He'd better buck his ideas up and toe the line during his work experience."

"He's a good boy. Why are his career aspirations such an issue for you? Are you worried you'll feel inferior or something?"

Dave raised his hand.

"Go on, hit me. It wouldn't be the first time, would it?"

Dave lowered his hand and then turned his head away in apparent acknowledgement of his shame and guilt, and retreated into the kitchen.

Brett had heard the shouting from upstairs, although had not heard the content. He didn't want to leave his mother to the inevitable but he needed to leave the house.

"I'm going out," Brett said as he trudged down the stairs.

"Where are you going?" Alice said.

"Just out. I want to get out for a walk," Brett said as he closed the door behind him.

"I hope he didn't hear what you said," Alice said. "I'll never forgive you if he did, you hear me?" but Dave ignored her comment.

Speed and danger had appealed to Lyle from a young age. His parents bought him a cabinet for his bedroom to store all the trophies from his go-karting competitions. He'd always outpace the competition. He excelled at the Police Advanced Driver course where he finished top of his class. He got a thrill out of high-speed pursuits that ended in him catching the criminals. Not because he was interested in apprehending the suspects, but because he was fiercely competitive.

"Where are you taking us?" Will said, as Lyle floored the accelerator pedal of the funeral car.

"You'll see," Lyle said as he took out his mobile phone and called the boss.

"What's the update?" the boss said.

"Tash is dead, as are the rest. That's the update."

"Why, what happened? And what about the Leidenstraums?"

"I'm with them now. A rival group, that's what happened. We were ambushed. They're all dead as well."

"And yet you survived?"

"What's your point?"

"Don't be so defensive. It's just an observation."

"It sounds like you're questioning my loyalty. I've just killed three people to ensure my survival. I couldn't have saved Tash or the others, I wish I could."

"Ok, I trust you. So, to clarify, we have the Leidenstraums but we don't have the robots and we have a lot of dead people, some of whom were close associates of mine. Any update on known connections for that RT we can lean on, not that I've got too many people left to do the leaning by the sounds of it."

"You surely don't have to be a qualified detective to work out that's who ambushed us."

"Really?"

"Yes. Just how many crime groups do you think are interested in these German kids?"

"We're British," Sarah said.

"Shut up," Lyle said. "No, I wasn't talking to you. Look, the guy that led the ambush and killed Tash was part of the group that took the robots. He's been identified by an eyewitness. The most important thing is that he is, sorry was, Nathan from Nathan's garage."

"I've never heard of him."

"There's no real reason why you would. I don't think he's someone you'd have encountered directly. I think his garage is legitimate, but if you don't know it, it is on a spacious plot of land with a secure compound and building at the back. My instincts are telling me RT had Nathan store the robots there."

The boss reclined in his chair. "Well, if you're right, that'll be the missing piece of the jigsaw. I suggest you get over there sharpish before word gets out."

"Already on my way. I'll speak to you soon," Lyle said and ended the call. Lyle turned and looked at Will. "In answer to your question, I'm taking you to Nathan's garage. With a bit of luck, we'll get this car repaired and find ourselves some robots."

Automobile repair was dirty work. Nathan's garage was dirtier than most, and not just because of the manual labour sustaining the mobility of Oxford's population. Brett walked into the office and was met by one of Nathan's mechanics who was covered almost head to toe in dirt and grease.

"Can I help you?" the mechanic said, as he futilely cleaned his hands with a cloth. The cloth was dirtier than he was.

"I'm Brett. Dave's son. I'm going to be doing work experience here."

"Oh right. Well, I hope you don't mind getting your hands dirty."

"No, I'm looking forward to it. Is Nathan here? I just wanted to thank him for sending flowers to my neighbour's funeral today."

"He's not I'm afraid. He went out in the truck a while ago. He should be back soon, otherwise I don't know who's going to lock up, as we're due to finish for the day. You're welcome to come and watch us working for a bit if you want to wait."

"Thanks. I'll do that. It'll be useful for my work experience."

Both were blissfully unaware Lyle had parked a short distance away and was conducting a more thorough assessment than one of their MOTs.

"Now what?" Will said.

"Shut up. I'm thinking," Lyle said. He then called the boss. "I'm here. But there are a few workers on site in the garage. I don't want to cause a scene."

"Ok," the boss said. "It's Friday afternoon. I reckon they'll be finishing up soon. Hang tight and see what happens. Keep me updated." The call ended.

"Where's my sister?" Tariq said.

"She's with your father," Lyle said and sniggered.

"I've done as I was asked. I want to see her."

"All in good time, all in good time."

"I'm so sorry," Sarah said, as she cradled Aunt Janice in her arms.

Will and Tariq watched silently. Lyle fixed his sights firmly on the garage.

Marcia was parked further away from the garage but was perfectly placed to watch the car and the garage without Lyle seeing her.

"Ok, I will take the blindfolds off and untie your hands now,"

Johannes said to Riz and Zams.

"Was this really necessary?" Riz said.

"Absolutely. You're on a need to know only basis, and you didn't need to see where I was bringing you for the meeting."

Zams and Riz smudged their eyes with their hands as they adjusted to the light and found themselves in a large open plan office that was bright and airy. They were in the centre of the room and the view from the windows ahead, to the side and behind them gave nothing away of their location.

"What is this meeting about?" Zams said.

"You'll find out but it is time for your work to begin, gentle-men," Johannes said, as he and Barry ushered them towards a desk located in front of a wall-mounted television tuned into a news channel, although the sound was muted.

"Take a seat," Johannes said.

Riz and Zams sat down at the desk in black leather chairs facing the television. Riz sat to the left and Zams to the right.

"These chairs are well comfortable aren't they, Riz?"

"Yes, they're not bad."

"Perfect for watching the news, bruv, if someone would turn the sound up. You know, the Ganja here is a lot stronger than in Oxford. I'm still completely stoned."

"I told you to go easy last night, Zams. We need to keep our wits about us."

"I'm not on about last night. I'm on about this morning. I had a spliff as long as a cucumber, bruv."

Riz shook his head.

There was a knock at the door.

"Stand up you two, you must show some respect." Johannes said.

"We've just sat down," Zams said.

"He told you to stand up so do it," Barry said.

Riz and Zams reluctantly complied and turned to face the door, which Johannes was walking towards.

Johannes opened the door and into the room walked three Asian men dressed immaculately in three-piece grey suits with white shirts, navy blue ties, and brown shoes. They proceeded to the desk where Riz and Zams were stood. The first man pulled out the black leather seat facing Riz and Zams; which the second male sat in. The first and third males stood behind the male and flanked him from either side.

Zams then went to take a seat.

"I didn't say you could sit down, did I?" the seated male said in Urdu.

Zams froze and looked at him nervously before stepping backwards and standing straight to attention. The male stared at him in silence for what seemed like hours but was a matter of seconds.

"You may both sit down," the male said, again in Urdu.

"I wish he'd make up his mind," Zams said in English.

"Shut up, Zams," Riz said as they both sat down and shuffled in their seats.

"I don't have any trouble making up my mind," the male said in English. "Riz is right, Zams, you really should shut up." The male then laughed. "I'm messing with you. As-Salaam-Alaikum."

"Wa-Alaikum-Salaam," Riz and Zams said.

"It's time to talk business. Barry doesn't speak Urdu so we'll conduct the meeting in English. That way, he can translate everything back to RT when he speaks to him."

"Maybe Barry should learn Urdu," Zams said.

"Be fair now, Zams. Barry struggles enough with English." Everyone laughed, except Barry, who looked on forlornly. "Sorry, Barry. As-Salaam-Alaikum."

"Walkumslam," Barry said.

"You see, Barry's learning already," the male said. "In fact, I think he pronounced it better than you two."

"Why are we here?" Riz said.

The male looked at Riz and Zams and then looked at Johannes. "I'm getting a bit annoyed with these two, Johannes," the male said in Dutch. Riz and Zams looked at each other. Barry scratched his head. "The best Urdu speakers RT can send me are an impatient and disrespectful British-Pakistani Laurel and Hardy." The male then punched the desk in a fit of anger.

"They are a bit rough around the edges but RT wanted to show you he's committed to working with the Islamic community in the UK, as you'd asked," Johannes said.

"British-Pakistani Laurel and Hardy," Zams said and stood up angrily. The male stood behind the left shoulder of the male stepped forward and back-handed Zams across the face with such force he fell back into his seat.

"Yes, Johannes," the male said, as if nothing had happened. "I do want my people to be included, but surely he could do better than this dross."

Zams held his cheek. "That hurt, as did the insult."

"Shut up, you moron," the male said to Zams. "I am seriously considering sending you back to RT in pieces, with a note attached to one of your severed arms explaining you aren't the sort of people I want him or I to be working with."

Riz and Zams looked at each other nervously and back towards Johannes and Barry before turning back to face the male.

"Wait a minute. That looks like Oxford on the news. Turn the sound up," Zams said.

"What?" the male said.

"That's Oxford in England on the news. Where we're from. Can we please have some sound to hear what's happening?" Riz said.

"Very well. Turn the sound up," the male said. Johannes walked over and pressed the volume button on the side of the television.

"We can now go live to our London correspondent, Anika, for the full details," the news presenter said.

"Thank you, Jens. The pictures you're hopefully seeing on your screen are from Oxford, which is just over one hour's drive from London and famous around the world for its prestigious university. Today, it finds itself the centre of attention following an extraordinary gun battle in broad daylight on a busy street resulting in several deaths," the correspondent said.

"Wait a minute. That's Nathan's truck," Barry said.

"Who the hell is Nathan?" Riz said.

"One of the psychos that kidnapped me. It's his garage I was kept in overnight," Zams said.

"It doesn't look like he'll be kidnapping anyone again," Riz said.

"SHUT UP. He is my friend. He might still be alive," Barry said.

The room fell silent and everyone remained glued to the television.

"Is there any word from the police, Anika, as to the cause of today's horrific bloodshed?" Jens said.

"The police say they are keeping an open mind regarding today's events but speculation is rife that it may be connected to the death of a notorious gangster. Rupert Tarquin Walters, known as RT, was found shot dead in a nearby warehouse this morning. Police are again keeping an open mind but it looks like he was the victim of a gangland execution.

"RT IS DEAD. NO, NO, HE CAN'T BE," Barry said.

"I don't believe it," Riz said.

"I know. RT was called Rupert," Zams said.

"Back to you in the studio, Jens," Anika said.

"Thank you, Anika. We'll bring you more on that story when we have it. And now over to Elke for the weather report."

Barry held his head in his hands. The seated male and Johannes looked at each other and nodded. The seated male turned to face each of the males stood either side of him in turn and nodded. Both males walked over to Barry, grabbed an arm each and pulled it behind Barry's back before kicking a leg each away causing Barry to fall to the floor.

"What are you doing? Let me go," Barry said.

"I'm very sorry, Barry, but all of your associates are dead," Johannes said.

"But you can work with me until everything is cleared up. Why are you doing this to me?"

Riz and Zams watched in horror as one of the males placed Barry in a headlock whilst the other restrained him, and proceeded to suffocate the life out of him. Barry flapped around like a bird taking off into the sky before the male cruelly snapped his neck. Johannes and the seated male displayed no emotion.

"What did you do that for?" Zams said, as he looked at Barry's lifeless body sprawled out across the floor.

"It creates less mess and less noise than other methods," the seated male said.

"I didn't mean how you killed him, I meant why did you kill him?"

"With his crime group decimated, he has no place anymore. It's merely a case of tying up loose ends."

Riz and Zams looked at each other petrified.

"Don't worry, we're not going to kill you. There is now a gap in the market which needs to be filled."

"Gap in the market?" Riz said.

"Yes. Obviously, you two were going to be working for RT. As RT and his group are sadly no more, we need to create a new distribution network on the UK side. Of course, you may feel this opportunity isn't for you and we'll understand completely, won't we Johannes?"

"Yes, completely. We'll understand that there's two places next to Barry on the van that need to be filled," Johannes said.

"So, our choice is work for you or die?" Riz said.

"I'm afraid so. Assuming you choose to live, sorry work, with us, I'm afraid I'm going to have to maintain the original plan as agreed with RT."

"What's that and why?" Zams said.

"You two will be returning to England in a vehicle with two

hundred and fifty kilograms of sweet brown powder, and no, it isn't cocoa." Riz and Zams eyes widened. "I need to ensure your commitment to our partnership from the beginning and this will do it."

"What if we get caught?" Riz said.

"That's very negative thinking," Johannes said.

"You'll go to jail owing us a lot of money and it will be bad news all round," the seated male said. "You would owe RT money as well for what he's paid into this venture already, but I don't think you'll need to worry about that debt somehow."

Riz and Zams looked at each other aghast.

"Johannes, I think you should get some champagne, non-alcoholic of course. We can toast our new business partners and the fact we're going to make more money."

"Why will you be making more money?" Zams said.

"The terms of our agreement won't be anything like the percentage RT and his group were getting. That's another good reason why we needed to sever ties with Barry. Thanks, Barry," the seated male said as he callously looked over and waved at Barry.

"Right now, you may not think I'm a particularly fair man," the seated male said as Barry's body was being dragged unceremoniously across the floor by his associates.

"Well, whatever would give us that impression?" Zams said.

"But you must understand, RT was established with a structured network and you two are not. That is why you can't possibly have the same percentage. There will be more work and increased overheads for Johannes and I to support you in filling the gap in the market."

Johannes nodded.

"Riz sells weed. To me and a few others. You can't say he isn't established," Zams said. Riz elbowed Zams as if to encourage him to be quiet.

"No offence, Riz, but selling a few ounces of weed is hardly evidence of the ability to operate as a wholesaler of heroin like RT. That's a bit like comparing a small shop with a giant supermarket."

"Why do you want us to do it then?" Riz said.

"I don't particularly. The plan was for you two to help RT, Johannes, and myself in forging some new markets in the British Pakistani community. You were never meant to be frontmen. As I have already expressed quite clearly, I am very sceptical of RT's choice but, in the current situation I think Johannes and I have little option but to proceed with you."

"How are we going to operate without the required infrastructure?" Riz said.

"Barry is, sorry was, one of the connections from RT and the rest of the group to the middle market," Johannes said. "You'll step in and we'll need you to build with considerable support from us from there."

"As such, I'm afraid your share has to be dramatically reduced, at least to begin with."

"To what?" Zams said.

"What do you think Johannes?" the seated male said. "Shall we say five percent?"

"WHAT. EACH?" Johannes said.

"No, between them."

"Ok. I think we can do that."

"What was RT getting?" Zams said.

"None of your business," Johannes said. "Whatever agreement we had with RT doesn't apply to you."

"Ok, if we agree this reduced rate of five percent then I don't think we should have to drive the gear home," Zams said.

"Zams is right," Riz said and nodded.

"This business relationship we are entering into will need to be based on trust and a display of your competence to work with us. The first example of that is you taking the drugs back to the UK as planned, and then managing the security and distribution of it," the seated male said. "The unfortunate demise of RT creates a lot of extra work for us and so frankly, you should be delighted at five percent. It is most generous."

Every Friday after work, the mechanics at Nathan's Garage went to the King's Arms for a few swift halves to wash away the week in the bar with bricklayers, roofers, and plasterers. Office workers drank in the Red Lion. The distinction was clear. A man had dared to go in the King's Arms and complain about a hard week researching and writing an academic paper. He'd been picked up by his silk tie and despatched outside by a man with plaster dried into his forehead.

"Brett, I've tried calling Nathan but there's no answer," the mechanic said. "We're due to finish for the day soon. I don't suppose you'd stay here and hold the fort, would you? He's got the keys to lock up, you see."

"Of course. Not a problem at all."

"Thanks," the mechanic said as he pulled the shutters down. Both mechanics collected their things and left via the office. Brett followed them out.

"Goodbye," Brett said and waved.

The mechanics waved back and gave a thumbs up. Each of them got into their vehicles and drove away. Brett retreated to the office, unaware he was being closely watched by an eagle-eyed Lyle.

Lyle drove the vehicle into Nathan's compound and parked. "I'm going into the office to have a chat with that lad," Lyle said. "I'm locking you in the car as I don't trust you. Stay silent."

As Lyle walked towards the office, Brett stepped outside.

"I'm sorry sir, we're actually closed for the day," Brett said.

Lyle flashed his warrant card. "No, I'm afraid you'll have to stay open for business a bit longer."

"Well, the manager isn't here officer. Perhaps you can come back another time. Are you ok? Is that blood?"

"No, I'm afraid not. This has got to happen now. Don't worry it's not my blood. Now, step back into the office."

Will started banging on the car window in an attempt to get Brett's attention, but it didn't work and Brett did as Lyle had instructed. Lyle followed Brett into the office and closed the door behind him. "I need to search these premises," Lyle said.

"What for? Don't you need a warrant to do that?"

"You're right, I do. Here. Here's my warrant," Lyle said as he took out a handgun and pointed it at Brett, who placed his hands in the air. Lyle made a call. "I have control of the garage," he said, and looked menacingly at Brett.

18

Chapter Eighteen: Disbelief

DI Jarvis and DS Radcliffe were apoplectic as news of events filtered through. Jarvis kicked a swivel chair in frustration, which served only to hurt his foot. The chair slid across the room in what looked like a victory lap of honour. He stormed to the CID room and burst angrily into Johnson's office.

"I think you have some explaining to do, Acting ACC Johnson," DI Jarvis said brusquely.

"How dare you come in here without knocking, and thinking you can speak to me in such an aggressive and disrespect-ful tone. I will not tolerate such flagrant insubordination, Inspector, do you hear me?" Johnson said, as he took to his feet authoritatively. "It is still Inspector, isn't it? You haven't suddenly been promoted a few grades? If I have any explaining to do, it will be to people superior to you. Perhaps you will be permitted to take the minutes or make the tea or something."

"I prefer use of the word senior to superior, sir."

"Do you now? Well, I prefer superior. In fact, senior and superior, in my humble opinion."

"I don't think you know the meaning of the word, sir."

"That's enough, Inspector Jarvis. I don't want to hear another single word out of you until I speak to your management."

"You won't have to wait long sir. I understand ACC George Nicholls and Chief Superintendent Anne Kelly are on their way here."

"What? Nicholls and Kelly, on their way here. Why? Surely, I can just speak to them on the phone?"

"With all due respect, sir, this is a very serious situation and not really the sort of event that can be dealt with on the phone."

"I know it is a serious matter," Johnson said. He gently sat back down in his chair and contemplated for a moment. "Please let me know when they arrive, Inspector. I've not seen either of them in such a long time."

"Will do, sir. I apologise for my behaviour. I'm just shocked by what's happened. I let the emotions get the better of me. It was very inconsiderate and disrespectful. You must be absolutely devastated by the death of one of your officers and the disappearance–"

"Yes, thank you Inspector. I am in shock. I haven't taken it all in yet." At that moment, a phone began vibrating on Johnson's desk.

"I'll leave you to answer that, sir?"

Johnson nodded. Jarvis left the office and closed the door behind him.

"Yes?" Johnson said.

"Lyle is at Nathan's garage. He thinks the robots are there. I thought you'd like to know," the boss said.

"Like to know. Like to know. I'd like to know why Natasha Herbert is dead. I'd like to know why the media, who were already crawling all over my police station because of Clare Stevens, are multiplying in number and Oxford has become worldwide news. I'd like to know how on earth I'm going to survive the scrutiny that is coming my way. I'd like to—"

"I'd like you to keep it together. It's important you don't lose the plot now. I'm sorry if it sounds insensitive, but Herbert and the others were just collateral damage."

"Collateral damage? I liked Natasha. We kissed the other day."

"Kissed. You sound like a lovestruck teenager. Get a grip of yourself—"

"No, you get a grip. This is your fault. I met my end of the bargain and your poor planning has cost lives–"

"Don't you dare talk to me like that, do you hear me? I've no objection to reuniting you with your dear beloved Natasha, if that's what you'd like? Do we understand each other? I'm not happy either. I've lost a number of people I trusted and loyalty isn't that easy to come by. But ultimately, you and I can still come out of this unscathed, provided you are convincing. If you can't be convincing, Paul, I will have to conclude you're a liability to me, and you really don't want me to draw that conclusion."

As Johnson was poised to respond, the boss ended the call. Johnson launched the mobile phone across his office in frustration, just as Jarvis returned and knocked the door.

"WHAT IS IT NOW?" Johnson said.

Jarvis stepped through the door. "Sorry, I thought you'd want to know. ACC Nicholls and Chief Superintendent Kelly have arrived."

"Already?" Johnson said in an exasperated tone. Jarvis nodded. "Fine, I will be down shortly. Give me a moment please." Johnson inhaled a deep breath and took to his feet. From his office window, he surveyed the scores of people milling about outside the police station. He straightened his tie and nodded to himself in determination and defiance.

Lyle was perplexed as to why Nathan's employees had left a teenager alone at the garage.

"What's your name, lad?" Lyle said.

"It's Brett."

"Brett what?"

"Sadler."

"What are you doing here, Brett Sadler? Why have you been left in charge of the garage?"

"I'm doing work experience next week. The mechanics needed to leave so I agreed to wait here for Nathan the owner to return."

"You'll be waiting a long time. Nathan's dead."

"What are you talking about? He can't be."

"He is. And I should know, because I'm the one that killed him."

"What, why?"

"He shot my colleague dead, that's why. I had no choice. Do you know what's in that building over there, Brett? Tell me the truth."

"I don't know. Nathan wouldn't let me go over there. He said something about looking after precious cargo for someone."

"Did he now?"

"Yes, is that what you're looking for?"

"I am looking for some very precious cargo, Brett. You've been most helpful."

"Shall we go over and have a look?"

"There's no 'we' in this equation, Brett. I'm going to go over and have a look. You can stay here. Now, I don't want you getting any ideas of following me or trying to leave. So, I'm going to handcuff you to this desk, ok?"

"Are you going to kill me, like you did Nathan?"

"No, Brett. Not unless you disobey me. Now, sit in the chair while I handcuff you." Lyle proceeded to handcuff Brett's left hand to the table leg. "Don't you be trying anything, do you understand me, Brett?" He looked angrily at Lyle. Lyle put the gun to Brett's temple and pressed hard.

"You're hurting me."

Lyle slowly released the gun's pressure from Brett's head. "Sit still and keep your mouth shut," Lyle said. He stepped back from Brett and retrieved Nathan's keys from his pocket. "I just need to find which of these is the right key to that building," he said, before turning and walking purposefully out of the office.

Marcia watched as Lyle swaggered across the compound with keys jangling in his hand. Her hands furiously gripped the steering wheel in anticipation as Lyle tried key after key, and then finally, the door opened, and Lyle stepped through with trepidation before closing the door behind him. Marcia sent a text message from her phone before starting the engine and driving as slowly and quietly as she could into the compound and parked. Will, Sarah, and Tariq were overjoyed to see her.

The bright orange sign said 'Parkeerplaaats', Dutch for 'car park.' Three men entered under the direction of the only one of them that could read, let alone understand the sign.

"This is the vehicle you will return to the UK in," Johannes said removing blindfolds from Riz and Zams, who found themselves stood in an open-air car park that was sparsely filled with vehicles.

"You've got to be kidding me," Zams said. "A black van with white Arabic writing scrawled over it. We wouldn't be any more of a target to be stopped at UK Customs if we had a sign up in bright lights saying 'Drugs on board'."

"Don't be ridiculous. The writing says 'Charitable Donations.'

You won't be stopped."

"It says it in Arabic," Riz said. "Even if the Customs Team are oddly diverse enough to have an Arabic speaker, which I doubt they are, we're still going to get stopped. Knowing our luck, it's probably the Asian guy's day off anyway."

"It would be racist to stop two young Asian men driving a charity van. They wouldn't dare."

"In what pasty-faced equality fantasy land have you appeared from? We won't be racially profiled. Oh no, they'll stop Sheila and Terry instead of us, because they've overloaded their Rover with duty free wine and cigarettes from a French Supermarket. We are doomed," Zams said.

"Two things if I may. Firstly, you two don't know the first thing about drug trafficking. It's the less conspicuous people they're looking out for now. Think about it. Two UK citizens of Asian Pakistani origin driving a Dutch registered vehicle purporting to be conducting charity work. Nobody would be so stupid as to attempt such a thing. Who would invest a quarter of a tonne of heroin in such a venture? It's much more sophisticated these days. This is why you two really can't get more than five percent, you don't have the required strategic and tactical thought processes. But you will. If by remote chance you are stopped though, you will need a very good story as a defence."

"Like what? 'Sorry officer, there's a quarter of a tonne of heroin on board but we thought it was cocoa powder.' We're taking it to our uncle in Birmingham who works at Cadbury World because we thought they'd turn it into chocolate bars we could sell at the mosque to raise money for charity," Zams said shaking his head.

"I think that's a great idea," Johannes said. Riz and Zams were astonished. "A backstory you can both repeat easily that would be hilarious when you got to court. Now, if you'd let me finish. Secondly, you aren't going back to the UK via France. You will be going direct from Holland, to the magical city of Hull."

"Hull?" Riz said.

"Yes. Now, stop worrying about getting stopped and prepare to start driving."

"Can we have a look at the gear in the back first?" Zams said.

"No, I'm afraid not."

"Why not?" Riz said.

"Plausible deniability. If you are unfortunate enough to be stopped, which I'm sure you won't be, you will be more convincing when questioned. Now, which one of you will be driving?"

"I'll do it," Riz said.

"No. I think we should take it in turns," Zams said.

"How about one of you does the driving Holland side, and one of you does the driving UK side. Do I have to think of everything for you two?"

"Shall we play paper, rock, scissors to decide?" Zams said.

"We don't have time for you two to play stupid games. Riz shouted up first so he can drive now and you can drive when you're in the UK."

Johannes then threw the keys to Riz who caught them. "There you go. Now, the details of where you're going and the ferry you'll be on are in the glove compartment. Have fun gentlemen. We shall speak soon."

Riz and Zams looked at each other resigned to their fate, reluctantly climbed into the vehicle, and set off.

There were people from his past that Johnson would be delighted to be reunited with. Mainly women. ACC Nicholls and Chief Superintendent Kelly were two people he'd prefer to leave in the past, but that decision was out of his sweaty palms.

"Hello, Chief Superintendent Johnson, it has been a very long time. In some ways, not nearly long enough."

"Well, hello George. How lovely to see you, and it's Acting ACC Johnson, actually."

"Is it now? Well, congratulations, Paul," ACC Nicholls said. "I'd like to say it's thoroughly deserved but..."

"And how are you, Anne?" Johnson said, completely ignoring Nicholls's remark.

"Very well thank you, Paul," Chief Superintendent Kelly said.

"I'd prefer it if you called me, sir, Anne. Protocols are important."

"They are Paul. They are."

"Is there a room available where we can talk in private?" ACC Nicholls said.

"Yes, there is. Please follow me." They arrived at the room, Johnson opened the door to allow Nicholls and Kelly through but then prevented Jarvis from entering the room. "Not a conversation for you to be present for, Inspector. Perhaps you could go and get us some drinks or something."

"No, Paul, Inspector Jarvis will be joining us," ACC Nicholls said. "And we're fine for drinks, thank you." Jarvis smirked at Johnson and entered the room.

"Chief Superintendent Kelly and I will be interviewing you, with Inspector Jarvis taking notes," ACC Nicholls said.

"It seems a bit unnecessary. And, not that I want to raise it. But it seems a bit strange that you would interview me, what with our history. Perhaps don't write that down Jarvis."

"Please feel free to write everything down Inspector Jarvis. I found Paul in bed with my wife when I worked In Oxford as a Detective Inspector and Paul was a Detective Sergeant. I transferred to London after that happened. It's a long time ago and has no bearing on the current matter whatsoever."

"But I did take the vacant Detective Inspector's job after you left and you divorced your wife so—"

"Moving to London boosted my career immeasurably, and it's where I met my second wife. So, if anything Paul, I should be thanking you. But, to the point in hand, this is for us to gain a first-hand account from you of everything that has happened and present that to the Complaints Oversight Unit to review. Any further action will be taken by them, not me. So, please rest assured Paul, this will be entirely fair and transparent."

"Why don't the Complaints Unit come here themselves and speak to me, if they think this is necessary?"

"They're rather busy, Paul," Chief Superintendent Kelly said.

"For the second time, Anne, I think, no, I know, and I insist you address me as sir. Inspector Jarvis, please ensure the Chief Superintendent's insubordination is fully documented."

"Sorry, sir, my mistake. I must say, you do seem a bit on edge though," Chief Superintendent Kelly said.

"On edge. Well, of course I am. One of my officers has been cruelly gunned down in the line of duty in the prime of her life, with her colleague believed kidnapped along with members of the public we were protecting. Another one of my officers, who I had the utmost respect for, is corrupt and has killed another police officer, all while working on the highly sensitive, high-profile investigation that has cost my officer her life. I have murder scenes, crime scenes, dead bodies, bullet ridden streets, terrified citizens, traumatised shop staff. And you wonder why I'm on edge. Never mind coming here to interview me. What are you going to do to support me?"

Nicholls, Kelly, and Jarvis looked at each other and then back at a despairing Johnson who held out his hands and said: "I need your help, not your criticism."

"I'm not sure why you think we're here to criticise you, Paul," ACC Nicholls said. "We just need to piece together what has happened and understand your version of events. I'm sure that you, more than anyone, want justice for Natasha Herbert, and to hopefully preserve the life of Simon Lyle."

"Of course, that's exactly what I want," Johnson said, feigning crocodile tears.

"Well then please answer the following three questions," ACC Nicholls said.

"One. How is it, following concerns raised during the initial investigation into the activities of Dr Robert Leidenstraum by Oxfordshire Constabulary's Confidential Unit, a unit you were formerly a Superintendent of, you, in your role as Oxfordshire Constabulary's appointed Chief Superintendent senior responsible officer, overseeing the highly confidential counter investigation led by Superintendent Ray Wright at Reading Constabulary's Confidential Unit, nominated an Oxfordshire-based detective be seconded to that investigation, who it now transpires is a highly corrupt, ruthless cop killer?

"Two. Why did you delay redeploying aerial resource to the armed incident in the City Centre when this would have assisted ground units in identifying and apprehending those offenders?

"Three. Why were two extremely valuable subjects who you were responsible for the security of, left with the protection of one unarmed unit which has resulted in several deaths, including that of one, possibly two police officers.

"We are not here to criticise Paul; we are simply here to understand."

Johnson sank into his chair, gulped, and thought of a suitable response.

Will, Sarah, and Tariq watched as Marcia opened the boot of her car. They were thrilled to see Clare climb out, swiftly followed by John.

"Our neighbour Brett is in there," Will said pointing towards the office.

"I'll go and get him and some tools from the garage to break into the vehicle and free them," John said.

"Fine, the guns you and Clare took from the officers at the hospital are in the glove compartment. Clare and I will take them and apprehend Lyle," Marcia said.

"Ok, be careful. We'll come and help as soon as we can," John said.

"No, it's best you all wait out here or in the office," Clare said.

John nodded and headed for the office as Clare and Marcia armed and prepared themselves.

"DON'T SHOOT," John said, as he walked into the office and was confronted by Brett pointing a gun at him with one hand, whilst his other hand was still handcuffed to the table leg. "I'm here to help, please don't shoot," John said placing his hands in the air.

"Who are you and what are you doing here?" Brett said with his finger massaging the trigger.

"I've come to help. I'm with some police officers who are going to apprehend Lyle."

"Really? I didn't hear any sirens or seeing any flashing lights."

"We're in a plain car and we're trying not to startle Lyle. Where did you get that gun from?"

"I've just found it in the bottom drawer of this table. In his panic to handcuff me, he didn't check what might be in these desk drawers. It's nothing personal, but I'm not entirely convinced I can trust you. I'm going to shoot this handcuff off and then we'll go and find these police friends of yours."

"No, don't do that. That's way too dangerous. Plus, we don't want to alert Lyle. Let me go and get some tools from the garage, then I can free you and I can get Will, Sarah, and Tariq out of the car as well."

"Will, Sarah, and Tariq? My neighbours Sarah and Will?"

"Yes, it's them."

"What the hell are they doing here?"

"Lyle brought them here."

"You're not making sense. You're lying to me."

"I'm not lying to you, Brett. Please let me get some tools."

"Ok. Move slowly and keep your hands up. Stay where I can see you. Any sudden movements and I'll shoot."

John tentatively walked past the table Brett was attached to and into the garage. "Brett, I can see a hammer. Can I pick it up?"

"ONE HAND, you use one hand to pick it up and keep the other one up in the air."

"I've got it now, Brett."

"Good. Put your hand back up in the air with the hammer in it, turn around and walk back towards me very slowly. Ok, now I'm going to keep my gun pointed at you while you smash the chain off."

"What if you flinch and shoot me by mistake?"

"Don't give me a reason to flinch."

Lyle was wide-eyed with delight at what he had found in the compound.

"Who are you?" one of the figures said.

"I'm the police. Don't worry." Lyle then made a call to the boss. "I just thought you'd like to know, I've found the robots," he said with a smirk.

"Well done. I'll be over soon. You can tell young Tariq he can expect a family reunion," the boss said and ended the call.

Lyle continued to look in awe at the robots but was astonished to see the figure that was the exact replica of Brett Sadler.

"PUT YOUR HANDS UP LYLE, YOU'RE UNDER ARREST," Clare said, as she and Marcia burst into the building with guns drawn at Lyle who had his back facing them. Clare moved to the left and Marcia to the right.

"Is that you, Clare?" Lyle said as he placed his hands above his head with his mobile phone still in his right hand.

"Yes, it's me. Now turn around, slowly."

Lyle swivelled his head and body around and saw Clare out of the corner of his eye but was not yet able to see Marcia in his peripheral vision. In an instant he launched the mobile phone in Clare's direction and dived behind a shelving unit. Marcia fired at Lyle but the gun jammed and the bullet didn't release. The phone thrown by Lyle hit Clare on the head; she was temporarily stunned and dropped her gun. Lyle quickly retrieved his gun, and, from his position on the ground fired his gun twice in quick succession.

Will, Sarah, Tariq, John, and Brett all heard the gunshots.

"SMASH IT OFF NOW," Brett said. John executed the manoeuvre to perfection and with such force the table leg buckled under the pressure. With the cuff and partially snapped chain still attached to his left wrist, and with the gun in his other hand, Brett darted out of the office.

"Come back," John said. "It's too dangerous to go in there alone." But Brett ignored him and ran across the compound, ignoring the further pleas of Will, Sarah, and Tariq from inside the car.

John ran out with the hammer in his hand and approached the rear of the vehicle. "GET DOWN," he said, as he summoned all his strength to slam the hammer into the back window, causing it to smash partially. Brett stopped at the door of the building and turned around as John smashed the rest of it enabling Will, Sarah, and Tariq to climb out through the shards of glass onto the boot of the vehicle. Brett and John locked eyes. John shook his head but Brett turned around, determined to enter.

Johnson thought he'd given a convincing account of his actions, one even the boss would be proud of, but he was increasingly desperate for the scrutiny to end.

"Can I leave now?" he said. "I've told you everything I know."

"Well, let us recap the interview first Paul, to make sure we're absolutely clear," ACC Nicholls said. "You appointed DS Clare Stevens as you regarded her as a highly skilled and experienced officer with a distinguished record of service, someone whom you knew well and respected. You had no reason to suspect she could possibly be corrupt, and recent events have left you in a state of abject shock, questioning how this could have happened with such an esteemed officer, destroying your own confidence and belief in your colleagues and the police service." Johnson nodded with his head bowed. "You completed a full risk assessment for the funeral of Dr Leidenstraum and reacted to an unexpected and fast-moving situation at considerable pace, contemporaneously recording the rationale for the decisions you made in your policy book. You wholly stand by your resourcing and management of the event. The deployment of unarmed plain clothes resource is documented within your resource decision making. That resource was left alone in a perilous situation was a matter of considerable misfortune and, with hindsight, you would change none of your decisions." Johnson again nodded with his head bowed. "Not for me to advise you legally, Paul, but you may want to consider your use of the phrase 'considerable misfortune.' Johnson looked up at ACC Nicholls. "I don't think any future inquest or inquiry would look favourably upon such a statement as a plausible defence, do you?"

"What happens now?" said a stony-faced Johnson.

"You can go back to work for now. The Complaints Oversight Unit will review and will be in touch," said ACC Nicholls.

"Thank you," Johnson said and stood up.

"There is just one thing, Paul, if I may," ACC Nicholls said. "Pending the Oversight Unit's review, I'm going to insist that all of your decision making is overseen and ratified by either Anne or I.''

''I must protest that this is hugely undermining–''

''Paul, you are in a difficult enough situation as it is, and I must advise that you are in no position to protest whatsoever. Your decision making has resulted in tragic consequences, the full detail of which is not yet known. It would be remiss of me not to put assurances in place for the safety of both officers and the public which I am sure you would agree is paramount.'' Johnson reluctantly nodded and walked out of the room.

Lyle towered over Clare, poised to fire as Brett stepped through the door. Lyle turned to point his gun at Brett but Brett's reflexes were quicker. He fired a bullet into Lyle's left arm as Clare leapt up from the floor and ferociously grabbed Lyle's testicles. He squealed in excruciating pain, dropped his gun, and fell to his knees. Clare continued to grip tightly as Lyle tried to fight back and reach for his gun with tears streaming from his eyes. Brett ran over and kicked the gun away, before stamping on the bullet wound in Lyle's arm, and then viciously pistol whipping him across the face.

''Are you hurt?'' Brett said to Clare.

"No, the bullet grazed me, but Marcia..."

Brett turned to see Marcia slumped in the corner with blood trickling from under her body. He pistol-whipped Lyle again and Clare took the opportunity to pin him to the ground and handcuff him behind his back. Brett ran over to Marcia, who was still conscious and tried to stem the bleeding.

"We've got to get in there," Will said.

"We don't have any guns," John said.

"You two go in. Tariq and I will get some more weapons from the garage," Sarah said.

Will and John tentatively ventured into the building, with John still carrying the hammer in his hand. They saw Clare restraining Lyle and Brett tending to Marcia.

"Are you ok, Brett?" Will said and helped him with Marcia. Brett nodded. John went to help Clare. Will looked over at Clare who motioned with her eyes to get Brett out of the building.

"Brett, how does it feel to have a robot for a twin?" Lyle said.

"Shut up," John said, and punched him in the back of the head.

"What did he say?" Brett said.

"Nothing, Ignore him. Why don't you go and speak to Sarah and Tariq and make sure they're ok?" Will said.

"Go on Brett, go and take a real good look at yourself in the corner," Lyle said.

Clare grabbed Lyle's head, pulled it back and proceeded to smash it off the concrete floor, and then again, a touch harder than the first time.

Brett stood up and walked over towards the corner of the room.

"Don't do it Brett. Please don't go over there," Will said, but Brett ignored him.

Clare screamed and pulled Lyle's head back for a third time but John intervened and restrained Clare.

Sarah and Tariq walked in as Brett discovered the cloned robot of himself. The room fell eerily silent as everyone looked in sympathetic dismay at Brett.

Brett frantically shook his head and muttered to himself before pointing the gun in his hand at the version of himself.

"Don't do it, Brett. Please don't do it. We can explain. Please," Sarah said.

Brett kept his finger poised on the trigger but turned to face Sarah. "GO ON THEN, EXPLAIN TO ME WHAT IS GOING ON," he said, as his whole body trembled in shock.

19

Chapter Nineteen: Consequences

If the class system denoted the very fabric of British society, the underworld within it operated on a very different class system altogether. You'd got to be in a class of your own not only to reach, but to stay at the top of the pecking order of the criminal fraternity. They say crime doesn't pay, but try telling that to the boss.

As he strolled along the dark grey granite floor tiles of his spacious kitchen diner towards the bifold door with a breathtaking view of a finely manicured rear garden with a swimming pool, a phone vibrated on the white marble worktop peppered with black swirls.

"Yes?" the boss said, as he answered the call.

"We're outside in the van now. The cargo is on board," the voice said.

"Excellent. We'll be out shortly," the boss said and ended

THE DOCTOR'S HIDDEN PATIENTS

the call. "Did you hear that?" he said to the terrified woman stood before him. "Your daughter and that wretched husband of yours are here. And we're off to see your son, Tariq."

The female fell to her knees and screamed. She started to hyperventilate. The boss picked her up off the floor and slapped her hard around the face.

"As you've been so helpful and as I'm feeling nice, I'm not going to restrain you. But if you do anything stupid, I'll take it out on Tariq or Shabeela, maybe even both. Now, get your shoes on and get in the car." The female quickly did as she was told.

The boss nodded to the two henchmen seated in the van, as he and the female climbed into his car. They drove off in convoy through the knuckleduster-shaped electric gates.

Brett paced backwards and forwards tormented by his reflection. He screamed out in anger and disbelief at what he was witnessing.

"Hello Brett," the figure said.

"Don't talk to me, don't you dare talk to me," Brett said, his face contorted with confusion, anger, and sheer disbelief. "How are you going to explain this to me, Sarah, Will, how?"

374

"It's really difficult. We're still really struggling with it ourselves," Sarah said.

"Stay with me, Marcia," Will said, as Marcia grew increasingly weak. "We need to get her to a hospital," he said, as he walked over towards his sister.

They were all unaware that a car and van had arrived in the compound.

"I know she does, Will. Brett, our dad did experiments which he really shouldn't have done. I don't know what else to say."

The boss and the female watched from the car as the armed henchmen walked a bound, gagged, and blindfolded Tanveer and Shabeela from the van towards the building. The female screamed hysterically; the boss grabbed her around the throat, pulled her close to him and put his gun to her mouth.

"Not one more sound from you," he said, before letting go of her, jumping out of the vehicle and hurrying around to the passenger seat. He forcefully removed her from the passenger seat, but she remained perfectly silent as he marched her towards the building. With Tanveer as a human shield, the first henchman walked through the door with his gun drawn, closely followed by the second henchman with Shabeela, and with his gun drawn, with the boss and the female closely behind.

"Everyone put their hands up," the first henchman said. They all did as they were told, except Brett.

The boss closed the door behind him. "All of you keep your hands up and stand in a line on this back wall here," the boss said with his gun drawn.

"MUM!" Tariq screamed. The female nodded. Tariq, Shabeela, and their Mum all started to cry. Tariq tried to run over to her to her.

"Stop right there, Tariq," the boss said. "Nice to finally put a face to the name. What's that, Tanveer? You're a bit surprised your wife is here? I bet you are. Hello John, how's the wife and kids doing? What are you doing down there, Simon? I can't believe you let this lot get the better of you."

Tariq and John both scowled at the boss.

"Boss, what about the lad with the gun over there?" the first henchman said.

"Son, you really need to put that gun down. It's not playtime here," the boss said to Brett. "You don't want to get shot, do you?"

"You can shoot me if you want," Brett said. "But not before I put a bullet in this robot."

"I can't let you shoot the robots, son. They're too valuable."

"The one he's pointing the gun at looks just like him, boss," the second henchman said.

"You should be flattered the good doctor decided to use you as the subject for one of his robots. Now, put the gun down," the boss said.

"Urghh," the voice said faintly from directly behind where the boss was stood. The boss turned around and pointed his gun at Marcia.

"Oh dear. You don't look so well, love."

"She needs to get to a hospital," Will said.

"I'm afraid that's out of the question. She's just going to have to die there peacefully, Will. Pleasure to meet you, son." Will was stunned into silence. "And you must be Sarah, lovely to meet you, darling."

"I wish I could say the same. Please let us get her to a hospital."

"You greet me like that and then ask for my help. I don't think so, sweetheart."

"Do you want her moved from behind this door, boss?" the second henchman said.

"No, leave her there to die in peace. Show a bit of respect, will you? Look, son, you need to put that gun down. I'm going to count to ten and if that gun isn't out of your hand, I'm going to shoot you."

"What if I shoot the robot and then put the gun down?" Brett said.

"If you shoot the robot, I'm going to shoot you no matter what. One... two... three... four... five... six..."

"Put the gun down, Brett, please," Sarah said.

"Listen to her, Brett. Seven. You don't want to die a spotty, nerdy virgin, do you? Although if I shoot you and you live, you'll have a great tale to tell, and you'll be popular. The girls will think you're a real bad boy. And I should know. Eight... nine."

Brett lowered the gun, placed it on the ground and raised his hands in the air.

"A wise decision, young man. Now step back away from the gun. I'm going to come over and take a closer look at these robots."

"Are you going to let me out of these handcuffs?" Lyle said.

"Simon, I would love nothing more than to let you out of the handcuffs. But, I'm very sad to say that I no longer require your services."

"What, what... do you mean by that?"

"Firstly, your days in the police are numbered. Secondly, it's only a matter of time before they join the dots together, if they haven't already. You're going to jail. Which means you are of absolutely no use to me anymore. In fact, if anything you're a significant liability, which I can't have. I'm sorry, Simon," the boss said and pointed his gun at him.

Lyle wriggled around on the floor. "NO, YOU CAN'T DO THIS—"

The boss fired a single bullet into his temple, drawing gasps from the stunned witnesses. He then casually stepped over Lyle's lifeless body as blood seeped out from the wound in his head, and continued walking in the direction of Brett and the robots.

Unbeknownst to all whilst Lyle's execution was taking place, a weakening Marcia had summoned the strength to retrieve the phone from her pocket and sent a text message.

"These robots are amazing," the boss said to Brett, but Brett diverted his gaze away in the other direction. "And, priceless. I get it, you thought you were unique. Treat it as if it's the twin brother you never had. Now, walk over and stand by the others." Brett did as he was told.

The boss made a call. "I can confirm I have the merchandise," he said before abruptly ending the call.

"Take the blindfolds and gags off Tanveer and Shabeela," the boss said to the henchmen, who did as they were instructed.

"Mummy," Shabeela said tearfully as her eyes locked with her mother for the first time in months. Tanveer looked towards the ground unable to look anyone in the eye.

"YOU CAN LOOK TOWARDS THE GROUND, PATHETIC COW-ARD," Tariq said.

"Ok that's enough," the boss said. "Look at me, Tanveer," he said. Tanveer shook his head and refused to look up, so the boss grabbed him hard by the face and forced him to look up. "Now, look at your wife," the boss said as he forced Tanveer's head to face towards her direction.

She could barely look at Tanveer as he mouthed, 'I'm sorry.'

"Go on Tanveer, ask me in front of everyone how come your wife is still alive? No, I didn't think so. Your son's right, you're a coward. You see, Tanveer here let lust get the better of him, and he sought my services to get rid of his wife so he could be with his lady friend. Unfortunately, Tanveer couldn't afford to pay so he had to work for me—"

"YOU SET ME UP, HAD MY FAMILY KIDNAPPED AND DID ALL OF THIS BECAUSE OF YOUR AFFAIR WITH AMANDA. YOU PIECE OF—" John said.

"Oi, I was speaking. I understand you're angry with him. I would be if I was in your shoes, but you don't interrupt me John, ok?"

"YOU'RE WORSE THAN HE IS."

"That hurts my feelings, John, it really does. Anyway, as I was saying, Tanveer couldn't afford to pay. So, I told him I'd killed his wife here and that he'd have to work to pay me back. But then I decided she'd be an asset to me, so she's been held captive at my house in domestic servitude."

"YOU'RE SICK," Tariq said. "I'LL KILL YOU."

"Calm down, Tariq. She's been cooking and cleaning for me, nothing more sinister than that."

"That's bad enough. Keeping her hostage away from her children," John said.

"I'm just saying there's been nothing sexual. She's not my type. I don't mean that in a racist way."

"So, you're quite happy to be a cold-blooded killer but heaven forbid anyone should think you're a sex fiend or a racist. You have a truly warped perspective, you really do," John said.

"Thank you for your input, Sigmund Freud. The point is, her husband, their father, thought she was dead, and he let them believe she was still alive. He really is a monster. But I am a man of my word."

"What do you mean by that?" Tariq said.

"Tanveer has completed his work for me and so it's time I met my end of the agreement."

The boss pulled Tariq and Shabeela's mother close to him and then put a gun to her head.

"NOOOOOO," Tariq and Shabeela said.

"Don't do this," Clare said.

As the boss started to squeeze his finger on the trigger of the gun, Marcia summoned the strength to lift her body from the floor, pick up the gun which had been resting underneath her the entire time and fire a shot into the back of the boss. The boss fell forwards to the floor and dropped his gun. As the stunned henchmen turned to shoot Marcia, Shabeela bit the hand of the henchman next to her causing him to yelp loudly in pain, whilst Clare rugby tackled the henchman with Tanveer, knocking both to the ground.

Brett quickly retrieved Lyle's gun which he had earlier kicked away, and shot the henchman nursing his bite wound once in the head. Brett turned to see Clare and the other henchman on the floor wrestling for control of the henchman's gun. He fired one shot to the head and one to the body of the henchman before pointing the gun at Tanveer. Sarah and Will ran to attend to Marcia as everyone else in the room tried to digest the magnitude of the events that had unfolded in the preceding few seconds. Will immediately dialled 999 and called for an ambulance.

"No, please don't shoot him," Tariq and Shabeela's mum said.

"You want him to survive after all he's done?" Brett said.

"Yes. I want him to survive, but only to make him suffer. If you kill him, he will not suffer. Death is too good for him."

"She's right, Brett," John said. "He deserves to face the full wrath of the law and rot in a cell for the rest of his natural days."

"Ok," Brett said as he lowered the gun. He then raised the gun again and fired a single shot at Tanveer's left foot. Tanveer screamed in pain. The bullet had severed two of his toes and caused blood to squirt out like someone vociferously squeezing a ketchup bottle.

"BRETT," Clare said.

"What? Are you telling me he doesn't deserve to endure some physical pain for what he's done?"

"No, I'm not saying that," Clare said, as Tariq and Shabeela's mum screamed at the top of her voice, walked over towards a squealing Tanveer, and kicked him as hard as possible between the legs. She proceeded to slap and punch him in a frenzied fashion before Tariq restrained her, hugged her tightly and walked her over towards Shabeela, where the three of them embraced.

Brett walked back towards the robots and pointed the gun at his replica.

"NOOO," Clare said.

"No, please don't shoot me, Brett," the replica robot said.

"I told you not to speak to me," Brett said, his face contorted with anger. He pulled the trigger but the chamber was empty. He tossed the gun to one side and picked up the gun he had earlier placed on the floor when instructed to by the boss. He pointed it at the replica.

"No, Brett you can't," Will said as he ran over to stop him. Will stood between Brett and his target.

"Get out of my way, Will. I don't want to shoot you."

"Then don't. Please don't," Will said. "We're good friends and neighbours, Brett, please put the gun down. You don't need to do this."

"We are Will, but that doesn't mean I won't shoot you do you hear me?"

"He's more than your friend and neighbour, Brett," Sarah said.

Everyone looked at Sarah in shock, including a deteriorating Marcia.

"What do you mean?" Brett said.

"No, Sarah. Not like this," Will said.

"What is she talking about, Will?"

"Nothing, Brett. Please put the gun down."

"Stop lying to me, Will, or I'm going to shoot you."

"YOU'RE GOING TO SHOOT HIM, YOU'RE GOING TO SHOOT MY BROTHER, YOU'RE GOING TO SHOOT YOUR BROTHER, YOU'RE GOING TO SHOOT OUR BROTHER."

Brett lowered his gun, his mouth opened wide with shock. He turned to face Sarah, then back to face Will.

"W-w-w-what are you talking about?" Brett said.

"Our father is your father. That's why there's a robot replica of you," Sarah said.

Brett fainted on the spot and fell in a heap on the floor. Will tended to him. Sirens could then be heard approaching the building.

"That ambulance was quick," John said.

"We're going to need more than one," Clare said. She stood up, walked towards Marcia, and embraced her. "Hold on, help is coming," she said.

Sarah and John walked over to Will.

"Now what?" John said, as they all looked at each other,

looked at Brett and then at the robots.

A barrage of vehicles arrived outside the compound in quick succession. The main road was sealed off at all access points as a helicopter hovered overhead and surveyed the area. Heavily armed personnel prepared themselves and then made their way cautiously onto the premises, with some moving towards the garage and others towards the building.

"Is that a helicopter I can hear?" Tariq said.

At that, explosions could be heard and plumes of smoke filled the air as the main door to the building and its rear fire exit were forced open. Armed officers swooped in and barked their instructions at all inside to get down on the ground. All complied.

Steam escaped from the boiling kettle in the CID kitchen. Johnson stood over it and placed a teabag in the only clean mug available. The mug had 'NYPD' written on it. He needed something far stronger than a cup of tea, but for now it would have to do. He very much doubted a Police Officer in New York would ever drink out of a mug with 'Oxfordshire PD' written on it, more's the pity, he thought.

"Paul Johnson," the familiar voice of Superintendent Ray Wright said. Johnson turned around and was confronted by

Ray Wright and several other officers, including ACC Nicholls and Chief Superintendent Kelly.

"What's going on?" Johnson said.

"Paul, you are under arrest for Misconduct in Public Office, amongst a whole range of other offences. You do not have to say anything but it may harm your defence if you do not mention when questioned something which you later rely in court. Anything you do say may be given in evidence," Wright said.

Johnson suddenly launched to grab the hot kettle and was tackled to the ground and placed in handcuffs.

"It's over, Johnson," ACC Nicholls said. "Take him away."

The title of 'Foreign Secretary' conjured up an image of someone who constantly clocked up air miles whilst smiling and being frightfully polite to overseas politicians and investors. It was the ultimate sales job for Britain. Some days, though, paperwork was a must and this was one of those days. The Foreign Secretary was in her office, the glamour of taxpayer funded international travel substituted for a box of ministerial submissions littered with policy drivel. The door burst open and she was apprehended by police officers and arrested.

"What on earth is going on? Does the Prime Minister know that you are doing this?"

As she was led away, the Prime Minister and Home Secretary were stood in the corridor watching.

"Prime Minister, what is going on? Please put a stop to this madness?" the Foreign Secretary said.

The Prime Minister looked her firmly in the eye, shook his head and said nothing.

"I can't believe it, Prime Minister, I really can't," the Home Secretary said. "You think you know people."

"I know, I can scarcely believe it is true. This is a deeply disturbing revelation, it really is. It is going to be a feeding frenzy with the media, and what about the public? Our standing as a country on the global stage. We need to convene an urgent cabinet meeting."

"Yes, Prime Minister. I shall organise it immediately."

The warrant had been checked and checked again a hundred times by as many people to ensure it was correct. You must be accurate if you're going to arrest a Solicitor, because they most definitely will inspect the paperwork looking for so much as a word out of place. The most senior partner at the law firm was sat at his desk wearing a pin-striped navy suit, twill white shirt, a mustard-coloured tie with matching pocket handkerchief and brown shoes when the police stormed into his North London office and detained him. He remained remarkably calm and made no comment as he was placed in handcuffs and led away to a police van.

Tanya Parry had graduated from Oxford University with a first-class degree in Journalism and now she found herself live at the scene of unfolding drama that would be worldwide news. The reporter had craved a story that would elevate her career and satisfy her ambitions, and this was it. This was the moment in the spotlight she'd dreamed of.

"What are you doing?" an officer said to Tanya, who had taken up a position next to a section of 'Police Do Not Cross' tape. She had a microphone in her hand and was in company with a male operating a camera.

"I'm Tanya Parry. I'm a journalist," the female said.

"How have you got here so quickly? This is a serious situation. You can't film here."

"I'm a good journalist, that's how, and just you try stopping me. I've every right to film my report from here, unless it's unsafe, and if it's unsafe then I suggest you extend this cordon. Is the camera ready, Bill?"

"It's ready, Tanya. We're good to go. I just need to confirm they're ready in the studio."

The Prime Minister stood to his feet to address his cabinet when an aide rushed into the room and whispered in his ear.

"Oh, my good lord," the Prime Minister said. "Yes, switch it on immediately."

The aide switched on the television and put the news channel on as the anchor was finishing speaking.

"For more on this incredible breaking news story, we go live to our correspondent Tanya Parry in Oxford," the anchor said.

"Thank you, Harold. You join me here at a scene of complete and utter chaos. I can barely hear myself think over the noise from the helicopter overhead. A short time ago the emergency services descended upon Nathan's Garage, closing all access to the road outside to the public. Armed officers, along with what appeared to be military personnel swarmed the compound. What followed were a few explosions and smoke, the likes of which Oxford has never witnessed before. We're now waiting in anticipation of what is going to happen next."

"Tanya, thank you. Is this in any way connected to other events in Oxford that have occupied the news in recent days?" Harold said.

"That is yet to be confirmed but speculation is certainly growing of a possible connection between all the incidents that have taken place. One theory emerging is that events here are linked to a very large police presence for the funeral of Dr Robert Leidenstraum earlier today. Dr Leidenstraum, a specialist in biotechphilanthropical studies is believed to have been subject to a police investigation into unethical activities he had been carrying out in developing half human half robot hybrids. In fact, as I speak Harold, it looks like technicians in white laboratory coats are poised waiting to enter the compound, so maybe the robots are inside."

"How the hell does she know this?" the Prime Minister said.

"Tanya, I'm sorry to interrupt you but breaking news is reaching us in the studio here that the Foreign Secretary has been arrested, along with a solicitor, and a senior ranking officer from Oxfordshire Police, in what has been described as an ongoing linked fast-moving investigation."

"We're ruined, ruined I tell you..." the Prime Minister said.

"We've got to do something, Prime Minister, and quickly," the Home Secretary said.

"Yes, you are right. I think we should tell the media I have suspended the Foreign Secretary, pending the outcome of the investigation. Yes, do it now. Make calls to the broadcasters. I want this information on these bulletins now."

"Harold, you may be able to hear sirens in the background. We're just watching an ambulance drive away from the scene at speed. I'm sorry we're unable to provide any more information about that at this time," Tanya said.

"Tanya, thank you very much for now," Harold said, before directly addressing the viewers. "We're going to resume our normal programming and will bring you further details in our later bulletin. Hold on, just before we go, I'm getting information in my ear that the Prime Minister has just announced he has taken the decision to suspend the Foreign Secretary whilst this criminal investigation takes place."

"Well, that's something, Prime Minister," the Home Secretary said.

"Yes, but it is the equivalent of putting a small plaster on a large gaping wound. It will do little to stem the flow. I am going to have to address the public as soon as I can."

Superintendent Ray Wright was in the custody sergeant's rest room. He sipped a hot chocolate from a polystyrene cup and nibbled on a chocolate hobnob. A hot chocolate and a biscuit, or two as he plotted his interview tactics had been his modus operandi for years.

"While we are waiting for the legal reps for Johnson and the Foreign Secretary, let's interview this solicitor and see what he has to say," Superintendent Ray Wright said.

The solicitor was brought from his cell and taken to an interview room.

"Are you sure you will not require legal representation?" Superintendent Wright said.

"No, I will not. I will represent myself. I have a statement I would like to read out, following which I will be answering 'no comment' to any of your questions."

"Very well," Superintendent Wright said.

"I am the Foreign Secretary's brother-in-law. I am married to her eldest sister. I was telephoned by an unknown male who said he was contacting me on behalf of my sister-in-law to let me know that my sister-in-law had found out I was having an affair. The male told me that I must do as I was told or my wife would be informed of this fact. I was instructed to ask no questions and to act as the liaison point between this male and another male. I have been the conduit between the two and passed messages and calls back and forth. These messages have generally been quite cryptic and I haven't been able to establish what the activities are about. I hoped I wasn't helping to facilitate anything illegal, but was so desperate for my wife not to find out I have complied with all of the requests. I am truly sorry for my actions."

"Who are you having an affair with?" Superintendent Wright said.

"I'd rather not say. I mean no comment."

"You are truly sorry for your actions?"

"Yes, I am. No comment."

"Are you sorry you had an affair, sorry your sister-in-law found out, sorry you have participated in a criminal conspiracy or sorry for all of it?"

"No comment."

"I'm very pleased you've managed to work out how to say no comment."

"No comment."

"That wasn't a request for you to do it. You didn't need to answer that." Suddenly an alarm activated.

"Interview suspended. A panic alarm has been activated," Superintendent Wright said, and stopped the tape. "Wait here with him," he said to his colleague, before leaving the interview room to find out what was happening.

"It's Johnson," an officer said. "He's hung himself." Ray Wright buried his head in his hands.

The emergency services continued to process the scene at Nathan's compound.

"THIS MAN HAS A PULSE," a paramedic said. "IT'S FAINT BUT HE IS STILL ALIVE."

20

Chapter Twenty: Culmination

Saturday 10 July, 1999. 7.25am.

After twelve mind numbing hours floating across the North Sea, Riz and Zams prepared for their ferry to dock in Hull.

"Breathe in that fresh air, bruv," Zams said. "It's the last we're going to get for a while."

"Don't say that. Maybe we will get through," Riz said.

"You're having a laugh. Have you not noticed the funny looks we've been getting from other passengers? There will be a protest from them if we aren't stopped."

"That's just plain old-fashioned racism, Zams. That's nothing to do with the van. They'd be like that whether we were travelling in a vehicle or if we were foot passengers."

"Will all passengers travelling in a vehicle please now return to that vehicle pending arrival at the port," a voice announced across the loudspeaker.

"Riz, why don't we just depart as foot passengers, leave the van and declare we were kidnapped and forced to do this?"

"I think we've got a better chance with the story of our uncle working for Cadbury's in Birmingham. Come on, let's get back in the van. I'll drive us out of the port, you can drive home from there."

"We have now arrived in Hull. Drivers, you may now start your engines and prepare to disembark," a voice announced across the loudspeaker.

"Zams, will you stop shaking? You look guilty."

"I don't want to point out the obvious, Riz, but we are guilty."

"Well, yes. We are, sort of. But we need to at least try and look as if we're innocent. We don't need to give them any more reasons to think about stopping us."

As they emerged from the ferry onto land they sat perfectly still and smiled wholesomely at officials. They were immediately instructed to pull in for checking.

"Oh no Riz, I told you. And look, they've got a sniffer dog as well."

"Shut up, Zams. Let me do the talking." Riz wound down his

window. "Good morning, officer. How are you today?"

"Good morning. Interesting vehicle you have here Mr...?"

"Whatever name is on my passport I am travelling on. I can't remember. Just call me Riz."

The official stared at Riz and was clearly unamused.

"That's a great start that is, Riz," Zams said in Urdu.

"Speak English," the official said. "Out of the vehicle now, both of you. Stand alongside the van with your hands placed on the side and your feet spread a shoulder width apart."

Riz and Zams complied with the instruction. As they did so, they turned to face the nodding approval of their detention from other passengers.

"The sniffer dog is getting excited. I wonder why that is?" another official said.

"It's probably because he can smell the heroin in the back of our van, I mean cocoa. It's cocoa, not heroin. My uncle, I mean our uncle, he works at Cadbury's in Birmingham. They need cocoa not heroin. He'll get promoted to Chief Buyer," Zams said.

"Either you two are innocent or you've got a warped sense of humour," the first official said.

The official with the sniffer dog opened the back of the van. Riz and Zams closed their eyes and braced themselves.

"It looks like it's just cocoa, foodstuffs and toys," Riz and Zams heard a voice say. They both looked at each other, confused.

"We'll conduct a thorough search and a few field tests and if all is well, you two can be on your way," the first official said to Riz and Zams. A short time later they were released.

"I don't understand Riz. What are we going to do now?"

"Nothing. We're going to drive home and do nothing."

"Yes, but what about all the heroin we have on board? I can't believe they thought it was cocoa and have let us go."

"You idiot. It is cocoa. We don't have any heroin. Those people in Holland were obviously winding us up. I'll pull over shortly and you can drive us back to Oxford."

Marcia's eyes lit up with excitement as she watched Clare walk along the ward and stop at the foot of her bed.

"Good afternoon, DC Reynolds. How are you feeling?" Clare said.

"Clare. I'm so pleased to see you. How is everyone? How have you got out of the police station already?"

"Relax. I'll fill you in on everything I know."

"Before you do, you might like to know that the man I shot in the back is still alive, and he's in a bed a bit further down on the other side of the ward. From what I can gather he is going to live."

"Is he now? And I thought the armed officer outside the entrance to the ward was just for you?" Clare kissed Marcia on the forehead and held her hand. "I've not stopped thinking about you. I thought I was going to lose you."

"No, I'm going to be ok. Although I don't think I'll be running any marathons anytime soon."

"Probably for the best. They are very impactive on your joints anyway." They both laughed.

"So, are you going to tell me what's happened since I was drifting in and out of consciousness yesterday?"

"We were all arrested, even poor Shabeela. Fortunately, just before the police arrived, we had time to switch Brett the human with Brett the robot."

"Why did you do that?"

"I suggested it because of fingerprints and gunpowder residue.

With Brett having fired those weapons, there would be no way of devising a story that explained the scene forensically to keep him out of jail, and he didn't deserve that. Also, it provided leverage for all of us, but particularly Sarah and Will, to take a robot out of there as part of combatting any cover up the government might try and initiate. Although bizarrely, when I was interviewed, I was asked if I knew of anyone communicating with the media as they were already aware of the robots. They kept asking me if I knew a Tanya Parry and played a video of her reporting for the news from the scene yesterday."

Marcia looked awkward at the mention of the name Tanya Parry.

"It's front page of every newspaper today. I think my favourite headline is 'Dr Frankenstraum's monsters.' Not nice for poor Sarah and Will, though."

"No, it's not. So, the real Brett was taken away with the other robots?"

"Yes, I'd love to be a fly on the wall when the Ministry of Defence realise Brett actually is human. They probably have by now, but it's too late."

"How do you mean?"

"Well, apart from the robotic switch, oh and that Tanveer shot you, and Lyle, and the henchmen, but one of the henchmen managed to shoot Tanveer in the foot, we told the whole truth in interview, so they had no choice but to release all of us, except Tanveer. I've no idea what he said in interview. Even without our lies about him shooting people they should have enough to charge him for what he is guilty of. As for me, it turns out that the Police Complaints Oversight Unit were onto Johnson and somehow have established I'm innocent, although I've no idea how they've drawn that conclusion. Brett the robot was interviewed and even his mother as appropriate adult didn't have an inkling it wasn't human Brett, which is unbelievable. Mind you, teenagers are a bit robotic, aren't they? Anyway, they put the fact the robot was weakening down to Brett feeling tired. After our release, Sarah and Will managed to convince Brett's mum to let the robot that she thinks is her son spend time with them. We all went to Sarah and Will's aunt's house. Dr Leidenstraum's journals were seized from Sarah by the authorities, who will presumably use them to keep the other robots alive for now, but Sarah hadn't told anyone there was a floppy disk she had found with her father's journals. She stored it at their aunt's house ahead of the funeral. It also had information on it about how to conduct the process to keep the robots alive. Sarah and Will used it to successfully carry out the procedure on robotic Brett. That was quite an amazing thing to watch. The three of them, along with the Paterson family, Tariq, Shabeela and their mum have now gone to the German Embassy in London to claim political asylum and seek refuge from persecution in the UK. It's ironic, given all their father has put everyone through, that they are going to appeal to his homeland for support. It was quite an emotional goodbye. They were all eternally grateful for all we had done to help and asked me to pass on their sincere thanks to you. They'd loved to have come to see you in person."

"Wow, quite a lot happens when you're unconscious. I can't believe it."

"No, it really is incredible but, you know what's really incredible?"

"What's that?"

"After I parted ways with everyone, I went back to your flat to freshen up and collect a few things for you. And I noticed a photograph on your bedroom wall."

Marcia squirmed.

"Yes, it's an incredible coincidence that there's a photograph of you and some friends on holiday. And one of those friends just happens to be Tanya Parry."

"Ok, I admit Tanya is a good friend of mine," Marcia said.

"And you relayed sensitive information to her as a journalist?" Clare said. "I know you've not been a detective all that long Marcia but—"

"I haven't been truthful with you Clare. I think I should probably explain."

"Ok, now I'm worried."

"Before I explain, I just want you to know that I really do have feelings for you. I hope this won't change things, because I think, no, I know, I'm falling in love with you, but I'll understand if it does."

Clare looked pleased, but also confused and scared by Marcia's comments.

"I love you too Marcia," Clare said.

"I'm not a newly qualified detective for Oxfordshire Police. I'm an experienced detective and undercover operative for the Police Complaints Oversight Unit's Anti-Corruption Unit. I was deployed as part of an investigation into Johnson, Lyle, and Herbert. I'm really sorry."

Clare gasped open-mouthed at this revelation.

"The reason the police know you're innocent and have released you is because of my reporting into my superiors."

"You lied to me, Marcia, you lied to us all."

"Yes, I did. And I'm sorry for that but I'm not sorry for what I've done to help you, Will, Sarah, and the others."

"I don't believe it. I have feelings for you Marcia, but I question whether it was all an act."

"It was not an act, Clare, I promise you. My superiors don't know about me and you, and that's because that is real."

"Even though you're not?"

"I am real, Clare, just not quite what you thought."

"And what about the reporter? What would your superiors make of that?"

"They wouldn't understand my explanation. It would cost me my job, Clare."

"Try explaining to me first."

"After I eavesdropped on the conversation with the Security Minister at the station, I feared gravely for Sarah and Will's safety. I didn't know what I could do to protect them but felt compelled that I should. It wasn't a spur of the moment decision, Clare, it really wasn't. I gave it a lot of thought I promise you. I contacted Tanya and said I had a story for her but would let her know when the time was right. I messaged her when I was sat outside Nathan's compound. I figured the media attention would in a strange way offer Sarah and Will some sort of protection."

"You're right."

"Really?"

"Yes, your superiors wouldn't understand."

"Thanks for that."

"But I can see why you did it. Even if I'm not sure if it was the right decision. How much contact have you had with your superiors during this assignment?"

"A fair bit, although the last week has been a bit tricky to say the least. It's been tough balancing things out, knowing what to say to who and when, taking care not to get caught out. The most important contact was the final one, when I was lying on the floor having been shot."

"What do you mean?"

"I managed to send a message to say where we were and to get the emergency services to the scene as soon as possible."

"That's impressive considering your condition and the peril of the situation. You're a good undercover operative, Marcia, you've been very brave and have done an excellent job, even if I am furious with you."

"Thank you. Try not to be too angry with me, Clare, please. I never intended to hurt you."

"No, I'm sure you didn't. Mind you, could you not have done something to intervene in stopping me and my house from being plastered all over the news."

"I'm sorry. I wasn't happy with that decision either. My bosses were desperate to gather evidence against Johnson, Lyle, and Herbert. I think they thought it would be easier to clear you later as part of the case against them."

"I will be taking a grievance against that decision. They had no right to publicly besmirch my name as part of an investigation into corrupt officers."

"No, they didn't. I think you'd have a good case for compensation."

"I'm sure I have. To buy me a new house if nothing else."

"You could always come and live with me, if you want to that is?"

"I don't recall saying I'd forgiven you for your betrayal. Besides, shouldn't we at least go on a date before we consider moving in together? We've already taken things quite far enough."

"Is that your peculiar way of asking me out on a date?"

"Marcia, if that is your real name? Would you like to go on a date with me when you get out of hospital?"

"Marcia is my name; it is Reynolds that is an alias. I will think about it, Sarge, I'll think about it," Marcia said with a beaming smile.

A nurse walked up to Marcia's bed and checked her charts.

"How is she doing, nurse?" Clare said.

"She's doing well, all things considered."

"That's good news."

"Speaking of news, they have just announced on the television the Prime Minister has stepped aside due to this scandal with the Foreign Secretary and these robots."

"REALLY?" Clare and Marcia said.

"Yes. He's stepping aside with immediate effect. A press conference will be broadcast live later," the nurse said and walked away.

"I don't suppose you considered that as a possible consequence when you contacted Tanya?"

"No, definitely not. It is not every day you are involved in the removal of a Prime Minister. I am a bit worried."

"Yes, it is a bit of a concern, isn't it?"

"What do you think I should do, Clare?"

"I think you should... no, scrap that, I think *we* should consider we have some friends who are moving to Germany, and I can equally go on a date with you in Munich as I can in Oxford. What would you say to that?" Clare said, as she tenderly held Marcia's hand.

"Ja bitte," Marcia said as she firmly gripped Clare's hand and gazed into her eyes.

"Danke schön, Marcia, Danke schön," Clare said with a warm and loving smile.

The Oxford to Holland to Hull to Oxford adventure ended as Zams parked the van on the road outside his house.

"Home sweet home, bruv," Zams said applying the hand-brake.

"That's great, Zams but I thought you'd have dropped me off first," Riz said.

"No, I'll get out and you can take the van from here."

"What am I supposed to do with this van? I can't exactly park it up outside my house, can I?"

At that point, a phone in the van started to ring.

"Where's that sound coming from?" Zams said.

"I think it's coming from the glove box," Riz said. He opened the glove box, retrieved the phone, and passed it to Zams.

"Why should I answer it?"

"Just answer it."

"Hello, who is this?"

"Hello Zams, it is so good to speak to you again."

"Johannes, is that you?"

"It is indeed. I am so pleased you have made it back to Oxford. Many congratulations."

"Thanks Johannes, we're so glad to be... Wait a minute, how do you know we've made it back to Oxford?"

"I have some friends parked in a white van on the opposite side of the street from you. Perhaps a coincidence but I think they travelled from Holland to Hull and then drove to Oxford."

Zams was stunned.

"Please wave at my friends, Zams. Sorry, I should say our friends."

Zams waved politely in the direction of the white van.

"What are you doing, who are you waving at?" Riz said.

"Just smile and wave Riz, just smile and wave."

Riz reluctantly raised his left hand and started waving.

"So, I suppose you and Riz are wondering why the officials didn't find any heroin when you were stopped at Hull?"

"It had crossed our mind, Johannes, yes."

"We were sure you two would be stopped. Two young Asian men travelling from Holland in a van covered in Arabic writing. We couldn't possibly load that vehicle with heroin."

"But you said—"

"I know what I said Zams but I lied to you. I'm sorry. It would have been a miracle if you hadn't been stopped. Anyway, we're very proud of how brave the two of you were. And so, it will be an absolute pleasure going into business with you."

"Well, we don't have an uncle at Cadbury's so I don't know what we're going to do with all this cocoa."

Johannes laughed. "You are so funny, Zams. Don't worry about the cocoa. I'd suggest you focus on the heroin that is in the white van. You see, you were the perfect decoy. While the officials were dealing with you two, the van with the heroin in was able to sail through, if you'll excuse the pun. It's time to get to work, I'll be in touch," Johannes said and ended the call.

"Zams, what is going on? Why are we still waving at that van?"

"The heroin that we thought was in this van is in that van. Whilst the sniffer dog was licking my crotch in Hull, they were driving off unchallenged. Riz, we are international drug traffickers now. We are going to be involved in selling heroin."

"While also making copious amount of hot chocolate, it would seem. Whichever way you look at it, our future is brown powder."

In 307 days' time, not that he was counting, Superintendent Ray Wright was due to retire from the police. In a career spanning twenty-nine years, he'd interviewed people from just about all walks of life, but never had he interviewed a government minister. His heart was beating fast, and not just because he'd drank too much hot chocolate and polished off the chocolate hobnobs.

"Good afternoon, Foreign Secretary, how are you?" Superintendent Ray Wright said.

"Don't you 'good afternoon' me. How much longer am I going to be caged in this rat hole?"

"As long as it takes. In fact, I am hopeful the Superintendent will be extending your stay with us. Don't worry, it will be an independent Superintendent, not me conducting that process."

"Well, I am sure that Superintendent will see sense and let me out. I am the Foreign Secretary and there has clearly been a mistake, a career ending mistake, Superintendent."

"Well, that is rather ironic because I am afraid the Prime Minister has decided to suspend you, so you aren't currently the Foreign Secretary. Career ending mistake, indeed."

"He wouldn't. He can't."

"Perhaps you can take that up with him. For now, it is time we started this interview."

"My legal representative has advised me to answer 'no comment' to your questions. I don't know why. I've done nothing wrong, but I will be answering no comment."

"It's your interview, your choice. At what point did you decide to commit treason against the UK?"

"No comment," she said, shaking her head. "Treason, what utter nonsense."

"Tell me about your relationship with your older sister?"

"None of your business. No comment."

"What about her husband, your brother-in-law?"

"No comment. This is ridiculous," she said folding her arms defensively.

"When did you find out your brother-in-law was having an

affair?"

"W-what? No comment," she said and appeared visibly shocked.

"How do you think your sister will feel that you haven't told her about her husband's affair? Which betrayal do you think she will think is worse, his or yours?"

"I haven't betrayed. No comment."

"Who have you conspired with to blackmail your brother-in-law?"

"This is outrageous. I have done no such thing. I do not know where you've come up with these ludicrous and frankly preposterous questions from. Where is your evidence of any of this?"

"Evidence Foreign Secretary, sorry, former Foreign Secretary. You want evidence? I'll give you evidence," Superintendent Wright said.

"Go on then. I can't wait to hear it."

"Tell me what you know about a Nokia thirty-two ten with the telephone number ending six four four?"

"What? No comment."

"This phone has been in regular contact with another Nokia

thirty-two ten with the telephone number ending seven six eight. Who is the user of that device?"

"No idea. No comment. You tell me."

"We don't know yet. Anyway, the number ending seven six eight has been in contact with a Nokia thirty-two ten with the telephone number eight nine seven. What can you tell me about that?"

"The Nokia thirty-two ten is a very popular model."

"I would try and be less flippant if I were you. The Nokia thirty-two ten with the telephone number ending eight nine seven was found in the search of your brother-in-law's office."

The Foreign Secretary looked perplexed.

"Nothing to say about that. Well, the Nokia thirty-two ten with the number ending eight nine seven was in touch with a Motorola V thirty-six eighty-eight with the telephone number ending one nine one. And that belongs to a very well-known criminal who is currently in hospital with gunshot wounds."

"This is fascinating, officer, but what has this got to do with me?"

"It is Superintendent, actually. And I am drawing you a picture which will become ever clearer. The telephone number one nine one was in contact with an Ericsson S eight-six-eight with the telephone number ending four five five."

"I am tired of this now. Can't you do something?" the Foreign Secretary said to her legal representative."

"Superintendent, can you please get to the point as to how this connects to my client?" the legal rep said.

"Yes, I am getting there. The Ericsson S eight-six-eight with the telephone number ending four five five was known to be used by Detective Chief Superintendent Paul Johnson who tried to kill himself while in custody here yesterday and is currently recovering in hospital."

The Foreign Secretary remained bemused.

"So, I am going to summarise it for you. We have an unknown male who has contacted your brother-in-law and told him they are contacting him on your behalf because you have found out he's having an affair, which your brother-in-law has admitted to in interview. That male has blackmailed your brother-in-law to be a liaison point in a criminal enterprise."

"I don't know who that is and I didn't know my brother-in-law was having an affair."

"I put it to you that you are the user of Nokia thirty-two ten with the telephone number ending six four four. You directed an unknown male to blackmail your brother-in-law to help distance yourself from the criminal enterprise that was seeking to snare half human, half robot hybrids created by the late Dr Robert Leidenstraum on your behalf to sell to a rogue state."

"This is absolute drivel. How dare you?" the Foreign Secretary said.

"No, how dare you. I have not finished, not by a long way. The well-known criminal in hospital was found at a garage compound yesterday with the half human, half robot hybrid robots, along with the kidnapped children of Dr Leiden-straum, amongst others. A deceased, corrupt Police Officer was also found at that scene, Detective Constable Simon Lyle. He was working with Detective Chief Superintendent Paul Johnson, who was in contact with the well-known criminal, who was in contact with your brother-in-law, who was in contact with an unknown male who was in contact with you."

"This is very circumstantial, Superintendent," the Foreign Secretary's legal rep said.

"Is it? Ok, well let me see if I can outline why this is not circumstantial? Where did we find the Nokia thirty-two ten with the telephone number ending six four four?"

"I don't know," the Foreign Secretary said.

"We found it in your house. Explain that. Whilst you are explaining that, explain why the cell site analysis shows the calls from that phone to the unknown male using the number ending seven six eight were made exclusively from your house?"

"What? There must be some mistake."

"There is no mistake. If, by chance, you do not think that is evidence enough, then please explain receipt of six figure sums from Russia, China and Brazil into a business bank account belonging to you and your husband? The letter from the Venezuelan Ministry of Defence offering you political asylum which we found in your study, along with a Romanian passport. Foreign Secretary, if you have any plausible explanation for all of this then I suggest you say so now."

The Foreign Secretary was speechless.

"No, I didn't think so."

"Wait a minute. I don't know anything about this phone, this money, these documents. I must have been set up."

"Pull the other one. You might be able to lie to the public for a living but it won't wash in here, do you hear me?"

"I'm serious. When were these calls made? Show me?"

"Superintendent, my client is entitled to know when the calls were made."

"Very well." Superintendent Wright passed across the table a document with details of the calls between six four four and seven six eight.

The Foreign Secretary and the legal rep scrutinised the information thoroughly.

"Well, is there someone who could have been at your house on these dates and times to make these calls, leave the phone at your house, plant the documents in your study and therefore be responsible for all of this instead of you?"

The Foreign Secretary thought for a few moments, her eyes darted furtively around the room and then back to the document in front of her. Suddenly she gasped.

"OH MY GOD," she said. "OH MY GOD. I KNOW WHO IT IS."

"Tell me, who is it?"

"We interrupt this programme for a special news bulletin," the newscaster said. "Following the earlier announcement that the Prime Minister would be standing down in the wake of the scandal regarding the arrest of the Foreign Secretary and the discovery of half human, half robot hybrids, we now go live to our correspondent Tanya Parry who is outside Ten Downing Street.

"Thanks, Harold. We are waiting for a press conference to begin. Oh, the door is opening now. Hang on, that is the Home Secretary."

The Home Secretary walked up to the podium. The gathered photographers clicked away furiously on their cameras as the journalists stood with bated breath.

"Hello everyone. I will be reading a statement and will not be answering any questions. Following the Prime Minister's decision to stand down earlier today, it is with a mixture of great pride and sadness that I announce to you I am your new Prime Minister. This follows confirmation that I am the only candidate who has declared that they would like to be considered for the role. I want to pay tribute to the outgoing Prime Minister, who was a true friend and ally to me as well as a wonderful public servant to this magnificent country. By his own admission, his position had become untenable. To preserve the integrity and stability of the nation it is sadly necessary for him to walk away from a role he'd cherished and worked so incredibly hard for. I know the whole country will join me in thanking him for all he has done and wish him and his family well for the future. In the wake of the scandal that has cost the Prime Minister his job, I will be implementing measures to tighten the very foundations of our democracy and ensure no individual can operate so unethically and with such impunity for the length of time that Dr Leidenstraum did. Lessons must be learned, and this must be no token gesture. While this is not a time for party politics, I would like to stress that his actions for the most part took place under the opposition's government. So, questions must be asked as to how this was allowed to take place unchallenged for so long, and I announce today that an inquiry will be launched to root out the answers to those questions. I will also be seeking parliament's support in awarding compensation to the families of the teenagers affected by the abhorrent actions of Dr Leidenstraum. While I am not able to comment on the ongoing investigation into the suspended Foreign Secretary, I would like to assure the British public that it is my intention to draft as soon as possible a suite of recommendations that will overhaul parliamentary standards. I will commit to personally overseeing this and challenge ferociously anyone who does not hold office in this country with the dignity and honour that is required and expected by the British people and our allies overseas. I look forward to leading this great country with vigour into the new millennium. Thank you."

"Superintendent Wright, the only person who could have framed me and therefore be responsible for this is... the Home Secretary."

There was a knock at the door of the interview room.

"Sorry to interrupt, sir," an officer said. "But I thought you would like to know immediately. "The Home Secretary has just been announced as the new Prime Minister."

The room fell deathly silent as the Foreign Secretary and Superintendent Wright looked at each other, completely aghast.

"It's ok, he's made it clear he will do everything in his power to combat the sleaze that has brought terrific shame upon our country," the officer said.

21

Chapter Twenty One: Aftermath

Monday 12 July, 1999. 08:15am

As Haroon finished his second helping of Rice Krispies and placed his Spice Girls cereal bowl in the kitchen sink there was a knock at the door.

Haroon opened the front door to a uniformed female police officer and a female in a smart grey trouser suit.

"Good morning, I'm Detective Constable Jepson and this is Police Constable Morris. May we come in?" the non-uniformed female said.

"You're not going to arrest me, are you?" Haroon said. Panic was etched across his face due to his recent encounter with law enforcement.

"We're here to speak to you as a witness, given the fact your vehicle is at Nathan's Garage," DC Jepson said.

"We're hoping to be able to release the car back to you tomorrow," PC Morris said.

"Why would we be here to arrest you?" DC Jepson said.

"Well, Nathan was involved in kidnapping Zams who I'd taken to the warehouse, and detectives Lyle and Herbert were horrible to me at the police station on Thursday, but I phoned them on Friday to tell them I'd recognised Nathan when me and mum took the car to the garage. I've seen the news and they're all dead. I'm worried you're going to accuse me of more things I haven't done, like they did." Haroon stepped back pensively, sat down at the bottom of the stairs, and curled up into a ball.

PC Morris walked over and placed a reassuring hand on Haroon's shoulder. "Please don't be scared," PC Morris said.

"It is clear to me you have important information but I promise I'm going to treat you as a witness, not as a suspect," DC Jepson said. "I'm also troubled by whatever's happened to you at the police station. I'd like to help you resolve that as well."

Haroon looked at PC Morris and then at DC Jepson. "Thank you," he said smiling and nodding at them both.

The Prime Minister was sat in the exquisite, claret-coloured chair ready to get to work when there was a furious knock at the door.

"Come in," the Prime Minister said.

"Prime Minister. There is most urgent news," the Prime Minister's Principal Private Secretary said.

"What is it, Henry?"

"One of the robots seized isn't a robot, Prime Minister. He's just a teenage boy."

"WHAT?"

"The MOD think the robot version of him went with the Leidenstraums and the others to the Embassy."

"Get the German Chancellor on the phone, NOW. We need the decision to grant them temporary asylum overturned. Hurry, they're due to fly from Heathrow to Munich this morning."

"Yes, Prime Minister," Henry said running out of the room.

The plane stood proudly on the tarmac ready to undertake the relatively short flight from England to Germany. As passengers proceeded from the terminal, Sarah, Will, robot Brett, the Paterson family, Tariq, Shabeela and their mother were already sat comfortably on board within five rows at the rear of the plane which had been reserved for them. The engines stirred and the cabin crew communicated safety information as the pilot awaited confirmation the runway was ready.

"It all feels very real now that we're leaving, doesn't it?" Will said to his sister anxiously.

"Too real. I was on the phone in tears to Megan this morning. I don't know if or when I'll ever see my friends again. Missing Aunt Janice's funeral is breaking my heart."

"I'm devastated too, but without sounding selfish, if missing Aunt Janice's funeral prevents our own then that's a price I'm willing to pay."

"I agree. An uncertain future is better than no future at all."

The pilot proceeded to the runway as several Police Officers burst onto the tarmac. They ran in the direction of the plane waving their arms and shouting: "STOP THAT PLANE." The jet accelerated and left the runway.

"Look," Lucy said. "There's people on the ground waving us off."

They all looked out of their windows and waved back as they ascended the London skyline.